D0105612

Acclaim for *In the Lake of the Woods*

"O'Brien once more displays his enormous talent . . .
O'Brien's clean, incantatory prose always hovers on the
edge of dream, and his specialty is that twilight zone of chi-
meras and fears and fantasies where nobody knows what's
true and what is not . . . No one writes better about the fear
and homesickness of a boy adrift amid what he cannot understand, be it combat or love."
— *Time*

"A love story from Tim O'Brien? Well, yes . . . *In the Lake of
the Woods* is about hearts, all right — hearts of darkness . . .
O'Brien is a powerfully gifted storyteller."
— *San Diego Union-Tribune*

"Tim O'Brien is one of his generation's most deservedly ac-
claimed authors . . . He has written a risky, ambitious, perceptive, engaging, and troubling novel, full of unresolved
and unresolvable energies and powerful prose, a major at-
tempt to come to grips with the causes and consequences of
the late 20th century's unquenchable appetite for violence,
both domestic and foreign."
— *Chicago Tribune*

"O'Brien is like a painter, applying shading with this stroke,
depth with that one . . . O'Brien leaves us with the portrait
of a man who travels into his own heart of darkness. It's a
trip not many of us would choose to make, but O'Brien
makes the journey heart-rending, fascinating, and unfor-
gettable."   — *Minneapolis Star Tribune*

"An unrelenting exploration of the darkest recesses of the human heart and psyche. O'Brien's approach is bold, ambitious, and intriguing . . . By novel's end, you *will* know John and Kathy Wade; you will know them as intimately as you know the people you encounter every day of your life. They will haunt you as surely as John Wade's demons came back to haunt him."

—*Houston Chronicle*

"Tim O'Brien is an electrifying storyteller, a craftsman of the fictional form and a rhetorical master . . . *In the Lake of the Woods* is a dynamic read, chock-full of tension, expectation, speculation, and a burning desire for resolution . . . O'Brien, a true artist, has redefined the human self and has cast unmistakable shadows of doubt over the mind's ability to govern that self."

—*Virginian-Pilot/Ledger-Star*

"A riveting exploration of a tormented soul and wounded psyche . . . There are passages in *In the Lake of the Woods* that are almost too excruciating to read. O'Brien writes with a deceptive simplicity. His sentences are straightforward, his language unadorned. Reading his prose is like taking a punch on the chin from someone who looks harmless and finding yourself flat on your back."

—*Denver Post*

"A gripping novel of love and mystery . . . O'Brien is perhaps the best and most popular novelist and writer to emerge from the Vietnam War . . . Deception, magic, and the dark heart of My Lai seep into the soul of Tim O'Brien's spellbinding mystery, *In the Lake of the Woods*."

—*Oregonian*

"A story about love and a man's wanting it too much . . . One comes away from this novel with goosebumps."
— *Washington Times*

"A horror story and a love story, told by a brilliant writer— funny, awful, achingly sad."
— *Cosmopolitan*

"A tremendous achievement, a truly postmodern thriller . . . This is the rarest of thrillers, one that doesn't compete with cinematic conventions, instead crafting its suspense from literature's natural strength: the way in which an author can call on a reader's intelligence to help fashion a novel's effects."
— *Harper's Bazaar*

"O'Brien transformed the war—Our War—into a love story. He wrote books about violence that women would read. For two decades he has been developing a genre of fiction in which unspeakable atrocities are faithfully framed within human emotions. His turf is the heart at war . . . As in his earlier works, O'Brien keeps our eyes on life's mysteries."
— *Boston Magazine*

"Tim O'Brien is the best American writer of his generation."
— *San Francisco Examiner*

"At bottom, this is a tale about the moral effects of suppressing a true story, about the abuse of history, about what happens to you when you pretend there is no history."
— *New York Times Book Review*, Editors' Choice

"A relentless work full of white heat and dark possibility."
— *Boston Globe*

"*In the Lake of the Woods* is on par with O'Brien's second novel, *Going After Cacciato*, which won the National Book Award in 1979, and brilliant *The Things They Carried*, which was listed as one of the best books of 1990 by the *New York Times Book Review*."

—*Milwaukee Sentinel*

"For the long-time O'Brien fan, he's never been in better form." —*South Bend Tribune*

"*In the Lake of the Woods* is the one book I've read this year that keeps nagging at me. Did John Wade kill his wife? Does it matter? Isn't it as important, or more important, that O'Brien got up close to deception and what it does to the soul, to a marriage? . . . It will never be a title I look at without pausing." —*Detroit Free Press*

"One of the most haunting and true evocations of moral trouble to be published since Theodore Dreiser's *Sister Carrie* . . . This novel is about many things—marriage, Vietnam, American politics, the devil—but O'Brien does not force conclusions, does not cover up contradictions, doesn't try to tie his many loose themes neatly into one. He trusts language; he lets words play. And language rewards this trust." —*LA Weekly*

"A gut-punch of a novel . . . O'Brien turns the thriller from inside out, replacing answers with plausible hypotheses as he provides a harrowing glimpse of a married couple dancing on the precipice of disintegration, with all the past deceits of their lives suddenly coming unraveled."

—*Seattle Post-Intelligencer*

"*In the Lake of the Woods* probes a menacing and unmappable physical landscape for clues to the geography of the human heart . . . As he masterfully removes veil after veil from the mystery of John Wade and Vietnam, only to reveal more veils into infinity, O'Brien allows neither glib justification nor the comfort of simple villainy. Alas, evil comes unbidden and faceless from the jungle and the pines. Clearly, that's the mystery that has driven O'Brien's work."

—*Indianapolis Star*

"*In the Lake of the Woods* is a mystery—oh, is it ever a mystery, one that the Agatha Christies of this earth never glimpse, or if they do, they thrust into a hole so deep and dark and far away that even the existence of the hole is hidden, much less what's in it." —*Seattle Times*

"One of the imperatives driving any serious writer is the willingness to take chances, and Tim O'Brien has never shrunk from that requirement. His latest novel, *In the Lake of the Woods*, may represent his most audacious leap so far. It's an unflinching look into the cauldron of a tormented heart . . . You can read *In the Lake of the Woods* as a mystery, but that's almost too superficial to bother doing. Far better to follow Tim O'Brien into the unbearably stressed interstices of the human heart: If he could take that chance, can a reader do less?" —*Santa Barbara News-Press*

IN THE LAKE OF THE WOODS

Books by Tim O'Brien

TIM O'BRIEN

In the Lake of the Woods

MARINER BOOKS
HOUGHTON MIFFLIN HARCOURT
Boston • *New York*

First Mariner Books edition 2006

Copyright © 1994 by Tim O'Brien

ALL RIGHTS RESERVED

For information about permission to reproduce selections from
this book, write to trade.permissions@hmhco.com or to Permissions,
Houghton Mifflin Harcourt Publishing Company, 3 Park Avenue,
19th Floor, New York, New York 10016.

www.hmhco.com

Library of Congress Cataloging-in-Publication Data
O'Brien, Tim, date.
In the Lake of the Woods / Tim O'Brien
p. cm.
ISBN 978-0-395-48889-8
1. Married people—Minnesota—Fiction. 2. Missing
persons—Minnesota—Fiction. 3. Politicians—
Minnesota—Fiction. I. Title.
PS3565.B7515 1994
813'.54—dc20 94-5395 CIP

ISBN 978-0-618-70986-1 (pbk.)

Printed in the United States of America

DOC 20 19

4500645587

Portions of this book have appeared, in substantially different form,
in the *Atlantic Monthly*, *Boston Magazine*, and *Esquire*. The author
is grateful for permission to quote from the following: "Shame" by
Robert Karen, copyright © 1992 by Robert Karen, as first published
in the *Atlantic Monthly*, February 1992; "Homeless My Lai Vet
Killed in Booze Fight," from the *Boston Herald*, September 13, 1988,
reprinted with permission of the *Boston Herald*.

With thanks to John Sterling, Larry Cooper, Michael Curtis, Les Ramirez, Carol Anhalt, Lori Glazer, Lynn Nesbit, and my loving family. Sam Lawrence, who died in January 1994, was my publisher, advocate, and friend for more than two decades. I will always happily recall his faith in me.

IN THE LAKE OF THE WOODS

1

How Unhappy They Were

In September, after the primary, they rented an old yellow cottage in the timber at the edge of Lake of the Woods. There were many trees, mostly pine and birch, and there was the dock and the boathouse and the narrow dirt road that came through the forest and ended in polished gray rocks at the shore below the cottage. Then there were no roads at all. There were no towns and no people. Beyond the dock the big lake opened northward into Canada, where the water was everything, vast and very cold, and where there were secret channels and portages and bays and tangled forests and islands without names. Everywhere, for many thousand square miles, the wilderness was all one thing, like a great curving mirror, infinitely blue and beautiful, always the same. Which was what they had come for. They needed the solitude. They needed the repetition, the dense hypnotic drone of woods and water, but above all they needed to be together.

At night they would spread their blankets on the porch and lie watching the fog move toward them from across the lake. They were not yet prepared to make love. They had tried once, but it had not gone well, so now they would hold each other and talk quietly about having babies and perhaps a house of their own. They pretended things were not so bad. The election had been lost, but they tried to believe it was not the absolute and crushing thing it truly was. They were careful with each other; they did not talk about the sadness or the sudden trapdoor feeling in their stomachs. Lying still under their blankets, they would take turns thinking up names for the children they wanted—funny names, sometimes, so they could laugh—and then later they would plan the furnishings for their new house, the fine rugs they would buy, the antique brass lamps, the exact colors of the wallpaper, all the details, how they would be sure to have a giant sun porch and a stone fireplace and a library with tall walnut bookcases and a sliding ladder.

In the darkness it did not matter that these things were expensive and impossible. It was a terrible time in their lives and they wanted desperately to be happy. They wanted happiness without knowing what it was, or where to look, which made them want it all the more.

As a kind of game they would sometimes make up lists of romantic places to travel.

"Verona," Kathy would say, "I'd love to spend a few days in Verona." And then for a long while they would talk about Verona, the things they would see and do, trying to make it real in their minds. All around them, the fog moved in low and fat off the lake, and their voices would seem to flow away for a time and then return to them from somewhere in the woods beyond the porch. It was an echo, partly. But inside the echo there was also a voice not quite their own—like a whisper, or a nearby breathing, something feathery and alive. They would stop to listen, except the sound was never there when listened for. It mixed with the night. There were rustlings in the timber, things growing and things rotting. There were night birds. There was the lap of lake against shore.

And it was then, listening, that they would feel the trapdoor drop open, and they'd be falling into that emptiness where all the dreams used to be.

They tried to hide it, though. They would go on talking about the fine old churches of Verona, the museums and outdoor cafés where they would drink strong coffee and eat pastries. They invented happy stories for each other. A late-night train ride to Florence, or maybe north into the mountains, or maybe Venice, and then back to Verona, where there was no defeat and where nothing in real life ever ended badly. For both of them it was a wishing game. They envisioned happiness as a physical place on the earth, a secret country, perhaps, or an exotic foreign capital with bizarre customs and a difficult new language. To live there would require practice and many changes, but they were willing to learn.

At times there was nothing to say. Other times they tried to be brave.

"It's not really so terrible," Kathy told him one evening. "I mean, it's bad, but we can make it better." It was their sixth night at Lake of the Woods. In less than thirty-six hours she would be gone, but now she lay beside him on the porch and talked about all the ways they could make it better. Be practical, she said. One day at a time. He could hook up with one of those fancy law firms in Minneapolis. They'd shop around for a cheap house, or just rent for a while, and they'd scrimp and draw up a budget and start paying off the debts, and then in a year or two they could jump on a plane for Verona, or wherever else they wanted, and they'd be happy together and do all the wonderful things they'd never done.

"We'll find new stuff to want," Kathy said. "Brand-new dreams. Isn't that right?" She waited a moment, watching him. "Isn't it?"

John Wade tried to nod.

Two days later, when she was gone, he would remember the sound of mice beneath the porch. He would remember the rich forest smells and the fog and the lake and the curious motion Kathy made with her fingers, a slight fluttering, as if to dispel all the things that were wrong in their lives.

"We'll do it," she said, and moved closer to him. "We'll go out and make it happen."

"Sure," Wade said. "We'll get by fine."

"Better than fine."

"Right. Better."

Then he closed his eyes. He watched a huge white mountain collapse and come tumbling down on him.

There was that crushed feeling in his stomach, yet even then he pretended to smile at her. He said reassuring things, resolutely, as if he believed, and this too was something he would later remember—the pretending. In the darkness he could feel Kathy's heartbeat, her breath against his cheek. After a time she turned beneath the blankets and kissed him, teasing a little, which was irritating but which meant she cared for him and wanted him to concentrate on everything they still had or someday could have.

"So there," she said. "We'll be happy now."

"Happy us," he said.

It was a problem of faith. The future seemed intolerable. There was fatigue, too, and anger, but more than anything there was the emptiness of disbelief.

Quietly, lying still, John Wade watched the fog divide itself into clusters over the dock and boathouse, where it paused as if to digest those objects, hovering for a time, then swirling and changing shape and moving heavily up the slope toward their porch.

Landslide, he was thinking.

The thought formed as a picture in his head, an enormous white mountain he had been climbing all his life, and now he watched it come rushing down on him, all that disgrace. He told himself not to think about it, and then he was thinking again. The numbers were hard. He had been beaten nearly three to one within his own party; he had carried a few college towns and Itasca County and almost nothing else.

Lieutenant governor at thirty-seven. Candidate for the United States Senate at forty. Loser by landslide at forty-one.

Winners and losers. That was the risk.

But it was more than a lost election. It was something physical. Humiliation, that was part of it, and the wreckage in his chest and stomach, and then the rage, how it surged up into his throat and how he wanted to scream the most terrible thing he could scream—*Kill Jesus!*—and how he couldn't help himself and couldn't think straight and couldn't stop screaming terrible things inside his head, because nothing could be done, and because it was so brutal and sad and final. He felt crazy sometimes, real depravity. Late at night an electric sizzle came into his blood, a tight pumped-up killing rage, and he couldn't keep it in and he couldn't let it out. He wanted to hurt things. Grab a knife and start slashing and never stop. All those years. Climbing like a son of a bitch, clawing his way up inch by fucking inch, and then it all came crashing down at once. Everything, it seemed, his sense of purpose, his pride, his career, his honor and reputation, his belief in the future he had so grandly dreamed for himself.

John Wade shook his head and listened to the fog. A single moth played against the screened window behind him.

Forget it, he thought. Don't think.

And then later, when he began thinking again, he took Kathy up against him, holding tight. "Verona," he said firmly, "we'll do it. Deluxe hotels. The whole tour."

"That's a promise?"

"Absolutely," he said. "A promise."

Kathy smiled at this. He could not see the smile, but he could hear it passing through her voice when she said, "What about babies?"

"Everything," Wade said. "Especially that."

"Maybe I'm too old. I hope not."

"You're not."

"I'm thirty-eight."

"We'll have thirty-eight babies," he said. "Hire a bus in Verona."

"There's an *idea*. Then what?"

"I don't know, just drive and see the sights and be together. You and me and a busload of babies."

"You think so?"

"For sure. I promised."

And then for a long while they lay quietly in the dark, waiting for these things to happen, some sudden miracle. All they wanted was for their lives to be good again.

Later, Kathy pushed back the blankets and moved off toward the railing at the far end of the porch. She seemed to vanish into the heavy dark, the fog curling around her, and when she spoke, her voice came from somewhere far away, as if lifted from her body, unattached and not quite authentic.

"I'm not crying," she said.

"Of course you're not."

"It's just a rotten time, that's all. This stupid thing we have to get through."

"Stupid," he said.

"I didn't mean—"

"No, you're right. Damned stupid."

Things went silent. Just the waves and woods, a delicate in-and-out breathing. The night seemed to wrap itself around them.

"John, listen, I can't always come up with the right words. All I meant was—you know—I meant there's this wonderful man I love and I want him to be happy and that's all I *care* about. Not elections."

"Fine, then."

"And not newspapers."

"Fine," he said.

Kathy made a sound in the dark, which wasn't crying. "You do love me?"

"More than anything."

"Lots, I mean?"

"Lots," he said. "A whole busful. Come here now."

Kathy crossed the porch, knelt down beside him, pressed the palm of her hand against his forehead. There was the steady hum of lake and woods. In the days afterward, when she was gone, he would remember this with perfect clarity, as if it were still happening. He would remember a breathing sound inside the fog. He would remember the feel of her hand against his forehead, its warmth, how purely alive it was.

"Happy," she said. "Nothing else."

2

Evidence

He was always a secretive boy. I guess you could say he was
obsessed by secrets. It was his nature.[1]
  —Eleanor K. Wade (Mother)

Exhibit One: Iron teakettle
Weight, 2.3 pounds
Capacity, 3 quarts

Exhibit Two: Photograph of boat
12-foot Wakeman Runabout
Aluminum, dark blue
1.6 horsepower Evinrude engine

He didn't talk much. Even his wife, I don't think she knew the
first damn thing about . . . well, about *any* of it. The man just
kept everything buried.[2]
  —Anthony L. (Tony) Carbo

---

1. Interview, December 4, 1989, St. Paul, Minnesota.
2. Interview, July 12 and July 16, 1993, St. Paul, Minnesota.

Name: Kathleen Terese Wade

Date of Report: 9/21/86

Age: 38

Height: 5'6"

Weight: 118 pounds

Hair: blond

Eyes: green

Photograph: attached

Occupation: Director of Admissions, University of Minnesota, Minneapolis, Minnesota

Medical History: pneumonia (age 16), pregnancy termination (age 34)

Current Medications: Valium, Restoril

Next of Kin: John Herman Wade

Other Relatives: Patricia S. Hood (sister), 1625 Lockwood Avenue, Minneapolis, Minnesota[3]

   —Extract, Missing Persons Report

After work we used to do laps together over at the Y every night. She'd just swim and swim, like a fish almost, so I'm not worried about . . . Well, I think she's fine. You ever hear of a fish drowning?[4]

   —Bethany Kee (Associate Admissions Director,
    University of Minnesota)

3. Missing Persons File Declaration, DS Form 20, Office of the Sheriff, Lake of the Woods County, Baudette, Minnesota. Kathleen Wade was reported missing on the morning of September 20, 1986. The search lasted eighteen days, covered more than 800 square miles, and involved elements of the Minnesota State Highway Patrol, the Lake of the Woods County Sheriff's Department, the United States Border Patrol, the Royal Canadian Mounted Police (Lakes Division), and the Ontario Provincial Police.

4. Interview, September 21, 1991, Edina, Minnesota.

He was not a fat child, not at all. He was husky. He had big bones. But sometimes I think his father made him feel—oh, made him feel—oh—maybe overweight. In sixth grade the boy wrote away for a diet he'd seen advertised in some silly magazine . . . His father teased him quite a lot. Constant teasing, you could say.
—Eleanor K. Wade

You know what I remember? I remember the flies. Millions of flies. That's what I mostly remember.[5]
—Richard Thinbill

Exhibit Three: Photograph of houseplant debris
Remains of six to eight plants (1 geranium, 1 begonia, 1 caladium, 1 philodendron, others unidentified)
Plant material largely decomposed

John loved his father a lot. I suppose that's why the teasing hurt so bad . . . He tried to keep it secret—how much it hurt—but I could always tell . . . Oh, he loved that father of his. (What about *me?* I keep thinking that.) Things were hard for John. He was too young to know what alcoholism is.
—Eleanor K. Wade

5. Interview, July 19, 1990, Fargo, North Dakota. Former PFC Thinbill, a Native American (Chippewa), served with John Wade as a member of the First Platoon, Company C, 1st Battalion, 20th Infantry, 11th Infantry Brigade, Task Force Barker, Americal Division, Republic of Vietnam.

Exhibit Four: Polling Data

> *July 3, 1986*
> Wade—58%
> Durkee—31%
> Undecided—11%

> *August 17, 1986*
> Wade—21%
> Durkee—61%
> Undecided—18%[6]

Landslide isn't the word. You saw the numbers? Three to one, four to one—a career-ender. Poor guy couldn't get elected assistant fucking dogcatcher on a Sioux reservation . . . Must've asked a trillion times if there was anything that could hurt us, scum or anything. Man never said one single word. Zero. Which isn't how you run a campaign. . . Did I betray him? Fuck no. Other way around. I worked like a Mexican to get him elected.
> —Anthony L. (Tony) Carbo

Exhibit Five: Photographs (2) of boathouse (exterior), Lake of the Woods

Exhibit Six: Photographs (3) of "Wade cottage" (exterior), Lake of the Woods

6. *Minneapolis Star-Tribune*, The Minnesota Poll, July 3, 1986, and August 17, 1986, p. 1.

I'll bet she's on a Greyhound bus somewhere. Married to that creep, that's where I'd be. She liked buses.
> —Bethany Kee (Associate Admissions Director, University of Minnesota)

I can't discuss this.[7]
> —Patricia S. Hood (Sister of Kathleen Wade)

Engine trouble. That old beat-up Evinrude. Busted cord probably, or the plugs went bad. Give it time, she'll walk right through that door over there. I bet she *will*.[8]
> —Ruth Rasmussen

I was working down at the Mini-Mart and they come in and I served them both coffee at the counter and then after a while they started having this argument. It went on for a while. She was mad. That's all I know.[9]
> —Myra Shaw (Waitress)

A politician's wife, so naturally you try extra hard. We did everything except empty out the goddamn lake. I'm not done yet. Every day goes by, I keep my eyes open. You never know.[10]
> —Arthur J. Lux (Sheriff, Lake of the Woods County)

The guy offed her.[11]
> —Vincent R. (Vinny) Pearson

7. Interview, May 6, 1990, Minneapolis, Minnesota.
8. Interview, June 6, 1989, Angle Inlet, Minnesota.
9. Interview, June 10, 1993, Angle Inlet, Minnesota.
10. Interview, January 3, 1991, Baudette, Minnesota.
11. Interview, June 9, 1993, Angle Inlet, Minnesota.

That's preposterous. They loved each other. John wouldn't hurt a fly.
　　　—Eleanor K. Wade

Fucking flies!
　　　—Richard Thinbill

3

The Nature of Loss

When he was fourteen, John Wade lost his father. He was in the junior high gymnasium, shooting baskets, and after a time the teacher put his arm around John's shoulder and said, "Take a shower now. Your mom's here."

What John felt that night, and for many nights afterward, was the desire to kill.

At the funeral he wanted to kill everybody who was crying and everybody who wasn't. He wanted to take a hammer and crawl into the casket and kill his father for dying. But he was helpless. He didn't know where to start.

In the weeks that followed, because he was young and full of grief, he tried to pretend that his father was not truly dead. He would talk to him in his imagination, carrying on whole conversations about baseball and school and girls. Late at night, in bed, he'd cradle his pillow and pretend it was his father, feeling the closeness. "Don't be dead," he'd say, and his father would wink and say, "Well, hey, keep talking," and then for a long while they'd discuss the right way to hit a baseball, a good level swing, keeping your head steady and squaring up your shoulders and letting the bat do the job. It was pretending, but the pretending helped. And so when things got especially bad, John would sometimes invent elaborate stories about how he could've saved his father. He imagined all the things he could've done. He imagined putting his lips against his father's mouth and blowing hard and making the heart come alive again; he imagined yelling in his father's ear, begging him to please stop dying. Once or twice it almost worked. "Okay," his father would say, "I'll stop, I'll stop," but he never did.

In his heart, despite the daydreams, John could not fool himself. He knew the truth. At school, when the teachers told him how sorry they were that he had lost his father, he understood that lost was just another way of saying dead. But still the idea kept turning in his mind. He'd picture his father stumbling down a dark alley, lost, not dead at all. And then the pretending would start again. John would go back in his memory over all the places his father might be—under the bed or behind the bookcases in the living room—and in this way he would spend many hours looking for his father, opening closets, scanning the carpets and sidewalks and lawns as if in search of a lost nickel. Maybe in the garage, he'd think. Maybe under the cushions of the sofa. It was only a game, or a way of coping, but now and then he'd get lucky. Just by chance he'd glance down and suddenly spot his father in the grass behind the house. "Bingo," his father would say, and John would feel a hinge swing open. He'd bend down and pick up his father and put him in his pocket and be careful never to lose him again.

4

What He Remembered

Their seventh day at Lake of the Woods passed quietly. There was a telephone but it never rang. There were no newspapers, no reporters or telegrams. Inside the cottage, things had a fragile, hollowed-out quality, a suspended feeling, and over the morning hours a great liquid silence seemed to flow in from the woods and curl up around their bodies. They tried to ignore it; they were cautious with each other. When they spoke, which was not often, it was to maintain the pretense that they were in control of their own lives, that their problems were soluble, that in time the world would become a happier place. Though it required the exercise of tact and willpower, they tried to find comfort in the ordinary motions of life; they simulated their marriage, the old habits and routines. At the breakfast table, over coffee, Kathy jotted down a grocery list. "Caviar," she said, and John Wade laughed and said, "Truffles, too," and they exchanged smiles as proof of their courage and resolve. Often, though, the strain was almost impossible to bear. On one occasion, as she was washing the breakfast dishes, Kathy made a low sound in her throat and began to say something, just a word or two, then her eyes focused elsewhere, beyond him, beyond the walls of the collage, and then after a time she looked down at the dishwater and did not look back again. It was an image that would not go away. Twenty-four hours later, when she was gone, John Wade would remember the enormous distance that had come into her face at that instant, a kind of travel, and he would find himself wondering where she had taken herself, and why, and by what means.

He would never know.

In the days ahead he would look for clues in the clutter of daily detail. The faded blue jeans she wore that morning, her old tennis shoes, her white cotton sweater. The distance in her eyes. The way she rinsed the breakfast dishes and dried her hands and then walked out of the kitchen without looking at him.

What if she'd spoken?

What if she'd leaned against the refrigerator and said, "Let's do some loving right here," and what if they had, and what if everything that happened could not have happened because of those other happenings?

Some things he would remember clearly. Other things he would remember only as shadows, or not at all. It was a matter of adhesion. What stuck and what didn't. He would be quite certain, for instance, that around noon that day they put on their swimsuits and went down to the lake. For more than an hour they lay inert in the sun, half dozing, then later they went swimming until the cold drove them back onto the dock. The afternoon was large and empty. Brilliant patches of red and yellow burned among the pines along the shore, and in the air there was the sharp, dying scent of autumn. There were no boats on the lake, no swimmers or fishermen. To the south, a mile away, the triangular roof of the Forest Service fire tower seemed to float on an expansive green sea; a narrow dirt road cut diagonally through the timber, and beyond the road a trace of gray smoke rose from the Rasmussen cottage off to the west. Northward it was all woods and water.

He would remember a gliding, buoyant feeling in his stomach. The afternoons were always better. Waves and reflections, the big silver lake planing out toward Canada. Not so bad, he was thinking. He watched the sky and pretended he was a winner. Handshakes and happy faces—it made a nice picture. A winner, sure, and so he lay basking in the crisp white sunlight, almost believing.

Later, Kathy nudged him. "Hey there," she said, "you all right?"

"Perfect," he said.

"You don't seem—"

"No, I'm perfect."

Kathy's eyes traveled away again. She put on a pair of sunglasses. There was some unfilled time before she said, "John?"

"Oh, Christ," he said.

He would remember a movement at her jaw, a locking motion.

They swam again, taking turns diving from the dock, going deep, then they dried themselves in the sun and walked up to the cottage for a late lunch. Kathy spent the remainder of the afternoon working on a book of crossword puzzles. Wade sat over a pile of bills at the kitchen table. He built up neat stacks in order of priority, slipped rubber bands around them, and dropped them in his briefcase.

His eyes ached.

There was that electricity in his blood.

At three o'clock he put in a call to Tony Carbo, who wasn't available. A half hour later, when he tried again, Tony's secretary said he'd gone out for the day.

Wade thanked her and hung up.

He unplugged the telephone, carried it into the kitchen, and tossed it in a cupboard under the sink.

Maybe he dozed off. Maybe he had a drink or two. All he would remember with any certainty was that late in the afternoon they locked up the cottage and made the six-mile drive into town. He would remember an odd pressure against his ears—an underwater squeeze. They followed the dirt road west to the Rasmussen cottage, where the road looped north and crossed an iron bridge and turned to loose gravel. Wade would remember giant pines standing flat-up along the roadbed, the branches sometimes vaulting overhead to form shadowed tunnels through the forest. Kathy sat with her hands folded in her lap; after a mile or two she switched on the radio, listened for a moment, then switched it off again. She seemed preoccupied, or nervous, or something in between. If they spoke at all during the ride, he would have no memory of it.

Two miles from town the land began to open up, thinning into brush and scrub pine. The road made a last sharp turn and ran straight west along the shoreline into Angle Inlet. Like a postcard from the moon, Wade thought. They passed Pearson's Texaco station, a small white schoolhouse, a row of lonely looking houses in need of paint. Somebody's cat prowled away the afternoon on the post office steps.

Wade parked and went in to pick up their mail: a statement from his accountant, a letter from Kathy's sister in Minneapolis.

They crossed the street, did the grocery shopping, bought aspirin and booze and tanning lotion, then sat down for coffee at the little sandwich counter in Amdahl's Mini-Mart. A revolving Coca-Cola clock put the time at 5:12. In nineteen hours, almost exactly, Kathy would be gone, but now the corners of her eyes seemed to relax as she skimmed the letter from her sister. At one point she snorted and made a tossing motion with her head. "Oh, God," she moaned, then chuckled, then folded the letter and said, "Here we go again."

"What's that?"

"Patty. Double trouble, as usual—two new guys on the line. Always the juggler."

Wade nodded at the counter and said, "Good for Patty. More power to her." There was that sizzle in his blood, the smell of fish and sawdust sweating up from the Mini-Mart floorboards. An aluminum minnow tank near the door gave off a steady bubbling sound.

"Power's fine," Kathy said, "but not more *men*. No kidding, it seems like they always come in pairs—for Patty, I mean. They're like snakes or politicians or something." She flicked her eyebrows at him. "That's a joke."

"Good one."

"John—"

"Clever."

A muscle moved at her cheek. She picked up a glass salt shaker, tapped it against the counter.

"It's not my fault."

Wade shrugged. "Sorry."

"So stop it," she said. "Just please stop."

20

Kathy spun around on her stool, got up, went over to the magazine rack, and stood with her back to him. Dusk was settling in fast. A cold lake breeze slapped up against the Mini-Mart's screen door, startling the plump young waitress, causing a spill as she refilled their cups.

It was 5:24.

After a time Kathy sat down again and studied the frosted mirror behind the counter, the ads for Pabst and Hamm's and Bromo-Seltzer. She avoided eye contact, sliding down inside herself, and for an instant, watching her in the mirror, John Wade was assaulted by the ferocity of his own love. A beautiful woman. Her face was tired, with the lax darkening that accompanies age, but still he found much to admire. The green eyes and brown summer skin and slim legs and shapely little fingers. Other things, too—subtle things. The way her hand fit precisely into his. How the sun had turned her hair almost white at the temples. Back in college, he remembered, she used to lie in bed and grasp her own feet like a baby and tell funny stories and giggle and roll around and be happy, all those things and a million more.

Presently, Wade sighed and slipped a dollar bill under his saucer.

"Kath, I am sorry," he said. "I mean it."

"Fine, you're sorry."

"All right?"

"Sorry, sorry. Never ends." Kathy waited for the young waitress to scoop up their cups. "Stop blaming me. We lost. That's the truth—we *lost*."

"It was more than that."

"John, we can't keep doing this."

Wade looked at the revolving clock. "Mr. Monster."

———

They had a light supper, played backgammon for dimes, sat listening to records in the living room. Around eight o'clock they went out for a short walk. There was a moon and some stars, and the night was windy and cool. The fog had not yet rolled in off the lake. In the coming days John Wade would remember how he reached out to take her hand, the easy lacing of their fingers. But he would also remember how Kathy pulled away after a few steps. She folded her arms across her chest and walked up to the yellow cottage and went inside without waiting for him.

They did not take their blankets to the porch that night. They did not make love. For the rest of the evening they concentrated on backgammon, pushing dimes back and forth across the kitchen table.

At one point he looked up at her and said, "Kath, that stuff in the newspapers—"

Kathy passed him the dice.

"Your move," she said.

As near as he could remember, they went to bed around eleven. Kathy snapped off the lamp. She turned onto her side and said, "Dream time," almost cheerfully, as if it did not matter at all that she was now going away.

5

Hypothesis

The purest mystery, of course, but maybe she had a secret lover. Marriages come unraveled. Pressures accumulate. There was precedent in their lives.

In the kitchen that morning, when her eyes traveled away, maybe Kathy Wade was imagining a hotel room in Minneapolis, or in Seattle or Milwaukee, a large clean room with air-conditioning and fresh flowers and no politics and no defeat. Maybe she saw someone waiting for her. Or someone driving north toward Lake of the Woods, moving fast, coming to her rescue. An honest, quiet man. A man without guile or hidden history. Maybe she had grown tired of tricks and trapdoors, a husband she had never known, and later that night, when she said "Dream time," maybe it was this she meant—an escape dream, a dream she would now enter.

Among the missing, as among the dead, there is only the flux of possibility.

Maybe a heaven, maybe not.

Maybe she couldn't bear to tell him. Maybe she staged it. Not likely, but not implausible either. The motives were plentiful—fed up, afraid, exhausted by unhappiness. Maybe she woke early the next morning and slipped out of bed and got dressed and moved out to the porch and quietly closed the door behind her and walked up the narrow dirt road to where a car was waiting.

6

Evidence

We called him Sorcerer. It was a nickname.
        —Richard Thinbill

Exhibit Seven: Photograph of John Wade, age 12
Smiling
Husky, not fat
Waving a magician's wand over four white mice

He used to practice down in the basement, just stand in front of that old mirror of his and do tricks for hours and hours. His father didn't think it was healthy. Always alone, always shut up by himself. A very secretive boy, I think I mentioned that.
        —Eleanor K. Wade

Exhibit Eight: John Wade's Box of Tricks, Partial List
Miser's Dream
Horn of Plenty
Spirit of the Dark
The Egg Bag
Guillotine of Death

Silks
Pulls
Wands
Wires
Duplicates (6) of father's necktie

My sister seemed almost scared of him sometimes. I remember this one time when Kathy . . . Look, I don't think it's something we should talk about.
  —Patricia S. Hood

What did she so desire escape from? Such a captive maiden, having plenty of time to think, soon realizes that her tower, its height and architecture, are like her ego only incidental: that what really keeps her where she is is magic, anonymous and malignant, visited on her from outside and for no reason at all.

Having no apparatus except gut fear and female cunning to examine this formless magic, to understand how it works, how to measure its field strength, count its line of force, she may fall back on superstition or take up a useless hobby like embroidery, or go mad, or marry a disk jockey. If the tower is everywhere and the knight of deliverance no proof against its magic, what else?[1]
  —Thomas Pynchon (*The Crying of Lot 49*)

To study psychological trauma is to come face to face both with human vulnerability in the natural world and with the capacity for evil in human nature.[2]
  —Judith Herman (*Trauma and Recovery*)

---

1. Thomas Pynchon, *The Crying of Lot 49* (1965; reprint, New York: Perennial Library, 1990), pp. 21–22.

2. Judith Herman, *Trauma and Recovery* (New York: Basic Books, 1992), p. 7.

There is no such thing as "getting used to combat" . . . Each moment of combat imposes a strain so great that men will break down in direct relation to the intensity and duration of their exposure. Thus psychiatric casualties are as inevitable as gunshot and shrapnel wounds in warfare.[3]

—J. W. Appel and G. W. Beebe (Professors of Psychiatry)

It wasn't just the war that made him what he was. That's too easy. It was everything—his whole *nature* . . . But I can't stress enough that he was always very well behaved, always thoughtful toward others, a nice boy. At the funeral he just couldn't help it. I wanted to yell, too. Even now I'll go out to my husband's grave and stare at that stupid stone and yell Why, why, why!

—Eleanor K. Wade

You know, I think politics and magic were almost the same thing for him. Transformations—that's part of it—trying to change things. When you think about it, magicians and politicians are basically control freaks. [Laughter] I should know, right?

—Anthony L. (Tony) Carbo

The capacity to appear to do what is manifestly impossible will give you a considerable feeling of personal power and can help make you a fascinating and amusing personality.[4]

—Robert Parrish (*The Magician's Handbook*)

---

3. J. W. Appel and G. W. Beebe, "Preventive Psychiatry: An Epidemiological Approach," *Journal of the American Medical Association* 131 (1946), p. 1470.

4. Robert Parrish, *The Magician's Handbook* (New York: Thomas Yoseloff, 1944), p. 10.

Pouring out affection, [Lyndon Johnson] asked—over and over, in every letter, in fact, that survives—that the affection be reciprocated.[5]

   —Robert A. Caro (*The Years of Lyndon Johnson*)

There surely never lived a man with whom love was a more critical matter than it is with me.[6]

   —Woodrow Wilson

When his father died, John hardly even cried, but he seemed very, very angry. I can't blame him. I was angry, too. I mean —you know—I kept asking myself, Why? It didn't make sense. His father had problems with alcohol, that's true, but there was something else beneath it, like this huge sadness I never understood. The sadness caused the drinking, not the other way around. I think that's why his father ended up going into the garage that day . . . Anyway, John didn't cry much. He threw a few tantrums, I remember that. Yelling and so on. At the funeral. Awfully loud yelling.

   —Eleanor K. Wade

After a traumatic experience, the human system of self-preservation seems to go onto permanent alert, as if the danger might return at any moment. Physiological arousal continues unabated.[7]

   —Judith Herman (*Trauma and Recovery*)

---

5. Robert A. Caro, *The Years of Lyndon Johnson: The Path to Power* (New York: Alfred A. Knopf, 1982), p. 228.

6. Woodrow Wilson, in Richard Hofstadter, *The American Political Tradition* (1948; reprint, New York: Vintage Books, 1989), p. 310.

7. Herman, *Trauma and Recovery*, p. 35.

It wasn't insomnia exactly. John could fall asleep at the drop of a hat, but then, bang, he'd wake up after ten or twenty minutes. He couldn't *stay* asleep. It was as if he were on guard against something, tensed up, waiting for . . . well, I don't know what.

   —Eleanor K. Wade

Sometimes I am a bit ashamed of myself when I think how few friends I have amidst a host of acquaintances. Plenty of people offer me their friendship; but, partly because I am reserved and shy, and partly because I am fastidious and have a narrow, uncatholic taste in friends, I reject the offer in almost every case; and then am dismayed to look about and see how few persons in the world stand near me and know me as I am.[8]

   —Woodrow Wilson

Show me a politician, I'll show you an unhappy childhood. Same for magicians.

   —Anthony L. (Tony) Carbo

My mother was a saint.[9]

   —Richard M. Nixon

I remember Kathy telling me how he'd wake up screaming sometimes. Foul language, which I won't repeat. In fact, I'd rather not say anything at all.

   —Patricia S. Hood

---

8. Woodrow Wilson, in Hofstadter, *The American Political Tradition*, pp. 310–311.

9. Richard M. Nixon, *The Memoirs of Richard Nixon* (New York: Grosset and Dunlap, 1978), p. 1088.

For some reason Mr. Wade threw away that old iron teakettle. I fished it out of the trash myself. I mean, it was a perfectly good teakettle.

    —Ruth Rasmussen

The fucker did something ugly.

    —Vincent R. (Vinny) Pearson

Vinny's the theory man. I deal in facts. The case is wide open.[10]

    —Arthur J. Lux (Sheriff, Lake of the Woods County)

---

10. Yes, and I'm a theory man too. Biographer, historian, medium—call me what you want—but even after four years of hard labor I'm left with little more than supposition and possibility. John Wade was a magician; he did not give away many tricks. Moreover, there are certain mysteries that weave through life itself, human motive and human desire. Even much of what might appear to be fact in this narrative—action, word, thought—must ultimately be viewed as a diligent but still imaginative reconstruction of events. I have tried, of course, to be faithful to the evidence. Yet evidence is not truth. It is only evident. In any case, Kathy Wade is forever missing, and if you require solutions, you will have to look beyond these pages. Or read a different book.

7

The Nature of Marriage

When he was a boy, John Wade's hobby was magic. In the basement, where he practiced in front of a stand-up mirror, he made his mother's silk scarves change color. He cut his father's best tie with scissors and restored it whole. He placed a penny in the palm of his hand, made his hand into a fist, made the penny into a white mouse.

This was not true magic. It was trickery. But John Wade sometimes pretended otherwise, because he was a kid then, and because pretending was the thrill of magic, and because for a while what seemed to happen became a happening in itself. He was a dreamer. He liked watching his hands in the mirror, imagining how someday he would perform much grander magic, tigers becoming giraffes, beautiful girls levitating like angels in the high yellow spotlights—naked maybe, no wires or strings, just floating there.

At fourteen, when his father died, John did the tricks in his mind. He'd lie in bed at night, imagining a big blue door, and after a time the door would open and his father would walk in, take off his hat, and sit in a rocking chair beside the bed. "Well, I'm back," his father would say, "but don't tell your mom, she'd kill me." He'd wink and grin. "So what's new?"

And then they'd talk for a while, quietly, catching up on things, like cutting a tie and restoring it whole.

He met Kathy in the autumn of 1966. He was a senior at the University of Minnesota, she was a freshman. The trick then was to make her love him and never stop.

The urgency came from fear, mostly; he didn't want to lose her. Sometimes he'd jerk awake at night, dreaming she'd left him, but when he tried to explain this to her, Kathy laughed and told him to cut it out, she'd never leave, and in any case thinking that way was destructive, it was negative and unhealthy. "Here I am," she said, "and I'm not going anywhere."

John thought it over for several days. "Well, all right," he said, "but it still worries me. Things go wrong. Things don't always last."

"We're not *things*," Kathy said.

"But it can happen."

"Not with us."

John shrugged and looked away. He was picturing his father's big white casket. "Maybe so," he said, "but how do we know? People lose each other."

In early November he began spying on her. He felt some guilt at first, which bothered him, but he also found satisfaction in it. Like magic, he thought—a quick, powerful rush. He knew things he shouldn't know. Intimate little items: what she ate for breakfast, the occasional cigarette she smoked. Finesse and deception, those were his specialties, and the spying came easily. In the evenings he'd station himself outside her dormitory, staring up at the light in her room. Later, when the light went off, he'd track her to the student union or the library or wherever else she went. The issue wasn't trust or distrust. The whole *world* worked by subterfuge and the will to believe. And so he'd sometimes make dates with her, and then cancel, and then wait to see how she used the time. He looked for signs of betrayal: the way she smiled at people, the way she carried herself around other men. In a way, almost, he loved her best when he was spying; it opened up a hidden world, new angles and new perspectives, new things to admire. On Thursday afternoons he'd stake out women's basketball practice, watching from under the bleachers, taking note of her energy and enthusiasm and slim brown legs. As an athlete, he decided, Kathy wasn't much, but he got a kick out of the little dance she'd do whenever a free throw dropped in. She had a competitive spirit that made him proud. She was a knockout in gym shorts.

Down inside, of course, John realized that the spying wasn't proper, yet he couldn't bring himself to stop. In part, he thought, Kathy had brought it on herself: she had a personality that lured him on, fiercely private, fiercely independent. They'd be at a movie together, or at a party, and she'd simply vanish; she'd go out for a pack of gum and forget to return. It wasn't thoughtlessness, really, but it wasn't thoughtful either. Without reason, usually without warning, she'd wander away while they were browsing in a shop or bookstore, and then a moment later, when he glanced up, she'd be cleanly and purely gone, as if plucked off the planet. That fast—here, then gone—and he wouldn't see her again for hours, or until he found her holed up in a back carrel of the library. All this put a sharp chill in his heart. He understood her need to be alone, to reserve time for herself, but too often she carried things to an extreme that made him wonder. The spying helped. No great discoveries, but at least he knew the score.

And it was fun, too—a challenge.

Occasionally he'd spend whole days just tailing her. The trick was to be patient, to stay alert, and he liked the bubbly sensation it gave him to trace her movements from spot to spot. He liked melting into crowds, positioning himself in doorways, anticipating her route as she walked across campus. It was sleight-of-body work, or sleight-of-mind, and over those cool autumn days he was carried along by the powerful, secret thrill of gaining access to a private life. Hershey bars, for instance—Kathy was addicted, she couldn't resist. He learned about her friends, her teachers, her little habits and routines. He watched her shop for his birthday present. He was there in the drugstore when she bought her first diaphragm.

"It's weird," Kathy told him once, "how well you *know* me."

To his surprise Kathy kept loving him, she didn't stop, and over the course of the spring semester they made plans to be married and have children and someday live in a big old house in Minneapolis. For John it was a happy time. Except for rare occasions, he gave up spying. He was able to confide in her about his ambitions and dreams. First law school, he told her, then a job with the party, and then, when all the pieces were in place, he'd go for something big. Lieutenant governor, maybe. The U.S. Senate. He had the sequence mapped out; he knew what he wanted. Kathy listened carefully, nodding at times. Her eyes were green and smart, watchful. "Sounds fine," she said, "but what's it all for?"

"For?"

"I mean, *why?*"

John hesitated. "Because—you know—because it's what I want."

"Which is what?"

"Just the usual, I guess. Change things. Make things happen."

Kathy lay on her back, in bed. It was late April of 1967. She was nineteen years old.

"Well, I still don't get it," she said. "The way you talk, it sounds calculating or something. Too cold. Planning every tiny detail."

"And that's bad?"

"No. Not exactly."

"What then?"

She made a shifting motion with her shoulders. "I don't know, it just seems strange, sort of. How you've figured everything out, all the angles, except what it's *for.*"

"For us," he said. "I love you, Kath."

"But it feels—I shouldn't say this—it feels manipulating."

John turned and looked at her. Nineteen years old, yes, but still there was something flat and skeptical in her eyes, something terrifying. She returned his gaze without backing off. She was hard to fool. Again, briefly, he was assailed by the sudden fear of losing her, of bungling things, and for a long while he tried to explain how wrong she was. Nothing sinister, he said. He talked about leading a good life, doing good things for the world. Yet even as he spoke, John realized he was not telling the full truth. Politics *was* manipulation. Like a magic show: invisible wires and secret trapdoors. He imagined placing a city in the palm of his hand, making his hand into a fist, making the city into a happier place. Manipulation, that was the fun of it.

He graduated in June of 1967. There was a war in progress, which was beyond manipulation, and nine months later he found himself at the bottom of an irrigation ditch. The slime was waist-deep. He couldn't move. The trick then was to stay sane.

His letters from Kathy were cheerful and newsy, full of spicy details, and he found comfort in her chitchat about family and friends. She told funny stories about her sister Pat, about her teachers and roommates and basketball team. She rarely mentioned the war. Though concerned for his safety, Kathy also had doubts about his motives, his reasons for being there.

"I just hope it's not part of your political game plan," she wrote. "All those dead people, John, they don't vote."

The letter hurt him. He couldn't understand how she could think such things. It was true that he sometimes imagined returning home a hero, looking spiffy in a crisp new uniform, smiling at the crowds and carrying himself with appropriate modesty and decorum. And it was also true that uniforms got people elected. Even so, he felt abused.

"I love you," he wrote back, "and I hope someday you'll believe in me."

John Wade was not much of a soldier, barely competent, but he managed to hang on without embarrassing himself. He kept his head down under fire, avoided trouble, trusted in luck to keep him alive. By and large he was well liked among the men in Charlie Company. In the evenings, after the foxholes were dug, he'd sometimes perform card tricks for his new buddies, simple stuff mostly, and he liked the grins and bunched eyebrows as he transformed the ace of spades into the queen of hearts, the queen of hearts into a snapshot of Ho Chi Minh. Or he'd swallow his jackknife. He'd open up the blade and put his head back and make the moves and then retrieve the knife from somebody's pocket. The guys were impressed. Sorcerer, they called him: "Sorcerer's our man." And for John Wade, who had always considered himself a loner, the nickname was like a special badge, an emblem of belonging and brotherhood, something to take pride in. A nifty sound, too—Sorcerer—it had magic, it suggested certain powers, certain rare skills and aptitudes.

The men in Charlie Company seemed to agree.

One afternoon in Pinkville, when a kid named Weber got shot through the kidney, Sorcerer knelt down and pressed a towel against the hole and said the usual things: "Hang tight, easy now." Weber nodded. For a while he was quiet, flickering in and out, then suddenly he giggled and tried to sit up.

"Hey, no sweat," he said, "I'm aces, I'm golden." The kid kept rocking, he wouldn't lie still. "Golden, golden. Don't mean zip, man, I'm *golden.*"

Weber's eyes shut. He almost smiled. "Go on," he said. "Do your magic."

In Vietnam, where superstition governed, there was the fundamental need to believe—believing just to believe—and over time the men came to trust in Sorcerer's powers. Jokes, at first. Little bits of lingo. "Listen up," somebody would say, "tonight we're invisible," and somebody else would say, "That's affirmative, Sorcerer's got this magic dust, gonna sprinkle us good, gonna make us into spooks." It was a game they played—tongue-in-cheek, but also hopeful. At night, before heading out on ambush, the men would go through the ritual of lining up to touch Sorcerer's helmet, filing by as if at Communion, the faces dark and young and solemn. They'd ask his advice on matters of fortune; they'd tell each other stories about his incredible good luck, how he never got a scratch, not once, not even that time back in January when the mortar round dropped right next to his foxhole. Amazing, they'd say. Man's plugged into the spirit world.

John Wade encouraged the mystique. It was useful, he discovered, to cultivate a reserved demeanor, to stay silent for long stretches of time. When pressed, he'd put on a quick display of his powers, doing a trick or two, using the everyday objects all around him.

Much could be done, for example, with his jackknife and a corpse. Other times he'd do some fortune-telling, offering prophecies of things to come. "Wicked vibes," he'd say, "wicked day ahead," and then he'd gaze out across the paddies. He couldn't go wrong. Wickedness was everywhere.

"I'm the company witch doctor," he wrote Kathy. "These guys listen to me. They actually *believe* in this crap."

Kathy did not write back for several weeks. And then she sent only a postcard: "A piece of advice. Be careful with the tricks. One of these days you'll make *me* disappear."

It was signed, Kath. There were no endearments, no funny stories.

Instantly, John felt the old terrors rise up again, all the ugly possibilities. He couldn't shut them off. Even in bright daylight the pictures kept blowing through his head. Dark bedrooms, for instance. Kathy's diaphragm. What he wanted was to spy on her again—it was like a craving—but all he could do was wait. At night his blood bubbled. He couldn't stop wondering. In the third week of February, when a letter finally arrived, he detected a new coolness in her tone, a new distance and formality. She talked about a movie she'd seen, an art gallery she'd visited, a terrific Spanish beer she'd discovered. His imagination filled in the details.

February was a wretched month. Kathy was one problem, the war another. Two men were lost to land mines. A third was shot through the neck. Weber died of an exploding kidney. Morale was low. As they plodded from ville to ville, the men talked in quiet voices about how the magic had worn off, how Sorcerer had lost contact with the spirit world. They seemed to blame him. Nothing direct, just a general standoffishness. There were no more requests for tricks. No banter, no jokes. As the days piled up, John Wade felt increasingly cut off from the men, cut off from Kathy and his own future. A stranded sensation—totally lost. At times he wondered about his mental health. The internal terrain had gone blurry; he couldn't get his bearings.

"Something's wrong," he wrote Kathy. "Don't do this to me. I'm not blind—Sorcerer can *see*."

She wrote back fast: "You scare me."

And then for many days he received no letters at all, not even a postcard, and the war kept squeezing in on him. The notion of the finite took hold and would not let go.

In the second week of February a sergeant named Reinhart was shot dead by sniper fire. He was eating a Mars bar. He took a bite and laughed and started to say something and then dropped in the grass under a straggly old palm tree, his lips dark with chocolate, his brains smooth and liquid. It was a fine tropical afternoon. Bright and balmy, very warm, but

John Wade found himself shivering. The cold came from inside him. A deep freeze, he thought, and then he felt something he'd never felt before, a force so violent it seemed to pick him up by the shoulders. It was rage, in part, but it was also illness and sorrow and evil, all kinds of things.

For a few seconds he hugged himself, feeling the cold, and then he was moving.

There was no real decision. He'd lost touch with his own volition, his own arms and legs, and in the hours afterward he would remember how he seemed to glide toward the enemy position—not running, just a fast, winging, disconnected glide—circling in from behind, not thinking at all, slipping through a tangle of deep brush and keeping low and letting the glide take him up to a little man in black trousers and a black shirt.

He would remember the man turning. He would remember their eyes colliding.

Other things he would remember only dimly. How he was carried forward by the glide. How his lungs seemed full of ashes, and how at one point his rifle muzzle came up against the little man's cheekbone. He would remember an immense pressure in his stomach. He would remember Kathy's flat eyes reproaching him for the many things he had done and not done.

There was no sound at all, none that Sorcerer would remember. The little man's cheekbone was gone.

Later, the men in Charlie Company couldn't stop talking about Sorcerer's new trick.

They went on and on.

"Poof," somebody said. "No lie, just like that—*poof!*"

At dusk they dragged the sniper's body into a nearby hamlet. An audience of villagers was summoned at gunpoint. A rope was then secured to the dead man's feet, another to his wrists, and just before nightfall Sorcerer and his assistants performed an act of levitation, hoisting the body high into the trees, into the dark, where it floated under a lovely red moon.

John Wade returned home in November of 1969. At the airport in Seattle he put in a long-distance call to Kathy, but then chuckled and hung up on the second ring.

The flight to Minneapolis was lost time. Jet lag, maybe, but something else, too. He felt dangerous. In the gray skies over North Dakota he went back into the lavatory, where he took off his uniform and put on a sweater and slacks, then carefully appraised himself in the mirror. His eyes looked unsound, a little tired, a little frayed. After a moment he winked at himself. "Hey, Sorcerer," he murmured. "How's tricks?"

In the Twin Cities that evening, he took a bus over to the university. He carried his duffel to the plaza outside Kathy's dorm, found a concrete bench, and sat down to wait. It was shortly after nine o'clock. Her window was dark, which seemed appropriate, and for a couple of hours he compiled mental lists of the various places she might be, the things she might be doing. Nothing wholesome came to mind. His thoughts then gathered around the topics he would address once the occasion was right. Loyalty, for example, steadfastness and fidelity and trust and all the related issues of sticking power.

It was late, almost midnight, when Kathy turned up the sidewalk to her dorm.

She carried a canvas tote bag over her shoulder, a stack of books in her right arm. She'd lost some weight, mostly at the hips, and in the dark she seemed to move with a quicker, nimbler, more impulsive stride. It made him uneasy. After she'd gone inside, John sat very still for a time, not quite there, not quite anywhere; then he picked up his duffel and walked the seven blocks to a hotel.

He was still gliding.

That dizzy, disconnected sensation stayed with him all night. Exotic fevers swept through his blood. He couldn't get traction on his own dreams. Twice he woke up and stood under the shower, letting the water beat against his shoulders, but even then the dream-reels kept unwinding. Crazy stuff. Kathy shoveling rain off a sidewalk. Kathy waving at him from the wing of an airplane. At one point, near dawn, he found himself curled up on the floor, wide awake, conversing with the dark. He was asking his father to please stop dying. Over and over he kept saying please, but his father wouldn't listen and wouldn't stop, he just kept dying. "God, I *love* you," John said, and then he curled up tighter and stared into the dark and found himself at his father's funeral—fourteen years old, a new black necktie pinching tight—except the funeral was being conducted in bright sunlight along an irrigation ditch at Thuan Yen—mourners squatting on their heels and wailing and clawing at their eyes—John's mother and many other mothers—a minister crying "Sin!"—an organist playing organ music—and John wanted to kill everybody who was weeping and everybody who wasn't, everybody, the minister and the mourners and the skinny old lady at the organ—he wanted to grab a hammer and scramble down into the ditch and kill his father for dying.

"Hey, I *love* you," he yelled. "I *do*."

When dawn came, he hiked over to Kathy's dorm and waited outside on the concrete bench.

He wasn't sure what he wanted.

In mid-morning Kathy came out and headed down toward the classroom buildings. The routine hadn't changed. He followed her to the biology lab, then to the student union, then to the post office and bank and gymnasium. From his old spot under the bleachers he watched as she practiced her dribbling and free throws, which were much improved, and after lunch he spent a monotonous three hours in the library as she leaned over a fat gray psychology textbook. There was nothing out of the ordinary. Several times, in fact, he came close to ending his vigil, just grabbing her, holding tight and never letting go. But near dark, when she closed her book, he couldn't resist tailing her across campus to a busy kiosk, where she bought a magazine, then over to a pizza joint on University Avenue, where she ordered a Tab and a small pepperoni.

He stationed himself at a bus stop outside. His eyes ached—his heart, too—everything. And there was also the squeeze of indecision. At times he was struck by a fierce desire to believe that the suspicion was nothing but a demon in his head. Other times he wanted to believe the worst. He didn't know why. It was as though something inside him, his genes or his bone marrow, required the certainty of a confirmed betrayal: a witnessed kiss, a witnessed embrace. The facts would be absolute. In a dim way, only half admitted, John understood that the alternative was simply to love her, and to go on loving her, yet somehow the ambiguity seemed intolerable. Nothing could ever be sure, not if he spied forever, because there was always the threat of tomorrow's treachery, or next year's treachery, or the treachery implicit in all the tomorrows beyond that.

Besides, he liked spying. He was Sorcerer. He had the gift, the knack.

It was full dark when Kathy stepped outside. She passed directly behind him, so close he could smell the perfumed soap on her skin. He felt a curious jolt of guilt, almost shame, but for another ten minutes he tracked her back toward campus, watching as she paused to inspect the shop windows and Thanksgiving displays. At the corner of University and Oak she used a public telephone, mostly listening, laughing once, then she continued up toward the school. The evening had a crisp, leafy smell. Football weather, a cool mid-autumn Friday, and the streets were crowded with students and flower kids and lovers going arm in arm. Nobody knew. Their world was safe. All promises were infinite, all things endured, doubt was on some other planet.

Neptune, he thought, which gave him pause. When he looked up, Kathy was gone.

For a few moments he had a hard time finding focus. He scanned the sidewalks, shut his eyes briefly, then turned and made his way back to her dorm. He waited all night. He waited through dawn and into early morning.

By then he knew.

The knowledge was absolute. It was bone-deep and forever, pure knowing, but even then he waited. He was still there when she came up the sidewalk around noon. Arms folded, powerful, he stood on the steps and watched her move toward him.

"I was out," Kathy said.

Sorcerer smiled a small covert smile. "Right," he said. "You were out."

They married anyway.

It was an outdoor ceremony in the discreetly landscaped yard of her family's house in a suburb west of the Twin Cities.

44

Balloons had been tied to the trees and shrubs, the patio was decorated with Japanese lanterns and red carnations and crepe paper. Altogether, things went nicely. The minister talked about the shield of God's love, which warded off strife, and then recited—too theatrically, John thought—a short passage from First Corinthians. Oddly, though, it was not the solemn moment he had once imagined. At one point he glanced over at Kathy and grinned. "And though I have the gift of prophecy, and understand all mysteries, and all knowledge"—Her eyes were green and bright. She wrinkled her nose. She grinned back at him—"and though I have all faith, so that I could remove mountains . . ."A lawn mower droned a few houses down. A soft breeze rippled across the yard, and spikes of dusty sunshine made the trees glow, and pink and white balloons danced on their little strings. "For now we see through a glass, darkly; but then face to face: now I know in part; but then shall I know even as also I am known."

Then the minister prayed.

They promised to be true to each other. They promised other things, too, and exchanged rings, and afterward Kathy's sister opened the bar. Her mother gave them bed sheets. Her father presented them with the keys to an apartment in Minneapolis.

"It's scary," Kathy whispered, "how much I love you."

They drove away in a borrowed Chevy to the St. Paul Ramada, where they honeymooned for several days on a package deal. The secrets were his. He would never tell. On the second morning Kathy asked if he had any misgivings, any second thoughts, and John shook his head and said no. He was Sorcerer, after all, and what was love without a little mystery?

They moved into the apartment just after Easter.

"We'll be happy," Kathy said, "I know it."

Sorcerer laughed and carried her inside.

The trick then was to be vigilant. He would guard his advantage. The secrets would remain secret—the things he'd seen, the things he'd done. He would repair what he could, he would endure, he would go from year to year without letting on that there were tricks.

8

How the Night Passed

Twice during the night John Wade woke up sweating. The first time, near midnight, he turned and coiled up against Kathy, brain-sick, a little feverish, his thoughts wired to the nighttime hum of lake and woods.

A while later he kicked back the sheets and said, "Kill Jesus." It was a challenge—a dare.

He closed his eyes and waited for something terrible to happen, almost hoping, and when nothing happened he said it again, with authority, then listened for an answer. There was nothing.

Quietly then, John Wade swung out of bed. He moved down the hallway to the kitchen, ran water into an old iron teakettle, put it on the stove to boil. He was naked. His shoulders were sunburnt, his face waxy with sweat. For a few moments he stood very still, imagining himself kicking and gouging. He'd go for the eyes. Yes, he would. Tear out the eyeballs—fists and fingernails—just punch and claw and hammer and bite. God, too. He hoped there was a god so he could kill him.

The thought was inspiring. He looked at the kitchen ceiling

and confided in the void, offering up his humiliation and sorrow.

The teakettle made a light clicking noise.

"You too," he said.

He shrugged and got out the tea bags and lay down on the kitchen floor to wait. He was not thinking now, just watching the numbers come in. He could see it happening exactly as it happened. Minneapolis was lost. The suburbs, the Iron Range. And the farm towns to the southwest—Pipestone, Marshall, Windom, Jackson, Luverne. A clean, tidy sweep. St. Paul had been lost early. Duluth was lost four to one. The unions were lost, and the German Catholics, and the rank-and-file nobodies. The numbers were implacable. There was no pity in the world. It was all arithmetic. A winner, obviously, until he became a loser. Which was how it happened: that quick. One minute you're presidential timber and then they come at you with chain saws. It was textbook slippage. It was dishonor and disgrace. Certain secrets had been betrayed—ambush politics, Tony Carbo said—and so the polls went sour and in the press there was snide chatter about issues of character and integrity. Front-page photographs. Dead human beings in awkward poses. By late August the whole enterprise had come unraveled, empty wallets and hedged bets and thinning crowds, old friends with slippery new excuses, and on the first Tuesday after the second Monday in September he was defeated by a margin of something more than 105,000 votes.

John Wade saw it for what it was.

Nothing more to hope for.

Too ambitious, maybe. Climbing too high or too fast. But it was something he'd worked for. He'd been a believer. Discipline and tenacity. He had believed in those virtues, and in the fundamental justice of things, an everyday sort of fairness; that if you worked like a son of a bitch, if you stuck it out and didn't quit, then sooner or later you'd get the payoff. Politics, it was all he'd ever wanted for himself. Three years as a legislative liaison, six years in the state senate, four tedious years as lieutenant governor. He'd played by the rules. He'd run a good solid campaign, working the caucuses, prying out the endorsements—all of it—eighteen-hour days, late nights, the whole insane swirl of motels and county fairs and ten-dollar-a-plate chicken dinners. He'd done it all.

The teakettle made a brisk whistling sound, but John Wade could not bring himself to move.

Ambush politics. Poison politics.

It wasn't fair.

That was the final truth: just so unfair. Wade was not a religious man, but he now found himself talking to God, explaining how much he hated him. The election was only part of it. There were also those mirrors in his head. An electric buzz, the chemistry inside him, the hum of lake and woods. He felt the pinch of depravity.

When the water was at full boil, John Wade pushed himself up and went to the stove.

He used a towel to pick up the iron teakettle.

Stupidly, he was smiling, but the smile was meaningless. He would not remember it. He would remember only the steam and the heat and the tension in his fists and forearms.

"Kill Jesus," he said, which encouraged him, and he carried the teakettle out to the living room and switched on a lamp and poured the boiling water over a big flowering geranium near the fireplace. There was a hissing noise. The geranium seemed to vibrate for an instant, swaying sideways as if caught by a breeze. He watched the lower leaves blanch and curl downward at the edges. The room acquired a damp exotic stink.

Wade was humming under his breath. "Well now," he said, and nodded pleasantly.

He heard himself chuckle.

"Oh, my," he said.

He moved to the far end of the living room, steadied himself, and boiled a small spider plant. It wasn't rage. It was necessity. He emptied the teakettle on a dwarf cactus and a philodendron and a caladium and several others he could not name. Then he returned to the kitchen. He refilled the teakettle, watched the water come to a boil, smiled and squared his shoulders and moved down the hallway to their bedroom.

A prickly heat pressed against his face. The teakettle made its clicking sound in the night.

Briefly then, he let himself glide away. A ribbon of time went by, which he would not remember, then later he found himself crouched at the side of the bed. He was rocking on his heels, watching Kathy sleep.

Odd, he thought. That numbness inside him. The way his hands had no meaningful connection to his wrists.

For some time he crouched there, admiring the tan at Kathy's neck and shoulders, the wrinkles at her eyes. In the dim light she seemed to be smiling at something, or half smiling, a thumb curled alongside her nose. It occurred to him that he should wake her. Yes, a kiss, and then confess to the shame he felt: how defeat had bled into his bones and made him crazy with hurt. He should've done it. He should've told her about the mirrors in his head. He should've talked about the special burden of villainy, the ghosts at Thuan Yen, the strain on his dreams. And then later he should've slipped under the covers and taken her in his arms and explained how he loved her more than anything, a hard hungry lasting guile-less love, and how everything else was trivial and dumb. Just politics, he should've said. He should've talked about coping and enduring, all the clichés, how it was not the end of the world, how they still had each other and their marriage and their lives to live.

In the days that followed, John Wade would remember all the things he should've done.

He touched her shoulder.

Amazing, he thought, what love could do.

In the dark he heard something twitch and flutter, like wings, and then a low, savage buzzing sound. He squeezed the teakettle's handle. A strange heaviness had come into his arms and wrists. Again, for an indeterminate time, the night seemed to dissolve all around him, and he was somewhere outside himself, awash in despair, watching the mirrors in his head flicker with radical implausibilities. The teakettle and a wooden hoe and a vanishing village and PFC Weatherby and hot white steam.

He would remember smoothing back her hair.

He would remember pulling a blanket to her chin and then returning to the living room, where for a long while he lost track of his whereabouts. All around him was that furious buzzing noise. The unities of time and space had unraveled. There were manifold uncertainties, and in the days and weeks to come, memory would play devilish little tricks on him. The mirrors would warp up; there would be odd folds and creases; clarity would be at a premium.

At one point during the night he stood waist-deep in the lake.

At another point he found himself completely submerged, lungs like stone, an underwater rush in his ears.

And then later, in the starwild dark, he sat quietly at the edge of the dock. He was naked. He was all alone, watching the lake.

Later still, he woke up in bed. A soft pinkish light played against the curtains.

For a few seconds he studied the effects of dawn, the pale ripplings and gleamings. He'd been having a curious nightmare. Electric eels. Boiling red water.

John Wade reached out for Kathy, who wasn't there, then hugged his pillow and returned to the bottoms.

9

Hypothesis

Maybe it was something simple.

Maybe Kathy woke up scared that night. Maybe she panicked.

Just conjecture—maybe this, maybe that—but conjecture is all we have.

So something simple:

He was yelling bad things in the dark, and she must've heard him, and maybe later she smelled the steam and wet soil. Almost certainly, she would've slipped out of bed. She would've moved down the hallway to the living room and stopped there and watched him empty the teakettle on a geranium and a philodendron and a small young spider plant. "Kill Jesus," he was saying, which would've caused her to back away.

The rest would have been automatic. She would've turned and moved to the kitchen door and stepped out into the night.

Why? she thought.

Kill Jesus. That brutal voice. It wasn't his.

And then for a long while she stood in the windy dark outside the cottage, afraid to move, afraid not to. She was barefoot. She had on a pair of underpants and a flannel night-gown, nothing else.

A good man. So *why?*

Clutching herself, leaning forward against the cold, Kathy watched him pad into the kitchen, refill the teakettle, and put it on the stove to boil. His movements seemed stiff and mechanical. Like a sleepwalker, she thought, and it occurred to her that she should step back inside and shake him awake. Her own husband. And she loved him. Which was the essential truth, all that time together, all the years, and there was nothing to be afraid about.

Except it wasn't right. *He* wasn't right. Filtered through the screen door, his face looked worn and bruised, the skin deeply lined as if a knife had been taken to it. He'd lost weight and hair. His shoulders had the stooped curvature of an old man's. After a moment he lay down near the stove, sunburnt and naked, conversing with the kitchen ceiling. This was not the man she'd known, or thought she'd known. She had loved him extravagantly—the kind of love she'd always wanted—but more and more it was like living with a stranger. Too many mysteries. Too much walled-up history. And now the fury in his face. Even through the screen, she could make out a new darkness in his eyes.

"Well, now," he was saying. "Is everybody happy?"

Then he said, *"You!"*

He chuckled at this.

He jerked sideways and clawed at his face with both hands, deep, raking the skin.

A bit later he said, "Beautiful."

Again, Kathy felt a gust of panic. She turned and looked up the narrow dirt road. The Rasmussen cottage was barely a mile away, a twenty-minute walk. Find a doctor, maybe; something to settle him down. Then she shook her head. Better just to wait and see.

What she mostly felt now was a kind of pity. Everything important to him had turned to wreckage. His career, his reputation, his self-esteem. More than anyone she'd ever known, John needed the conspicuous display of human love—absolute, unconditional love. Love without limit. Like a hunger, she thought. Some vast emptiness seemed to drive him on, a craving for warmth and reassurance. Politics was just a love thermometer. The polls quantified it, the elections made it official.

Except nothing ever satisfied him. Certainly not public office. And not their marriage, either.

For a second Kathy looked up at the night sky. It surprised her to see a nearly full moon, a stack of fast-moving clouds passing northward. She tried to inventory the events unfolding in her stomach. Not only pity, but also frustration, and the fatigue of defeat. The whole election seemed to have occurred in another century, and now she had only the vaguest memory of those last miserable weeks on the road. All through August and early September, after the newspapers broke things wide open, it was a matter of waiting for the end to come exactly as it had to come. No hope and no pretense of hope. Over the final week they'd worked a string of towns up on the Iron Range, going through the motions, waving at crowds that weren't crowds anymore. Accusing eyes, perfunctory applause. A freak show. On primary day they'd made the short flight back to Minneapolis, arriving just before dark, and even now, in memory, the whole scene had the feel of a dreary Hollywood script—the steady rain, the threadbare little crowd gathered under umbrellas at the airport. She remembered John moving off to shake hands along a chain fence, his face rigid in the gray drizzle. At one point, as he stepped back, a lone voice rose up from the crowd—a woman's voice—not loud but extraordinarily pure and clear, like a small well-made bell. "Not true!" the woman cried, and for an instant the planes of John's face seemed to slacken. He didn't speak. He didn't turn or acknowledge her. There was a short quiet before he glanced up at the clouds and smiled. The haggard look in his eyes was gone; a kind of rapture burned there. "Not true!" the woman yelled again, and this time John raised his shoulders, a kind of plea, or maybe an apology, a gesture vague enough to be denied yet emphatic enough to carry secret meaning.

In the hotel that night she found the courage to ask about it. The early returns had come in, all dismal, and she remembered John's eyes locked tight to the television.

"I need to know," she said. "Is it true?"

"Is *what* true?"

"The things they're saying. About you."

"Things?"

"You know."

He switched channels with the remote, clasped his hands behind his head. Even then he wouldn't look at her. "Everything's true. Everything's not true."

"I'm your wife."

"Right," he said.

"So?"

"So nothing." His voice was quiet, a monotone. He turned up the volume on the TV. "It's history, Kath. If you want to trot out the skeletons, let's talk about your dentist."

She remembered staring down at the remote control.

"Am I right?" he said.

She nodded.

"Fine," he said, "I'm right."

A moment later the phone rang. John picked it up and smiled at her. Later that evening, in the hotel's ballroom, he delivered a witty concession speech. Afterward, they held hands and waved at people and pretended not to know the things they knew.

All that pretending, she thought.

The teakettle made a sharp whistling sound. She watched John push to his feet, lift the teakettle off the stove, and move down the hallway toward the bedroom. After a second she nudged the screen door open and stepped inside. A foamy nausea had risen up inside her. She glanced over at the kitchen counter, where the telephone should have been. For a while she stood motionless, considering the possibilities.

The gas burner was still on. She turned it off and went into the living room. At that point a wire snapped inside her. The smell, perhaps. The dead plants, the puddle of water spreading out across the floorboards.

Right then, maybe, she walked away into the night.

Or maybe not.

Maybe instead, partly curious, partly something else, she moved down the hallway to the bedroom. At the doorway she paused briefly, not sure about the formations before her — the steam, the dark, John crouched at the side of the bed as if tending a small garden. He didn't turn or look up. He seemed to be touring other worlds. Quietly, almost as a question, Kathy said his name and then watched as he leaned across the bed and raised up the teakettle. There was the scent of wet wool. A hissing sound. He was chuckling to himself, saying, "Well, well," and in that instant she must have realized that remedies were beyond her and always had been.

The rest had to follow.

She would've turned away fast. Not afraid now, thinking only of disease, she would've grabbed a sweater and a pair of jeans, hurried back to the kitchen, laced up her sneakers, and headed down the dirt road toward the Rasmussen place. Then any number of possibilities. A wrong turn. A sprain or a broken leg.

Maybe she lost her way.

Maybe she's still out there.

10

The Nature of Love

They were at a fancy party one evening, a political affair, and after a couple of drinks John Wade took Kathy's arm and said, "Follow me." He led her out to the car and drove her home and carried her into the kitchen and made love to her there against the refrigerator. Afterward, they drove back to the party. John delivered a funny little speech. He ended with a couple of magic tricks, and people laughed and clapped hard, and when he walked off the platform, Kathy took his arm and said, "Follow me."

"Where?" John said.

"Outside. There's a garden."

"It's December. It's Minnesota."

Kathy shrugged. They had been married six years, almost seven. The passion was still there.

It was in the nature of love that John Wade went to the war. Not to hurt or be hurt, not to be a good citizen or a hero or a moral man. Only for love. Only to be loved. He imagined his father, who was dead, saying to him, "Well, you did it, you hung in there, and I'm so proud, just so incredibly proud." He imagined his mother ironing his uniform, putting it under clear plastic and hanging it in a closet, maybe to look at now and then, maybe to touch. At times, too, John imagined loving himself. And never risking the loss of love. And winning forever the love of some secret invisible audience—the people he might meet someday, the people he had already met. Sometimes he did bad things just to be loved, and sometimes he hated himself for needing love so badly.

In college John and Kathy used to go dancing at The Bottle Top over on Hennepin Avenue. They'd hold each other tight, even to the fast songs, and they'd dance until they couldn't dance anymore, and then they'd sit in one of the dark booths and play a game called Dare You. The rules were haphazard. "I dare you," Kathy might say, "to take off my panty hose," and John would contemplate the mechanics, the angles and resistances, and then he'd nod and slide a hand under the table. It was a way of learning about each other, a way of exploring the possibilities between them.

One night he dared her to steal a bottle of Scotch from behind the bar. "No sweat at all," Kathy said, "it's way *too* easy," and she straightened her skirt and got up and said a few words to the bartender, who went into a back room, then she strolled behind the bar and stood studying the selections for what seemed a very long while. Finally she made a so-what motion with her shoulders. She tucked a bottle under her jacket and returned to the booth and smiled at John and dared *him* to order two glasses.

He was crazy with love. He pulled off one of her white tennis shoes. With a ballpoint pen he wrote on the instep: JOHN + KATH. He drew a heart around these words, tied the shoe to her foot.

Kathy laughed at his corniness.

"Let's get married," he said.

First, though, there was Vietnam, where John Wade killed people, and where he composed long letters full of observations about the nature of their love. He did not tell her about the killing. He told her how lonely he was and how he wanted more than anything to sleep with his hand on the bone of her hip. He said he was lost without her. He said she was his compass. He said she was his sun and stars. He compared their love to a pair of snakes he'd seen along a trail near Pinkville, each snake eating the other's tail, a bizarre circle of appetites that brought the heads closer and closer until one of the men in Charlie Company used a machete to end it. "That's how our love feels," John wrote, "like we're swallowing each other up, except in a *good* way, a perfect Number One Yum-Yum way, and I can't wait to get home and see what would've happened if those two dumbass snakes finally ate each other's heads. Think about it. The mathematics get weird." In other letters he wrote about the great beauty of the country, the paddies and mountains and jungles. He told her about villages that vanished right before his eyes. He told her about his new nickname. "The guys call me Sorcerer," he wrote, "and I sort of like it. Gives me this zingy charged-up feeling, this special power or something, like I'm really in control of things. Anyhow, it's not so bad over here, at least for now. And I love you, Kath. Just like those weirdo snakes—one plus one equals zero!"

When he was young, nine or ten, John Wade would lie in bed with his magic catalogs, drawing up lists of the tricks he wanted—floating glass balls, colorful fekes and tubes, exploding balloons with flowers inside. He'd write down the prices in a little notebook, crossing out items he couldn't afford, and then on Saturday mornings he'd get up early and take the bus across town to Karra's Studio of Magic in St. Paul, all alone, a forty-minute ride.

Outside the store, on the sidewalk, he'd spend some time working up his nerve.

It wasn't easy. The place scared him. Casually, or trying to be casual, he'd gaze into the windows and stroll away a few times and then finally suck in a deep breath and think to himself: Go—Now, he'd think—Go!—and then he'd step inside, fast, scampering past the glass display cases, letting his head fill up with all the glittering equipment he knew by heart from his catalogs: Miser's Dream and Horn of Plenty and Chinese Rings and Spirit of the Dark. There were professional pulls and sponge balls and servantes—a whole shelf full of magician's silks—but in a way he didn't see anything at all.

A young orange-haired woman behind the counter would flick her eyebrows at him.

"*You!*" she'd cry.

The woman made his skin crawl. Her cigarette voice, partly. And her flaming carrot-colored hair.

"You!" she'd say, or she'd laugh and yell, "Hocus-pocus!" but by that point John would already be out the door. The whole blurry trip terrified him. Especially the Carrot Lady. The bright orange hair. The way she laughed and flicked her eyebrows and cried, "You!"—loud—as if she *knew* things.

The ride home was always dreary.

When he walked into the kitchen, his father would glance up and say, "Little Merlin," and his mother would frown and put a sandwich on the table and then busy herself at the stove. The whole atmosphere would tense up. His father would stare out the window for a time, then grunt and say, "So what's new in magic land? Big tricks up your sleeve?" and John would say, "Sure, sort of. Not really."

His father's hazy blue eyes would drift back to the window, distracted and expectant, as if he were waiting for some rare object to materialize there. Sometimes he'd shake his head. Other times he'd chuckle or snap his fingers.

"Those Gophers," he'd say. "Basketball fever, right? You and me, pal, we'll catch a game tomorrow." He'd grin across the table. "Right?"

"Maybe," John would say.

"Just maybe?"

"I got things to do."

Slowly then, his father's eyes would travel back to the window, still searching for whatever might be out there. The kitchen would seem very quiet.

"Well, sure, anything you want," his father would say. "Maybe's fine, kiddo. Maybe's good enough for me."

Something was wrong. The sunlight or the morning air. All around him there was machine-gun fire, a machine-gun wind, and the wind seemed to pick him up and blow him from place to place. He found a young woman laid open without a chest or lungs. He found dead cattle. There were fires, too. The trees and hootches and clouds were burning. Sorcerer didn't know where to shoot. He didn't know what to shoot. So he shot the burning trees and burning hootches. He shot the hedges. He shot the smoke, which shot back, then he took refuge behind a pile of stones. If a thing moved, he shot it. If a thing did not move, he shot it. There was no enemy to shoot, nothing he could see, so he shot without aim and without any desire except to make the terrible morning go away.

When it ended, he found himself in the slime at the bottom of an irrigation ditch.

PFC Weatherby looked down on him.

"Hey, Sorcerer," Weatherby said. The guy started to smile, but Sorcerer shot him.

John Wade was elected to the Minnesota State Senate on November 9, 1976. He and Kathy splurged on an expensive hotel suite in St. Paul, where they celebrated with a dozen or so friends. When the party ended, well after midnight, they ordered steaks and champagne from room service. "Mr. Senator Husband," Kathy kept saying, but John told her it wasn't necessary, she could call him Honorable Sir, and then he picked up a champagne bottle and used it as a microphone, peeling off his pants, gliding across the room and singing *Regrets, I've had a few*, and Kathy squealed and flopped back on the bed and grabbed her ankles and rolled around and laughed and yelled, "Honorable Senator Sir!" so John stripped off his shirt and made oily Sinatra moves and sang *The record shows I took the blows*, and Kathy's green eyes were wet and happy and full of the light that was only Kathy's light and could be no one else's.

One evening Charlie Company wandered into a quiet fishing village along the South China Sea. They set up a perimeter on the white sand, went swimming, dug in deep for the night. Around dawn they were hit with mortar fire. The rounds splashed into the ocean behind them—a bad scare, nobody was hurt—but when it was over, Sorcerer led a patrol into the village. It took almost an hour to round everyone up, maybe a hundred women and kids and old men. There was much chattering, much consternation as the villagers were ushered down to the beach for a magic show. With the South China Sea at his back, Sorcerer performed card tricks and rope tricks. He pulled a lighted cigar from his ear. He transformed a pear into an orange. He displayed an ordinary military radio and whispered a few words and made their village disappear. There was a trick to it, which involved artillery and white phosphorus, but the overall effect was spectacular.

A fine, sunny morning. Everyone sat on the beach and oohed and ahhed at the vanishing village.

"Fuckin' Houdini," one of the guys said.

As a boy John Wade spent hours practicing his moves in front of the old stand-up mirror down in the basement. He watched his mother's silk scarves change color, copper pennies becoming white mice. In the mirror, where miracles happened, John was no longer a lonely little kid. He had sovereignty over the world. Quick and graceful, his hands did things ordinary hands could not do—palm a cigarette lighter, cut a deck of cards with a turn of the thumb. Everything was possible, even happiness.

In the mirror, where John Wade mostly lived, he could read his father's mind. Simple affection, for instance. "Love you, cowboy," his father would think.

Or his father would think, "Hey, report cards aren't everything."

The mirror made this possible, and so John would sometimes carry it to school with him, or to baseball games, or to bed at night. Which was another trick: how he secretly kept the old stand-up mirror in his head. Pretending, of course—he understood that—but he felt calm and safe with the big mirror behind his eyes, where he could slide away behind the glass, where he could turn bad things into good things and just be happy.

The mirror made things better.

The mirror made his father smile all the time. The mirror made the vodka bottles vanish from their hiding place in the garage, and it helped with the hard, angry silences at the dinner table. "How's school these days?" his father would ask, in the mirror, which would permit John to ramble on about some of his problems, little things, school stuff, and in the mirror his father would say, "No problem, that's life, that's par for the course. Besides, you're my best pal." After dinner John would watch his father slip out to the garage. That was the worst part. The secret drinking that wasn't secret. But in the mirror, John would be there with him, and together they'd stand in the dim light, rakes and hoses and garage smells all around them, and his father would explain exactly what was happening and why it was happening. "One quickie," his father would say, "then we'll smash these goddamn bottles forever."

"To smithereens," John would say, and his father would say, "Right. Smithereens."

In all kinds of ways his father was a terrific man, even without the mirror. He was smart and funny. People enjoyed his company—John, too—and the neighborhood kids were always stopping by to toss around a football or listen to his father's stories and opinions and jokes. At school one day, when John was in sixth grade, the teacher made everyone stand up and give five-minute speeches about any topic under the sun, and a kid named Tommy Winn talked about John's father, what a neat guy he was, always friendly and full of pep and willing to spend time just shooting the breeze. At the end of the speech Tommy Winn gave John a sad, accusing look that lasted way too long. "All I wish," Tommy said, "I wish he was *my* father."

Except Tommy Winn didn't know some things.

How in fourth grade, when John got a little chubby, his father used to call him Jiggling John. It was supposed to be funny. It was supposed to make John stop eating.

At the dinner table, if things weren't silent, his father would wiggle his tongue and say, "Holy Christ, look at the kid stuff it in, old Jiggling John," then he'd glance over at John's mother, who would say, "Stop it, he's *husky*, he's not fat at *all*," and John's father would laugh and say, "Husky my ass."

Sometimes it would end there.

Other times his father would jerk a thumb at the basement door. "That pansy magic crap. What's wrong with baseball, some regular exercise?" He'd shake his head. "Blubby little pansy."

In the late evenings, just before bedtime, John and Kathy often went out for walks around the neighborhood, holding hands and looking at the houses and talking about which one they would someday have as their own. Kathy had fallen in love with an old blue Victorian across from Edgewood Park. The place had white shutters and a white picket fence, a porch that wrapped around three sides, a yard full of ferns and flower beds and azalea bushes. She'd sometimes pause on the sidewalk, gazing up at the house, her lips moving as if to memorize all its details, and on those occasions John would feel an almost erotic awareness of his own good fortune, a fluttery rush in the valves of his heart. He wished he could make things happen faster. He wished there were some trick that might cause a blue Victorian to appear in their lives.

After a time Kathy would sigh and give him a long sober stare. "Dare you to rob a bank," she'd say, which was only a way of saying that houses could wait, that love was enough, that nothing else really mattered.

They would smile at this knowledge and walk around the park a couple of times before heading back to the apartment.

Sorcerer thought he could get away with murder. He believed it. After he'd shot PFC Weatherby—which was an accident, the purest reflex—he tricked himself into believing it hadn't happened the way it happened. He pretended he wasn't responsible; he pretended he couldn't have done it and therefore hadn't; he pretended it didn't matter much; he pretended that if the secret stayed inside him, with all the other secrets, he could fool the world and himself too.

He was convincing. He had tears in his eyes, because it came from his heart. He loved PFC Weatherby like a brother.

"Fucking VC," he said when the chopper took Weatherby away. "Fucking *animals.*"

In 1982, at the age of thirty-seven, John Wade was elected lieutenant governor. He and Kathy had problems, of course, but they believed in happiness, and in their power to make happiness happen, and he was proud to stand with his hand on a Bible and look into Kathy's eyes and take the public oath even as he took his own private oath. He would devote more time to her. He would investigate the market in blue Victorians. He would change some things.

At the inaugural ball that evening, after the toasts and speeches, John led her out to the dance floor and looked directly at her as if for the first time. She wore a short black dress and glass earrings. Her eyes were only her eyes. "Oh,

Kath," he said, which was all he could think of to say, nothing else, just "Oh, Kath."

One day near Christmas, when John was eleven, his father drove him down to Karra's Studio of Magic to pick out his present.

"Anything you want," his father said. "No sweat. Break the bank."

The store hadn't changed at all—the same display cases, the same carrot-haired woman behind the cash register. Right away, when they walked in, she cried, *"You!"* and did the flicking thing with her eyebrows. She was dressed entirely in black except for a pair of copper bracelets and an amber necklace and two sparkling green stars pasted to her cheeks.

"The little magician," she said, and John's father laughed and said, "Little Merlin," and then for a long time the two of them stood talking like old friends.

John finally made a noise in his throat.

"Come on," he said, "we'll miss *Christmas*." He pointed at one of the display cases. "Right there."

"What?" said his father.

"That one. That's it."

His father leaned down to look.

"*There*," John said. "Guillotine of Death."

It was a substantial piece of equipment. Fifteen or sixteen pounds, almost two feet high. He'd seen it a hundred times in his catalogs—he knew the secret, in fact, which was simple—but he still felt a rubbery bounce in his stomach as the Carrot Lady lifted the piece of apparatus to the counter. It was shiny black with red enamel trim and a gleaming chrome blade.

The Carrot Lady nodded, almost tenderly. "My favorite," she said. "My favorite, too."

She turned and went into a storeroom and returned with a large cucumber. The sucker move, John knew—prove that the blade was sharp and real. She inserted the cucumber into the guillotine's wooden collar, clamped down a lock, stepped back, pulled up the chrome blade and let it fall. The cucumber lay on the counter in two neat halves.

"Good enough," said the Carrot Lady. She squinted up at John's father. "What we need now is an arm."

"Sorry?"

"Your arm," she said.

His father chuckled. "No way on earth."

"Off with the jacket."

His father tried to smile—a tall, solid-looking man, curly black hair and blue eyes and an athlete's sloping shoulders. It took him a long while to peel off his jacket.

"Guillotine of Death," he muttered. "Very unusual."

"Slip your wrist in there. No sudden movements."

"Christ," he said.

"That's the spirit," she said.

The Carrot Lady's eyes were merry as she hoisted up the blade. She held it there for a few seconds, then motioned for John to step behind the counter.

"You know this trick?" she said.

His father's eyes swept sideways. "Hell *no*, he doesn't know it."

"I do," John said. "It's easy."

"The kid doesn't have the slightest—"

"Simple," John said.

His father frowned, curled up his fingers, and frowned again. His forearm looked huge and meaty in the guillotine collar.

"Listen, what about *instructions?*" he said. "These things come with instructions, right? Seriously. Written-down instructions?"

"Oh, for Pete's sake," John said, "she *told* you to relax."

He grasped the blade handle.

Power: that was the thing about magic.

The Carrot Lady folded her arms. The green stars on her cheeks seemed to twinkle with desire.

"Go on," she said. "Let him have it."

There were times when John Wade wanted to open up Kathy's belly and crawl inside and stay there forever. He wanted to swim through her blood and climb up and down her spine and drink from her ovaries and press his gums against the firm red muscle of her heart. He wanted to suture their lives together.

It was terror, mostly. He was afraid of losing her. He had his secrets, she had hers.

So now and then he'd play spy tricks. On Saturday mornings he'd follow her over to the dry cleaners on Okabena Avenue, then to the drugstore and post office. Afterward, he'd tail her across the street to the supermarket, watching from a distance as she pushed a cart up and down the aisles, then he'd hustle back to the apartment and wait for her to walk in. "What's for lunch?" he'd ask, and Kathy would give him a quick look and say, "You tell me."

Briefly then, as she put the groceries away, Kathy's eyes would darken up with little flecks of gray. Such eyes, he'd think. He'd want to suck them from their sockets. He'd want to feel their weight on his tongue, taste the whites, roll them around like lemon drops.

Instead, he'd watch Kathy fold the grocery bags.

"You know, maybe I'm way off," she'd say, "but I get this creepy feeling. Like you're always there. Always worming around inside me."

John would smile his candidate's smile. "Very true. Not worming, though. Snaking."

"You didn't go out today?"

"Out where?"

"I don't know where. It just seemed—"

He'd pin her against the refrigerator, tight. He'd run a hand along the bone of her hip. He'd whisper in her ear. "Boy," he'd say, "do I *love* you. Boy, oh, boy."

"So you didn't go out?"

"Let's be cobras. You and me. Gobble each other up."

Sorcerer was in his element. It was a place with secret trapdoors and tunnels and underground chambers populated by various spooks and goblins, a place where magic was everyone's hobby and where elaborate props were always on hand—exploding boxes and secret chemicals and numerous devices of levitation—you could *fly* here, you could make *other* people fly—a place where the air itself was both reality and illusion, where anything might instantly become anything else. It was a place where decency mixed intimately with savagery, where you could wave your wand and make teeth into toothpaste, civilization into garbage—where you could intone a few syllables over a radio and then sit back to enjoy the spectacle—pure mystery, pure miracle—a place where every object and every thought and every hour seemed to glow with all the unspeakable secrets of human history. The jungles stood dark and unyielding. The corpses gaped. The war itself was a mystery. Nobody knew what it was about, or why they were there, or who started it, or who was winning, or how it might end. Secrets were everywhere—booby traps in the hedgerows, bouncing betties under the red clay soil. And the people. The silent papasans, the hollow-eyed children and jabbering old women. What did these people want? What did they feel? Who was VC and who was friendly and who among them didn't care? These were all secrets. History was a secret. The land was a secret. There were secret caches, secret trails, secret codes, secret missions, secret terrors and appetites and longings and regrets. Secrecy was paramount. Secrecy *was* the war. A guy might do something very brave—charge a bunker, maybe, or stand up tall under fire—and afterward everyone would look away and stay quiet for a while, then somebody would say, "How the fuck'd you *do* that?" and the brave guy would blink and shake his head, because he didn't know, because it was one of those incredible secrets inside him.

Sorcerer had his own secrets.

PFC Weatherby, that was one. Another was how much he loved the place—Vietnam—how it felt like home. And there was the deepest secret of all, which was the secret of Thuan Yen, so secret that he sometimes kept it secret from himself.

John Wade knew he was sick, and one evening he tried to talk about it with Kathy. He wanted to unload the horror in his stomach.

"It's hard to explain," he said, "but I don't feel real sometimes. Like I'm not *here.*"

They were in the apartment, making dinner, and the place smelled of onions and frying hamburger.

"You're real to me," Kathy said. "Very real, and very good."

"I hope so. Except I'm afraid to look at myself. Literally. I can't even look at my own eyes in the mirror, not for long. I'm afraid I won't be there."

Kathy glanced up from the onion she was chopping.

"Well, I adore looking at you," she said. "It's my second favorite thing to do."

"Good. I still wonder."

John put the hamburgers on a platter. Kathy dumped on the onions. She seemed nervous, as if she were aware of certain truths but could not bear to know what she knew, which was in the nature of their love.

"If you want," she said, "we'll skip supper. Do my favorite thing."

"I'm serious."

"So am I."

"Kath, listen, I need to *tell* you this. Something's wrong, I've *done* things."

"It doesn't matter."

"It does."

She smiled brightly at a spot over his shoulder. "We could catch a movie."

"Ugly things."

"A good movie wouldn't hurt."

"Christ, you're not—"

She picked up the hamburger platter. "We'll be fine. Totally fine."

"Sure," he said.

"Wait and see."

"Sure."

They were quiet for a moment. He looked at her, she looked at him. Anything could've happened.

———

74

Sorcerer didn't say a word about PFC Weatherby. It was reflex, after all. But for many days he felt a curious discomfort, almost giddy at times, almost sad at other times. On guard at night, watching the dark, Sorcerer would see PFC Weatherby start to smile, then topple backward, then make a funny jerking motion with his hand.

Like a hitchhiker, Sorcerer thought. A poor bum who couldn't catch a ride.

On the afternoon his father was buried, John Wade went down to the basement and practiced magic in front of his stand-up mirror. He did feints and sleights. He talked to his father. "I wasn't fat," he said, "I was *normal*." He transformed a handful of copper pennies into four white mice. "And I didn't jiggle. Not even once. I just *didn't*."

It was in the nature of their love that Kathy did not insist that he see a psychiatrist, and that John did not feel the need to seek help. By and large he was able to avoid the sickness down below. He moved with determination across the surface of his life, attending to a marriage and a career. He performed the necessary tricks, dreamed the necessary dreams. On occasion, though, he'd yell in his sleep—loud, desperate, obscene things—and Kathy would reach out and ask what was wrong. Her eyes would betray visible fear. "It wasn't even your *voice*," she'd say. "It wasn't *even you*."

John would force a laugh. He would have no memory beyond darkness.

"Bad dreams," he'd tell her, which he believed to be true, but which did not sound true, even to himself. He would hold her in his arms. He would lie there quietly, eyes wide open, taking from her skin what he needed.

And then later, sometimes for hours, Sorcerer would watch his wife sleep.

Sometimes he'd say things.

"Kath," he'd say, peering down at her, "Kath, my Kath," the palm of his hand poised above her lips as if to control the miracle of her breathing. In the dark, sometimes, he would see a vanishing village. He would see PFC Weatherby, and his father's white casket, and a little boy trying to manipulate the world. Other times he would see himself performing the ultimate vanishing act. A grand finale, a curtain closer. He did not know the technique yet, or the hidden mechanism, but in his mind's eye he could see a man and a woman swallowing each other up like that pair of snakes along the trail near Pinkville, first the tails, then the heads, both of them finally disappearing forever inside each other. Not a footprint, not a single clue. Purely gone—the trick of his life. The burdens of secrecy would be lifted. Memory would be null. They would live in perfect knowledge, all things visible, all things invisible, no wires or strings, just that large dark world where one plus one will always come to zero.

And so he'd lie watching her for much of the night.

"Kath, sweet Kath," he'd murmur, as if summoning her spirit, feeling the rise and fall of her breath against his hand.

11

What He Did Next

John Wade slept late the next morning, a jumpy electric sleep. It was almost noon by the time he'd showered and moved out to the kitchen. Still groggy, he brewed up a pot of coffee, scrambled three eggs, and carried his breakfast out to the porch. Another brilliant day: ivory clouds pinned to a glossy blue sky. He sat on the steps and ate his eggs. Little dream filaments kept unwinding in his head—hissing noises, a flapping sound.

At one point he glanced behind him, startled. "Hey, Kath," he said.

He listened.

Then he yelled, "Kath!"

Then he waited and yelled, "Kath, come *here* a minute!"

Inside, he rinsed the dishes and poured himself another cup of coffee. A half hour, he thought, and she'd show up. A nature hike or something. Most mornings she liked to head up along the shoreline or follow one of the trails out toward the fire tower.

Another half hour. An hour, tops.

Right now, he decided, it was time for some major house-cleaning. An unpleasant odor filled the air, a vegetable stink, and for starters he would do away with last night's debris. Tidy up the cottage, then go to work on his life. Wade compressed the idea into a firm resolution. Get up early from now on. Jog a few miles before breakfast, whittle off the campaign flab. Then sort through the larger mess. See if he could figure out a future for himself. Later in the day he'd sit down with Kathy and try to hammer out a few decisions; the first priority was their checkbook, a job of some sort. Make a few phone calls and see what pity could buy.

Shape up, he thought. Start now.

Moving briskly, Wade dug out a plastic garbage bag, marched into the living room, and collected the dead houseplants. He carried the bag outside and dumped it in one of the trash cans at the rear of the cottage. No doubt Kathy had discovered the wreckage that morning, or at least smelled it, and at some point soon he would have to come up with a fancy piece of defense work. Extenuating circumstances, he'd say. Which was the truth. A miserable night, nothing else, so he'd apologize and then prove to her that he was back in control. A solid citizen. Upright and virtuous.

The thought gave him energy.

He did a load of laundry, ran a mop across the kitchen floor. Already he felt better. A matter of willpower. For more than an hour he made his way through a stack of correspondence, setting aside a few items and junking the rest. Tidiness was paramount. He went through the bank statements, knocked off twenty sit-ups, put in another load of laundry, spent a few minutes wandering without aim from room to room. The place seemed curiously vacant. In the bedroom Kathy's slippers were aligned at the foot of the bed; her blue robe hung from its hook near the door. There was a faint scent of ammonia in the air. Quietly, afraid to disturb things, he moved down the hallway to the bathroom, where Kathy's toothbrush stood bristles-up in an old jelly jar. The water faucet was dripping. He turned it off. He listened for a moment, then returned to the kitchen.

It was a little after one-thirty. The fringes of the afternoon had already crossed into shadow.

Wade fixed himself a vodka tonic and carried it over to the kitchen window. Vaguely, without alarm, he wondered what was keeping her. Maybe payback. The plant thing would've turned her upside down, especially in light of other revelations, and no doubt she was now sending a message. Domestic screws: the contemplation of error and misdeed.

The thing to do, he reasoned, was maintain his resolve. Start by compiling a few lists. A self-improvement list, then a list of assets and debits, then a list of law firms in need of cheap labor. He poured another drink and sat down with a pencil and paper, letting the ideas come, cheerfully assembling a detailed list of all the fine lists he would make.

The booze was performing acrobatics on his nerves.

Nothing to it. Go with the lists.

At four o'clock he folded the laundry and did some random dusting. The afternoon had cooled fast. Restless, woozy at the margins, he freshened his drink and carried it out to the sofa in the living room. There was still that ammonia after-scent in the air, an operating room smell, and for a second he felt an illicit little tug at his memory. Something about the events of last night. Antiseptics and jungle smells.

He took a breath and lay back.

Gradually a nice calm came over him, the chemical somersaults, and for a considerable time he permitted himself the luxury of forgetfulness, no lists, no future at all, just the glide, exploring the void.

And then later, half dozing, John Wade detected movement in the room. Like a breeze, it seemed, as if a window had been left open, a motion so delicate he would both remember it and not remember it. A mind trick, for sure, but he could not ignore the pressure of Kathy's fingertips against the lids of his eyes. The surface tension was real. He heard her footsteps. He heard the low voice that could be only Kathy's voice. "So stupid," she said, "you could've *tried* me," and then came a fearful silence as she moved away, a drop in the temperature, a subtle relaxation in the magnetic force that one human body exerts upon another.

At six o'clock John Wade put on a jacket, fortified himself with a quick drink, and walked down to the dock. The evening had turned winter-cold. A wind was up, which put whitecaps on the lake, and the timber to the west had darkened to a dirty shade of gold.

What was necessary, Wade concluded, was the strictest allegiance to common sense. No cause for worry. Plenty of possibilities. He looked south toward the fire tower, then out at the whitecaps, then up at a sky painted in silky backlit blues. Already the first stars were out; in a half hour the darkness would be solid.

He stood still for a time, studying the shadows, trying to figure things.

"Okay," he said.

Something wobbled in his stomach. It wasn't right—he knew that.

Turning, he hustled back to the cottage, found a flashlight, and started up the dirt road toward the fire tower. He felt slippery inside, the vodka float.

Multiple calamities had come to mind. A bad fall. Lacerations, broken bones. Kathy was smart, yes, but she knew nothing about this wilderness. A suburb slicker. That was the joke between them: how she adored nature but didn't see why it had to be outside. Opposites were built into her personality. Contradiction was the rule. She enjoyed her morning stroll, the solitude and fresh air, but even then she conceived of nature as a department store with potted trees and a gigantic glass roof.

Which could turn unfortunate.

He moved fast, at times trotting, conscious of the approaching dark.

After ten minutes the road curved west and dipped down into a shallow ravine. Off to the left, a narrow footpath led into the woods toward the fire tower. Wade paused there, switched on the flashlight, scanned the cattails and deep brush. He edged forward a few steps, using the flashlight as a probe. Tempting, he thought. Plunge in and head for the fire tower. Except he was no trailblazer. The path wound off into soiled twilight purples, lavish and darkly tangled, vanishing altogether after a few yards. Everything blended with everything else, trees and brush and sky, and already he was on the edge of lost.

He stepped back onto the road and turned off his flashlight. There was a familiar breathing sound, something both distant and nearby.

"Kath?" he said.

He listened hard, shook his head.

Right now, he reasoned, she'd be back at the cottage. Not probably. For sure.

The notion calmed him. To be safe he hiked another quarter mile up the road, occasionally swinging the flashlight's yellow beam into the woods on both sides. At the old iron bridge over Tyne Creek, he stopped and called out her name a couple of times, softly at first, then louder, but there was only the near-far breathing in the dark.

Yo-yo, he told himself.

He turned back up the road.

It was a little past seven when he reached the cottage. He checked inside again, knowing she wasn't there, then transported a fresh drink out to the porch. The night was dull and ordinary, waves foaming up against the dock, a few tired loons. It was as if she'd gone next door to borrow something from a neighbor. Except there weren't any neighbors. A mile to the nearest occupied cottage, another eight miles to the nearest paved road. He looked down at the boathouse, then at the sky, then back to the boathouse. It occurred to him that he might call someone—Claude Rasmussen, maybe—but the idea seemed excessive. Any time now she'd come skipping up the road.

Absolutely.

It had to happen like that.

At nine o'clock he took a hot shower. At ten-thirty he finished off the vodka and switched to rum. Just after midnight a swell of nausea rose up into his throat, which turned to terror, and for the first time it came to him what must have happened.

He found the flashlight again and made his way down to the boathouse.

Not drunk, he told himself.

Unsteady, yes, but he could see things clearly. For more than an hour he'd been watching the image compose itself, a slow sharpening, the boathouse gradually taking shape. The tarpaper walls and sagging roof and stone foundation. The big double doors facing the lake.

There was no hurry. He knew exactly what he would find.

The night fog had settled in, which gave the earth a slick, mossy feel, and Wade found it necessary to assess each step for the possibility of hazard. He counted the reasons not to be afraid. She could handle herself. A good strong swimmer. And he loved her. That was the best reason, so much love, therefore nothing more could happen to them.

He nodded at this.

Ahead, the flashlight punched pale holes in the night. A gusty wind pressed in off the lake, and in the darkness there were numerous snappings and collisions. Oddly, he felt the desire to weep, but not the need.

Outside the boathouse, Wade paused to collect himself. The double doors stood partly open. The right panel dangled from its upper hinge, swaying slightly, its rusted hinge producing a soft, musical squeak.

It wasn't fear now. It was certainty.

He pulled the doors back, stepped inside, swung the flashlight across the dirt floor. There was no surprise. The boat was gone, as it had to be. The outboard was gone, too, and the gas can and the orange life vest and the two fiberglass oars.

Wade considered the facts. They had been married sixteen years, almost seventeen, and there was now the powerful certainty that the dominant track of his life had been permanently rerouted.

He stepped outside, closed the boathouse doors.

"So," he said, which sounded conclusive.

Briefly, he allowed Kathy's presence to make itself known —the trim, well-cared-for body, the campaign wrinkles at her eyes, the little-girl hands and summer skin and polished white smile. She knew things. No more secrets. She'd seen the headlines; she understood his capabilities.

In the dark she seemed to smile at him. Then she jerked sideways. Puffs of steam rose from the sockets of her eyes.

Impossible, of course.

He turned away, dug out his keys, and hurried up the slope to the Buick.

"I'm not drunk," Wade said.

"Who said drunk?"

"I'm *not*."

Ruth Rasmussen laid out a vinyl tablecloth, smoothed the edges, and brought over a mug of coffee. "Big swallow," she said. "It'll seal up the leaks."

"I'm sober."

"Sure you are. Down the happy hatch."

Ruth touched his shoulder and turned back to the stove. She was a large, sturdy woman in her mid-fifties, tall and rugged looking, with a graceful way of carrying the extra thirty pounds at her hips and belly. A spray of silvery black hair fell well below her shoulders.

"So just relax," she was saying. "Your wife's fine. One of those things."

"The boat, though. The boat's gone."

Ruth made an exasperated clucking sound. "Right, I believe

you mentioned the fact a couple thirty, forty times now. That's what boats are mostly *for*, they go places." She dropped a log into her wood cookstove, adjusted the flue valve, clanged down the iron cover. "Some dumb screw-up. The Evinrude clunked out on her, for sure that's what happened. Plugs or something. Cord got busted."

She turned and looked down at his coffee mug.

"Sugar?"

Wade shook his head. "It's not right. She wouldn't . . . It *feels* bad."

"Wait and see. Claude'll drive you back, check things out. Come on now, drain it."

The coffee was lukewarm and bitter, worse than bad, but Wade drank it down and started on another cup. After a minute Ruth put a loaf of bread in front of him.

"This much for sure," she said, "it don't help one bit to be negative. I bet it's that cruddy old outboard. Million times, I told Claude to spring cash money for a new one—billion times. Think he'd *do* it? No, sir. Not if it involves a wallet."

She chuckled at this and sat down across from him.

"Trick is to think positive. Think bad, get bad. Always works that way, seems to me."

Wade looked blankly at the table. His head hurt. His elbow joints, too, and other parts he couldn't locate. "It still feels wrong. Gone all day. Almost all night."

"Well, so the lady got herself stranded—so what? People run out of gas, lose an engine, all kinds of nutty stuff. Happens more than you think. Besides, your wife strikes me real solid, like somebody who can take care of herself." Ruth sprinkled brown sugar on a wedge of bread and slipped it across the table. "Great big bite, it'll soak up the poisons. Then we'll see what we see."

"Ruth, I don't think—"

"Eat."

Behind him, at the rear of the house, there was the sound of a toilet flushing. Claude Rasmussen came out carrying a pair of work boots and a corduroy hunting jacket. The old man went to the sink, hacked up some phlegm, spat, and bent forward to examine the discharge. He turned and looked up at Ruth.

"So how's our good senator?"

"Like a judge," she said. "Sober almost."

The old man grinned. He was pushing eighty, and showed it, but his eyes were still sharp and clear. After a moment he sat down and began lacing up his boots.

"Sober enough to navigate?"

"Just fine," Wade said.

"Sure you are. Finely lubricated, I'd say." Claude grinned again. "What we'll do is, we'll head down to the cottage, poke around a little. Ruth'll make a few calls into town." He shot a coded glance at his wife. "Try Vinny Pearson, the Mini-Mart, whoever else you can shake out."

Claude slid in a denture plate, bit down once, and pulled on a filthy Twins baseball cap.

"There's the program. Amendments, Senator?"

"Cute," Wade said.

"Well, yeah. I try."

Ruth slapped her big hands together. "Go on now. Things'll sort out."

Outside, Wade surrendered the keys and sat back as the old man swung the Buick into the fog. None of it seemed real. Like riding through someone else's life: the car and the road and the oncoming darkness. Claude drove one-handed, braking hard at the curves, his quick shrewd eyes scanning the road. The old man's health was failing—a bad heart and a half century of Pall Malls—but he still had the sly intelligence that had long ago made him a wealthy man. Though he found it convenient to pretend otherwise, Claude was no hick caretaker. He owned the cottage and plenty more—seven miles of shoreline, twelve thousand acres of prime timber butting up against state forest. He had the road access rights, too, which were leased out to Weyerhaeuser, and a major share in the two big resorts on the lake. Originally from Duluth, he'd made his money hauling taconite, trucks at first and then a small lake fleet, and for ten years Wade had known him casually as one of the old-time party contributors.

They were not friends in any meaningful sense. Barely acquaintances, really. But after the primary the only phone call that mattered had come from Claude Rasmussen. He'd offered the cottage and clean air and two weeks without newspapers. Which was enough. A tough bird, obviously, but right now toughness was a comfort.

At the cottage, where the road widened out, Claude cut the engine and let the car roll down the slope to the boathouse. For a few moments they sat quietly in the dark, letting their eyes adjust. The old man pulled a flashlight from the glove compartment. "How's the gyroscope? You can walk okay?"

"Perfect. I can walk *great*."

"Just a question." Claude made an indifferent motion with his shoulders. "Your breath, man—devil rum, smells like. Even an old goat like me, I can tell rum from crapola." He opened his door. "Let's see this terrific walk of yours."

The fog had stacked up thick along the shore, moist and

oily, and Wade felt an unpleasant weight in his lungs as he followed the old man over to the boathouse. Claude swung open the double doors and aimed his flashlight at the boat rack. Very pure, Wade thought. All that emptiness. After a time Claude tipped his cap back, squatted down, ran a hand along the dirt floor.

"Yeah, well," he said. "We got a gone boat."

"I told you."

"Sure, you told me." The old man stood up. He seemed to be listening for something. "Took herself a little ride. Don't mean diddly."

"She's not back yet."

"No kidding. That's what I admire about you, Senator. Plenty of optimism."

They went outside, checked the dock, then moved up through the rocks to the cottage. Inside, Wade snapped on the kitchen lights. Immediately he felt a new stiffness to the place, like a museum, everything frozen and hollow. He followed Claude from room to room, vaguely hopeful, but already a great stillness had entered the objects of their lives: her blue bathrobe, her slippers at the foot of the bed, the book of crossword puzzles folded open on the kitchen counter. That quick, Wade thought.

In the living room, Claude stopped and surveyed things. He looked puzzled. "The phone, man. Where's it at?"

"Around," Wade said. "I unplugged it."

"Unplugged?"

"What's the difference? We needed quiet, I put it away somewhere."

The old man sucked out his upper denture. He seemed to

be computing a run of numbers in his head. "Well, sure. Quiet's fine. Except I don't see why you had to go and hide the damn thing."

"I didn't *hide* it. I told you, it's here."

"Unplugged, though?"

"Yes."

Claude's eyes roamed. "So in other words there's no way your wife could've called? Like if she got stuck in town or got delayed or something?"

"I suppose not."

"You suppose?"

"Right. She couldn't."

Wade turned away. It took a few minutes to locate the telephone under the kitchen sink. He felt the old man's eyes tracking him as he carried it out to the living room and plugged it in.

Claude dialed, listened for a moment, and hung up.

"Busy," he said. "Ruth's probably got your lady on the horn right now."

"You think—"

"I think we cool our heels, don't get all panicked up."

"I'm not panicked," Wade said, "I'm worried."

"Fair enough, you're worried." The old man took off his cap and ran a hand across the top of his head, smoothing down hair that wasn't there. "No harm in worry, but I'll tell you a true fact. This place here, I've run it twenty-four straight years. Haven't lost one single paying customer. The factual truth. Not even one, except for a few dumbass fishermen, which I'm pissed to say wasn't permanent."

Wade shook his head. "Doesn't mean she's not in trouble."

"Right. It means we wait."

"Just sit?"

"Hell no, we don't just sit. Where's that knockout rum of yours?"

They moved out to the kitchen. Wade fixed a pair of drinks, passed one over to Claude, and looked up at the clock over the stove. Almost two in the morning. She'd been gone fifteen hours, maybe longer, and ugly pictures were beginning to form. Seaweed hair. A bottom-up boat.

Claude's voice seemed to come from Canada.

"I say, can she *swim?*"

"Swim?"

"Your wife."

Wade blinked and nodded. "Yes. Good swimmer."

"Well, there you are then, hey?"

"But it seems like—I don't know—like we should get out there and start looking."

"Look where?"

"Anywhere. Just look."

Claude was chewing on an ice cube. He squinted down at his drink, then sighed and swallowed. "Maybe you didn't notice," he said, "but it's dead dark out there. Black as sin—that's item one. Plus we got fog. Plus a couple thousand square miles of water, not to mention forest, not to mention God knows how many islands and sand bars and crap. Can't accomplish a damn thing."

"The police, then."

"What police? Vinny Pearson, he runs the Texaco station, Vinny's the police. Gets eighty bucks a month part-time—what's he gonna do? I'll *tell* you what. He's gonna say, 'Man, get your ass back to sleep,' which is pretty much what

I say. Nothing we can do till morning, that's a fact. Worst it can be, your wife's beached up somewhere."

"No way," Wade said.

"You sound awful certain."

"A feeling. I know."

"You know?"

"That's right."

Claude removed his cap again. He was silent for a while, studying a spot at the center of Wade's forehead. "One thing I'm curious about. You two lovebirds didn't . . . There wasn't like a fight or something?"

"No."

"A spat, I mean?"

"Of course not."

The old man frowned. "No big deal. Like with Ruth and me, sometimes we get itchy in the temper. She'll say something, I'll say something, pretty soon we're pitching hand grenades across the kitchen. It happens that way."

"Not with us," Wade said. "I woke up this morning, Kathy was gone."

"That's it?"

"Everything."

"Well, good. There we are." The old man leaned back in his chair. There was a question in his eyes, something that hadn't yet shaped itself. He gazed thoughtfully at a stack of empty flowerpots on the kitchen counter.

"No fight, no problem," he finally said. "I was you, Senator, I'd just give it time, see what Ruth comes up with."

"Let's dispense with the senator shit."

"Wasn't meant to offend."

"Just lay off. I'm no senator."

Claude smiled. "Got thumped pretty bad. Three to one, I guess."

"Close enough."

"Damn pity. Democrats, they're a tough bunch to please. Like with me, I'm what you call a real true-blue Minnesota DFLer. Hubert and Orville and Floyd B. Olson—that crew —the old kickass corn-farmer boys. Meat and potatoes, so to speak. Say what you mean, mean what you say. One thing I don't care for, it's pussyfoot politics."

There was silence while the old man refilled his glass.

"Anyhow," he said, "can't say I voted for you."

Wade shrugged. "Not many can."

"Nothing personal."

"No. It never is."

Claude gave him a sidelong glance, amused. "Other hand, I'm not saying I *didn't*. Maybe so, maybe not. What surprised me—the thing I don't get—you never once asked for help. Money-wise, I mean. You could've asked."

"And then what?"

"Hard to say. People claim I'm a sucker for lost causes." The old man hesitated. "Truth is, you didn't have a Chinaman's prayer, not after all that nasty shit hit the papers. Even so, I might've tossed in a few bucks."

"Well, good. The thought counts."

"A hatchet job. Made you look . . . I guess it's not something you care to talk about?"

"I guess not."

The old man nodded. He glanced at the clock and pushed himself up. "Sit tight, I'll try Ruth again."

Wade's head was pounding. That fuzzy, seasick feeling had settled back over him; he couldn't make the ugly pictures go away. The debris was bobbing up all around him. Ghosts and algae and bits of bone.

He listened as Claude dialed. The old man spoke quietly for a few minutes, then sighed and hung up. "No luck. Ruth'll keep at it, plenty more names to call."

"The police," Wade said.

"Maybe."

"Not maybe. Kathy's out there, we need to get something started. Right now."

The old man stuffed his hands in his back pockets. Absently, frowning slightly, he looked at the stack of clay pots near the sink. "Well, see, I already explained, Vinny ain't no Kojak. All he can do is call down to the sheriff in Baudette. Put out some boats, line up a plane or two."

"That's a start," Wade said. "It's something."

"I guess."

"So let's move."

Claude was still evaluating the empty pots. He waited a moment, then crossed over to the kitchen sink.

"Those flowers, man. What the hell happened?"

"Nothing," Wade said. "An accident."

"Yeah?"

"Claude, we're wasting time."

A little vein wobbled at the old man's forehead. He picked up one of the pots and turned it in his hands. "Some accident," he said.

12

Evidence

It has been said that a miracle is the result of causes with which we are unacquainted. Once these causes are discovered we no longer have a miracle, but natural law . . . In a way, all of us dislike the laws of nature. We should prefer to make things happen in the more direct way in which savage people imagine them to happen, through our own invocation.[1]
—Robert Parrish (*The Magician's Handbook*)

He actually *thought* of himself as Sorcerer, that's how it seemed to me, and Kathy was his main audience. I can't see how she put up with it. Maybe she hoped he'd pull off a real miracle or something. For her own life, I mean. I guess sometimes my sister thought of him as Sorcerer too.
—Patricia S. Hood

For the spectator there is the complementary pleasure of yielding passively to an omnipotent and mysterious force, of

---

1. Parrish, *The Magician's Handbook*, p. 15.

submitting helplessly to mounting swells of excitement where reason is overthrown and judgment scuttled.[2]
—Bernard C. Meyer (*Houdini: A Mind in Chains*)

He was a charmer. Literally. Wrap you up in charms till you couldn't fucking move.
—Anthony L. (Tony) Carbo

A nice, polite man, if you ask me.
—Ruth Rasmussen

Kathy *knew* he had these secrets, things he wouldn't talk about. She *knew* about the spying. Maybe I'm wrong but it was like she needed to be part of it. That whole sick act of his.
—Bethany Kee (Associate Admissions Director, University of Minnesota)

. . . you may find yourself crying in corners and vowing that his buddies may have died on him in Vietnam, the brass may have turned its collective back on him, but you will never desert him. He needs you. Whether he can say it or not, whether he can act like it or not, he needs you.[3]
—Patience H. C. Mason (*Recovering from the War*)

---

2. Bernard C. Meyer, *Houdini: A Mind in Chains* (New York: E. P. Dutton, 1976), p. 136.

3. Patience H. C. Mason, *Recovering from the War: A Woman's Guide to Helping Your Vietnam Vet, Your Family, and Yourself* (New York: Penguin, 1990), p. 12.

I guess Kathy loved him so much she couldn't see what was happening all around her. Like this pixie dust. Sprinkle on the love, you end up fooling yourself.

—Patricia S. Hood

Audiences want to believe what they see a magician do, and yet at the same time they know better and do not believe. Therein lies the fascination of magic to modern people. It is a paradox, a riddle, a half-fulfillment of an ancient desire, a puzzle, a torment, a cheat and a truth.[4]

—Robert Parrish (*The Magician's Handbook*)

Exhibit Eight: John Wade's Box of Tricks, Partial List
Chinese Rings
Lota Bowl
Sponge balls
Stripper deck
Magician's wax
Postcard from father (dated July 19, 1956, photograph of un-
    identified granite building, handwriting largely illegible,
    ". . . out of here soon . . . can't wait to . . . Dad")
Magician's milk (2 cans)
Silk load
Book: *Time Telepathy*
Book: *Tarbell Course in Magic, Vol. I*
Assorted catalogs, Karra's Studio of Magic

That summer when John was eleven it got to where I didn't have any choice. The drinking just got worse and worse. His father would be down at the American Legion all afternoon

---

4. Parrish, *The Magician's Handbook*, p. 16.

and half the night. Finally I got up the nerve to check him into the state treatment center up north. I hate to say it, but it was a relief to have him out of the house. John and I, we both adored the man, but suddenly all the tension was gone and we could have supper without sitting there on the edge of our seats . . . A couple of times we drove up to visit John's dad on weekends. We'd go out on this grassy lawn and eat picnic lunches and . . . Well, it was nice. I remember one time—we were getting ready to leave—I remember his father walked us over to the car and put his arms around me and kissed me and almost cried and said he loved me and he was sorry and everything would be better now. It wasn't, though. It never got much better.

—Eleanor K. Wade

In every trick there are two carefully thought out lines—the way it looks and the way it is. The success of your work depends upon your understanding the relationship of these lines.[5]

—Robert Parrish (*The Magician's Handbook*)

I'm no psychiatrist, but if you ask me, politicians in general are pretty insecure people. Look at me—fat as a pig. Love-starved. [Laughter] So we go public. We're performers. We get up on stage and sing and dance and do our little show, anything to please folks, anything for applause. Like children. Just suck up the love.

—Anthony L. (Tony) Carbo

---

5. Ibid., p. 122.

John used to come into the store a lot. Ten, eleven years old. At first he seemed frightened, but after a while he started spending almost every Saturday there. A nice kid, I thought. I'd show him the new effects that came in—effects, that's what we call tricks—and we'd practice them together . . . He always called me the Carrot Lady, even when he got older. I doubt if he even knew my real name.[6]

—Sandra Karra (Karra's Studio of Magic)

If you want to find help for your vet, avoid churches that ascribe evil to outside forces, the devil tempting or taking over people. One reason for this is that maintaining an external locus of control ("the devil made me do it") precludes adult responses such as growing and profiting from experience.[7]

—Patience H. C. Mason (*Recovering from the War*)

Millions of them. Big mean fuckers. These were some very pissed-off flies.

—Richard Thinbill

The fact that a person acted pursuant to order of his Government or of a superior does not relieve him from responsibility under international law . . .[8]

—The Nuremberg Principles

GLOSSARY

Load: A hidden packet or bundle of objects to be magically produced.

---

6. Interview, St. Paul, Minnesota, December 16, 1991.

7. Mason, *Recovering from the War: A Woman's Guide to Helping Your Vietnam Vet, Your Family, and Yourself*, p. 320.

8. The Nuremberg Principles, 1946, Principle IV.

Lota Bowl: A piece of magical apparatus which appears to be empty or filled with liquid, at the magician's whim.

Misdirection: Any technique used by a magician to divert the audience's attention from noticing some secret maneuver.[9]

Dear Kath,

This letter will be short because there's not much to say right now. All I can think about is hopping on that freedom bird and heading home and getting married and spending the next ten years in bed. (Horny, horny!) Basically, things have been pretty tense lately. We keep taking casualties, mostly booby traps and stuff, but we can't ever find old Victor Charlie. It gets frustrating and I guess everybody's kind of woundup. Hard to describe. Like this weird infection or something. Sometimes you can almost smell it, or taste it, like there's something wrong with the air. Anyhow, I've made it this far, so I guess I'll be okay. I love you. Just like those two weirdo snakes I mentioned. One plus one equals zero!

Eternally horny,
"Sorcerer"

—John Wade (Letter, January 13, 1968)

The point of greatest danger for an individual confronted with a crisis is not during the period of preparation for the battle, nor fighting the battle itself, but in the period immediately after the battle is over. Then, completely exhausted and drained emotionally, he must watch his decisions most carefully. There is an increased possibility of error because he

---

9. Marvin Kaye, *The Stein and Day Handbook of Magic* (New York: Stein and Day, 1973), pp. 303, 305.

may lack the necessary cushion of emotional and mental re-serve which is essential for good judgment.[10]
—Richard M. Nixon

[After his 1941 defeat] Johnson's frustration and rage erupted over hapless aides . . . [He was] screaming and hollering, and throwing his arms . . .[11]
—Robert A. Caro (*The Years of Lyndon Johnson*)

We knew it was coming, sure, but I guess John hoped he had one more miracle up his sleeve. Didn't pan out. That last night, when the returns started coming in, he had this blank expression on his face. I can't pin it down exactly. Just empty. Like a walking dead man. Defeat does things to people.
—Anthony L. (Tony) Carbo

He drank some, that's true. Clobbered like that—who wouldn't?[12]
—Ruth Rasmussen

A candidate who has lost an election for the presidency, after all he has gone through in the campaign, is literally in a state of shock for at least a month after the election.[13]
—Thomas E. Dewey

John called me that night. He sounded almost asleep. I guess the emotion came later—a delayed shock or something. He was always the type to stew, just like his father.
—Eleanor K. Wade

---

10. Richard M. Nixon, *Six Crises* (New York: Doubleday & Co., 1962), pp. 120–121.

11. Caro, *The Years of Lyndon Johnson: The Path to Power*, p. 740.

12. See Exhibit Nine.

13. Thomas E. Dewey, in Nixon, *Six Crises*, p. 423.

The cruel circumstances attending [Al Smith's] defeat caused the memory of it to rankle in him for a long time . . . Like everyone else, he wanted to be loved.[14]

> —Matthew and Hannah Josephson (*Al Smith: Hero of the Cities*)

Exhibit Nine: Primary Election Results, Democratic Farmer Labor Party, State of Minnesota, September 9, 1986

Durkee—73%

Wade—21%

Other—6%[15]

---

14. Matthew and Hannah Josephson, *Al Smith: Hero of the Cities* (Boston: Houghton Mifflin Co., 1969), p. 403.

15. Aren't we all? John Wade—he's beyond knowing. He's an other. For all my years of struggle with this depressing record, for all the travel and interviews and musty libraries, the man's soul remains for me an absolute and impenetrable unknown, a nametag drifting willy-nilly on oceans of hapless fact. Twelve notebooks' worth, and more to come. What drives me on, I realize, is a craving to force entry into another heart, to trick the tumblers of natural law, to perform miracles of knowing. It's human nature. We are fascinated, all of us, by the implacable otherness of others. And we wish to penetrate by hypothesis, by daydream, by scientific investigation those leaden walls that encase the human spirit, that define it and guard it and hold it forever inaccessible. ("I love you," someone says, and instantly we begin to wonder—"Well, how much?"—and when the answer comes—"With my whole heart"—we then wonder about the wholeness of a fickle heart.) Our lovers, our husbands, our wives, our fathers, our gods—they are all beyond us.

101

13

The Nature of the Beast

The war was aimless. No targets, no visible enemy. There was nothing to shoot back at. Men were hurt and then more men were hurt and nothing was ever gained by it. The ambushes never worked. The patrols turned up nothing but women and kids and old men.

"Like that bullshit kid's game," Rusty Calley said one evening. "They hide, we seek, except we're chasin' a bunch of gookish fucking ghosts."

In the dark someone did witch imitations. Someone else laughed. For Sorcerer, who sat listening at his foxhole, the war had become a state of mind. Not bedlam exactly, but the din was nearby.

"Eyeballs for eyeballs," Calley said. "One of your famous Bible regulations."

All through February they worked an AO called Pinkville, a chain of dark, sullen hamlets tucked up against the South China Sea. The men hated the place, and feared it. On their maps the sector was shaded a bright shimmering pink to signify a "built-up area," with many hamlets and paddy dikes and fields of rice. But for Charlie Company there was nothing bright about Pinkville. It was spook country. The geography of evil: tunnels and bamboo thickets and mud huts and graves.

On February 25, 1968, they stumbled into a minefield near a village called Lac Son.

"I'm killed," someone said, and he was.

A steady gray rain was falling. Thunder advanced from the mountains to the west. After an hour a pair of dustoff choppers settled in. The casualties were piled aboard and the helicopters rose into the rain with three more dead, twelve more wounded.

"Don't mean zip," Calley said. His face was childlike and flaccid. He turned to one of the medics. "What's up, doc?"

Three weeks later, on March 14, a booby-trapped 155 round blew Sergeant George Cox into several large wet pieces. Dyson lost both legs. Hendrixson lost an arm and a leg.

Two or three men were crying. Others wanted to cry but couldn't remember how.

In the late afternoon of March 15 John Wade received a short letter from Kathy. It was composed on light blue stationery with a strip of embossed gold running along the top margin. Her handwriting was dark and confident.

"What I hope," she wrote him, "is that someday you'll understand that I need things for myself. I need a productive future—a real life. When you get home, John, you'll have to treat me like the human being I am. I've grown up. I'm different now, and you are too, and we'll both have to make adjustments. We have to be looser with each other, not so wound up or something—you can't *squeeze* me so much—I need to feel like I'm not a puppet. Anyway, just so you know, I've been going out with a couple of guys. It's nothing serious. Repeat: nothing serious. I love you, and I think we can be wonderful together."

Sorcerer wrote back that evening: "What do you get when you breed VC with rats?"

He smiled to himself and jotted down the answer on a separate slip of paper.

"Midget rats," he wrote.

At 7:22 on the morning of March 16, 1968, the lead elements of Charlie Company boarded a flight of helicopters that climbed into the thin, rosy sunlight, gathered into assault formation, then banked south and skimmed low and fast over scarred, mangled, bombed-out countryside toward a landing zone just west of Pinkville.

Something was wrong.

Maybe it was the sunlight.

Sorcerer felt dazed and half asleep, still dreaming wild dawn dreams. All night he'd been caught up in pink rivers and pink paddies; even now, squatting at the rear of the chopper, he couldn't flush away the pink. All that color—it was wrong. The air was wrong. The smells were wrong, and the thin rosy sunlight, and how the men seemed wrapped inside themselves. Meadlo and Mitchell and Thinbill sat with their eyes closed. Sledge fiddled with his radio. Conti was off in some mental whorehouse. PFC Weatherby kept wiping his M-16 with a towel, first the barrel and then his face and then the barrel again. Boyce and Maples and Lieutenant Calley sat side by side in the chopper's open doorway, sharing a cigarette, quietly peering down at the cratered fields and paddies.

Pure wrongness, Sorcerer knew.

He could taste the sunlight. It had a rusty, metallic flavor, like nails on his tongue.

For a few seconds Sorcerer shut his eyes and retreated behind the mirrors in his head, pretending to be elsewhere, but even then the landscapes kept coming at him fast and lurid.

At 7:30 the choppers banked in a long arc and approached the hamlet of Thuan Yen from the southwest. Below, almost straight ahead, white puffs of smoke opened up in the paddies just outside the village. The artillery barrage swept across the fields and into the western fringes of Thuan Yen, cutting through underbrush and bamboo and banana trees, setting fires here and there, shirting northward as the helicopters skimmed in low over the drop zone. The door gunners were now laying down a steady suppressing fire. They leaned into their big guns, shoulders twitching. The noise made Sorcerer's eyelids go haywire.

"Down and dirty!" someone yelled, and the chopper settled into a wide dry paddy.

Mitchell was first off. Then Boyce and Conti and Meadlo, then Maples, then Sledge, then Thinbill and the stubby lieutenant.

Sorcerer went last.

He jumped into the sunlight, fell flat, found himself alone in the paddy. The others had vanished. There was gunfire all around, a machine-gun wind, and the wind seemed to pick him up and blow him from place to place. He couldn't keep his legs beneath him. For a time he lay pinned down by things unnatural, the wind and heat, the wicked sunlight. He would not remember pushing to his feet. Directly ahead, a pair of stately old coconut trees burst into flame.

Just inside the village, Sorcerer found a pile of dead goats.

He found a pretty girl with her pants down. She was dead too. She looked at him cross-eyed. Her hair was gone.

He found dead dogs, dead chickens.

Farther along, he encountered someone's forehead. He found three dead water buffalo. He found a dead monkey. He found ducks pecking at a dead toddler. Events had been channeling this way for a long while, months of terror, months of slaughter, and now in the pale morning sunlight a kind of meltdown was in progress.

Pigs were squealing.

The morning air was flaming up toward purple.

He watched a young man hobbling up a trail, one foot torn away at the ankle. He watched Weatherby shoot two little girls in the face. Deeper into the village, in front of a small L-shaped hootch, he came across a GI with a woman's black ponytail flowing from his helmet. The man wiped a hand across his crotch. He gave a little flip to the ponytail and smiled at Sorcerer and blooped an M-79 round into the L-shaped hootch. "Blammo," the man said. He shook his head as if embarrassed. "Yeah, well," he said, then shrugged and fired off another round and said, "Boom." At his feet was a wailing infant. A middle-aged woman lay nearby. She was draped across a bundle of straw, not quite dead, shot in the legs and stomach. The woman gazed at the world with indifference. At one point she made an obscure motion with her head, a kind of bow, inexact, after which she rocked herself away.

There were dead waterfowl and dead house pets. People were dying loudly inside the L-shaped hootch.

Sorcerer uttered meaningless sounds—"No," he said, then

after a second he said, "Please!"—and then the sunlight sucked him down a trail toward the center of the village, where he found burning hootches and brightly mobile figures engaged in murder. Simpson was killing children. PFC Weatherby was killing whatever he could kill. A row of corpses lay in the pink-to-purple sunshine along the trail—teenagers and old women and two babies and a young boy. Most were dead, some were almost dead. The dead lay very still. The almost-dead did twitching things until PFC Weatherby had occasion to reload and make them fully dead. The noise was fierce. No one was dying quietly. There were squeakings and chickenhouse sounds.

"Please," Sorcerer said again. He felt very stupid. Thirty meters up the trail he came across Conti and Meadlo and Rusty Calley. Meadlo and the lieutenant were spraying gunfire into a crowd of villagers. They stood side by side, taking turns. Meadlo was crying. Conti was watching. The lieutenant shouted something and shot down a dozen women and kids and then reloaded and shot down more and then reloaded and shot down more and then reloaded again. The air was hot and wet. "Jeez, come *on*," the lieutenant said, "get with it—*move*—light up these fuckers," but Sorcerer was already sprinting away. He ran past a smoking bamboo schoolhouse. Behind him and in front of him, a brisk machine-gun wind pressed through Thuan Yen. The wind stirred up a powdery red dust that sparkled in the morning sunshine, and the little village had now gone mostly violet. He found someone stabbing people with a big silver knife. Hutto was shooting corpses. T'Souvas was shooting children. Doherty and Terry were finishing off the wounded. This was not madness, Sorcerer understood. This was sin. He felt it winding through his own arteries, something vile and slippery like heavy black oil in a crankcase.

Stop, he thought. But it wouldn't stop. Someone shot an old farmer and lifted him up and dumped him in a well and tossed in a grenade.

Roschevitz shot people in the head.

Hutson and Wright took turns on a machine gun.

The killing was steady and inclusive. The men took frequent smoke breaks; they ate candy bars and exchanged stories.

A period of dark time went by, maybe an hour, maybe more, then Sorcerer found himself on his hands and knees behind a bamboo fence. A few meters away, in the vicinity of a large wooden turret, fifteen or twenty villagers squatted in the morning sunlight. They were chattering among themselves, their faces tight, and then somebody strolled up and made a waving motion and shot them dead.

There were flies now—a low droning buzz that swelled up from somewhere deep inside the village.

And then for a while Sorcerer let himself glide away. All he could do was close his eyes and kneel there and wait for whatever was wrong with the world to right itself. At one point it occurred to him that the weight of this day would ultimately prove too much, that sooner or later he would have to lighten the load.

He looked at the sky.

Later he nodded.

And then later still, snagged in the sunlight, he gave himself over to forgetfulness. "Go away," he murmured. He waited a moment, then said it again, firmly, much louder, and the little village began to vanish inside its own rosy glow. Here, he reasoned, was the most majestic trick of all. In the months and years ahead, John Wade would remember Thuan Yen the way chemical nightmares are remembered, impossible combinations, impossible events, and over time the impossibility itself would become the richest and deepest and most profound memory.

This could not have happened. Therefore it did not.

Already he felt better.

Tracer rounds corkscrewed through the glare, and people were dying in long neat rows. The sunlight was in his blood.

He would both remember and not remember a fleet human movement off to his left.

He would not remember squealing.

He would not remember raising his weapon, nor rolling away from the bamboo fence, but he would remember forever how he turned and shot down an old man with a wispy beard and wire glasses and what looked to be a rifle. It was not a rifle. It was a small wooden hoe. The hoe he would always remember. In the ordinary hours after the war, at the breakfast table or in the babble of some dreary statehouse hearing, John Wade would sometimes look up to see the wooden hoe spinning like a baton in the morning sunlight. He would see the old man shuffling past the bamboo fence, the skinny legs, the erect posture and the wire glasses, the hoe suddenly sailing up high and doing its quick twinkling spin and coming down uncaught. He would feel only the faintest sense of culpability. The forgetting trick mostly worked. On certain late-night occasions, however, John Wade would remember covering his head and screaming and crawling through a hedgerow and out into a wide paddy where helicopters were ferrying in supplies. The paddy was full of colored smoke, lavenders and yellows. There were loud voices, and many explosions, but he couldn't seem to locate anyone. He found a young woman laid open without a chest or lungs. He found dead cattle. All around him there were flies and burning trees and burning hootches.

Later, he found himself at the bottom of an irrigation ditch. There were many bodies present, maybe a hundred. He was caught up in the slime.

PFC Weatherby found him there.

"Hey, Sorcerer," Weatherby said. The guy started to smile, but Sorcerer shot him anyway.

14

Hypothesis

What happened, maybe, was that Kathy drowned. Something freakish: a boating accident. Maybe a sandbar. Maybe she was skimming along, moving fast, feeling the cold spray and wind and sunlight, and then came a cracking sound, a quick jolt, and she felt herself being picked up and carried—a moment of incredible lightness, an unburdening, a soaring sensation —and then the lake was all around her, and soon inside her, and maybe in that way Kathy was drowned and gone.

The purest speculation, just one possibility out of many, but Kathy might've awakened early that morning.

Maybe for a few moments she watched him sleep. It had been a bad night, like so many other nights, and the sockets of John's eyes looked dark and old. At times she barely recognized him. All that rage—it was like some terrible virus that kept multiplying inside him. She wished there was a cure she could offer, or words she could say, but of course there was nothing.

Maybe she leaned over and kissed him. Maybe she whispered something.

It was still dark, almost certainly, when she slipped out of bed. She showered, dried her hair, checked her eyes for new wrinkles, returned to the bedroom, and put on a pair of faded blue jeans and a white cotton sweater. She was careful not to wake him. She hung her bathrobe on its hook near the door, aligned her slippers at the foot of the bed. In her stocking feet, trying for silence, she moved out to the kitchen and went about her morning routine. Orange juice and vitamins. Strong black coffee. A bowl of Wheaties, no sugar. She ate slowly, content to be alone, enjoying the stillness all around her. This was her favorite part of the day: the unfolding light, the fragile gleamings and stirrings. After breakfast she brushed her teeth, vigorously, rinsing the brush and leaving it bristles-up in the old jelly jar on the bathroom sink. She washed her dishes, wiped the counter. All these were rituals, fixed and solid.

And then for fifteen minutes, over a second cup of coffee, she sat at the kitchen table with her book of crossword puzzles. This, too, was a ritual. She liked to start each day with a sense of accomplishment, solving what could be solved.

Outside, the first smoky light had spilled out over the lake, and for a few seconds Kathy gazed without focus out the kitchen window, maybe daydreaming, maybe hoping that today things might finally turn good again. Pack a picnic lunch. Go for a swim and lie in the sun and talk about their lives. Which was one of the problems—they never talked anymore. They never communicated, they never made love. They'd tried once, on their second night, but it had been an embarrassment for both of them, and now it seemed they were always guarding their bodies, always careful, touching only for comfort and closeness. What they needed, she thought, was to be honest. Talk about everything they'd never talked about—trust and love and hurt, their truest feelings. Get him to open up. And then if things went well, if she could find the nerve, maybe then she'd confide her own big secret, just blurt it out. Tell him she was glad it was over. A relief, she'd say. No more elections. All that was finished and now she could confess to how much she'd always hated it. The polls and cameras and crowds. Real hate, she'd say. She hated the speeches and petty conspiracies and fake smiles and greedy old pols with their Velcro votes and greasy hands. She hated the stink of cigarettes and betrayal. There were times, she'd tell him, when the hating made her stomach hurt; it was like a rock inside her, a huge heavy rock, and she'd *tell* him that. Maybe she'd break down. Maybe she'd cry. Probably not. For sure, though, she would be clear about how much she hated tying her self-esteem to the whims of idiots. And the public eye. How it made her feel exposed and naked. How she couldn't tolerate another convention hall or another baked bean dinner or another soggy paper plate. Hate, she'd say. Deep, thick, honest hate. She would present a long, detailed list of the things she hated, and at the end she'd tell him that what she despised more than anything was what politics had done to their lives, how it had taken away everything she most wanted. Ordinary peace. A decent house, a baby to love. To say these things might be difficult—it had to be—but she wouldn't hold back. She'd tell him how the landslide had come as a soft warm rush, a release, like carrying around an enormous weight for years and years and then suddenly putting it down and feeling an incredible new lightness flow into her chest and stomach.

Glad, she'd say. She couldn't help it. It was all over and she was glad.

Kathy closed her eyes.

Don't cry, she thought. Then she said it aloud: "You jerk, just *don't*."

She sighed and went to the stove, refilled her coffee cup, and stood motionless for a time before returning to the crossword puzzle. It was just after six o'clock. Flakes of speckled light filled the kitchen. "Well, that's better," she said, and then for five or ten minutes she sat filling in the grid of squares, effortlessly, almost without thought, as if the puzzle were solving itself.

She felt calm and alert, a locking sensation, things in balance.

And so maybe then, gradually at first, Kathy became attuned to a curious new odor in the air. A foul tartness, like spoiled fruit. The smell had been there all along, in her coffee and orange juice, but now it seemed to condense into something solid.

Maybe at first she ignored it. Maybe she frowned and went back to the puzzle.

Or maybe, instead, she put down her pencil and got up to check the refrigerator and garbage pail. She would've tested the air again, maybe squinting, maybe not, then quietly followed her nose out to the living room. At that point things would've accelerated. She would've said something—a question probably—then reached out to touch one of the scalded plants. She would've remembered the teakettle wailing in the night, and John's voice. After a second a kind of understanding would've become manifest.

Something must have stirred inside her.

Not panic. Just the need to breathe. Speed seemed essential—move and keep moving.

She left her book of crossword puzzles folded open on the kitchen counter. She did not pause for a jacket, or to leave a note.

She was outside before telling herself to go.

Half trotting, not thinking at all, she hurried down the slope to the boathouse and opened up the double doors and dragged the little aluminum boat out into shallow water, letting it fishtail there while she went back for the engine. The old Evinrude was heavy but she managed to lock it in. She loaded the oars and gas can and life vest, then turned to close the boathouse doors. The right panel hung loose at its upper hinge, partly jammed. Kathy muscled it with a shoulder, leaning in hard, but the panel was stuck solid. She shook her head and waded out to the boat and hopped in. Maybe then, just for an instant, she gave an irritated glance back at the jammed door. Maybe she forgot to put on the life vest.

A chain of events was established. All the rest had to follow.

She used the oars to pull out into the deep water beyond the dock. Pausing there, she worked the choke and yanked hard on the starter cord, and when the engine caught, she gave the throttle a quarter turn and swung the boat north toward Angle Inlet. A hundred yards out she gave it more power. Fleetingly, perhaps, Kathy noticed the life vest under the front seat, but she did not stop to put it on. Her mind was elsewhere.

Just go, she thought. She leaned forward and concentrated on speed.

And so what must've happened was that Kathy took the boat along the curving shoreline, past the Birchwood resort and Brush Island. She was at full throttle. The little boat seemed to pick itself up at the bow, the breeze stiffening to a wind, and for ten or fifteen minutes Kathy watched the great pine forests sweep by in liquid greens and yellows. The speed felt good to her. The wind and the sunlight, the cold spray against her skin. Maybe she was daydreaming. Maybe she shut her eyes for a moment and tried to tell herself that things might still end happily. Even now it was possible. Thirty-eight years old, which wasn't so bad, and with luck she could still have the child she wanted, and a house, and a big garden out back with lilacs and a white birdbath. All they needed was to be open with each other. Tell the truth. Later, she thought, she'd make herself do it. No evasions—tell him straight out about Harmon. And then recite a list of all the things she resented. Politics, for sure. But also the manipulation and secrecy and self-pity and paranoia. Tell him it had to end. Tell him she knew about the spying—years ago, she'd known—and she simply couldn't bear it any longer. She'd be blunt with him. Not accusing, just telling. All those years, she'd say, like a disease, but now everything was different. They were free. They could start over and do things right and make their marriage fresh and good.

She'd tell him that.

Yes, she would. Which was all she'd ever wanted. Just to be happy.

Kathy nodded to herself and swung the boat west into the channel off Magnuson's Island.

Maybe it happened there.

Or maybe a mile ahead, where the channel narrowed. She would've been gazing out on the expanses of pine and blue water, the boat bouncing hard against the whitecaps, and maybe for a few seconds she leaned back and gave herself over to sun and speed. Maybe she never saw the sandbar. Maybe she was imagining how their lives might still be good, how things could change, how they would carry their blankets to the porch and lie in the fog and just talk and talk. There was a shiver at the bottom of the boat—a snapping sound—

and for an instant she was free of everything, she was light and high, she was soaring through the glassy roof of the world and breaking out into another, and then the lake was all around her, and soon inside her, and maybe in that way Kathy drowned and was gone.

15

What the Questions Were

County Sheriff Art Lux flew in from Baudette at first light on the morning of September 20. By 7:00 A.M. he had set up a makeshift headquarters in the work bay at Pearson's Texaco station. Within an hour the first bulletins had been issued over marine-band radio, and by 8:30 more than a dozen search boats were out on the lake.

It was just after nine when Lux and Vinny Pearson pulled up outside Wade's cottage in an old Willys jeep. Claude Rasmussen showed them in. They removed their hats, shook hands with Wade, took seats in the living room while Claude and Ruth went out to the kitchen to make coffee. For John Wade, who sat stiffly on the couch, the physical world seemed flimsy and poorly made. He'd slept only in snatches, an hour at most; the fatigue was doing tricks with his vision. He went down inside himself briefly, just gliding, and when he surfaced, the sheriff was saying something about the need to stay patient.

Wade nodded. "Which means no news?"

"Not yet. Not for a while." Lux opened a small spiral notebook. His eyes were pale blue and sympathetic. "Thing is, sir, that's a big piece of lake out there, it'll take time." He hesitated. "Right now, if you don't mind, we've got a few quick questions. Provided you feel up to it."

"Whatever helps," Wade said.

Lux smiled and balanced the notebook on his knee. He was a short, gaunt man in his late fifties, tanned and windburnt, dressed in gray trousers and a soiled gray shirt. More like a dairy farmer, Wade thought, than an officer of the law. The badge on his shirt looked like a toy.

After a moment the man slipped on a pair of half-moon reading glasses.

"Just so you know," he said, "we've already got twelve boats out, plenty more to come. The Provincial Police up in Kenora, they'll be sending out their own patrol units, which helps a lot. By noon we'll have a couple spotter planes. Probably more later in the day. Everything's coordinated through my office—that's standard." He smiled again. "So we've got the buttons punched. Border Patrol, State Police. All kinds of help."

Wade tried to keep his eyes level. He felt like an actor.

"One thing you should keep in mind," Lux said. "A case like this, it's not all that unusual. We run into it six, seven times a year. Lost hunters, lost fishermen. Somehow things turn out happy most often." Lux glanced over at Vinny Pearson, who sat quietly to the side, his eyes half shut. "Almost always. Isn't that right, Vin?"

Pearson made an impatient motion with his hand. "Sure, I guess so. Ask the man why he never—"

"Relax. One thing at a time." The sheriff adjusted his glasses, flattened the notebook against his knee. "Now, sir, we've got the basic story from Mr. Rasmussen—the bare bones, so to speak—but I figure it's best to hear it straight from you. Helps us sort things out." His eyes went warm with concern. "If you don't feel up to it, we can always try later."

"Now's fine," Wade said.

"Mind if I write stuff down?"

Wade shook his head. Out in the kitchen, Claude and Ruth Rasmussen were doing something with cups and saucers, their voices fading in and out, and again he had the slippery sensation of a dream.

The sheriff clicked open a ballpoint pen. "First thing, before I forget, you don't have a picture handy? Your wife, I mean."

"For what? She's not—"

"No particular reason. Just in case."

"In case she's damp," Vinny Pearson said. "In case the lady turns up wet."

"For chrissakes, Vinny."

"The guy *asked*."

Wade turned and looked into Pearson's eyes, locking on, and for an instant something important seemed to pass between them. An acknowledgment of certain possibilities. Wade nodded at him and pulled a small photograph from his wallet. The snapshot was nearly four years old, cracked and grainy, but the sheriff studied it with appreciation.

"Gorgeous," he said. "Very pretty. And what about the vitals, sir? Weight, height, all that."

"You've got the photo there. Five-six, hundred eighteen pounds. She'll be thirty-nine in February."

"Identifying marks? Scars or anything?"

"No."

"Medical trouble?"

"No."

The sheriff looked at the snapshot again, slipped it into his breast pocket, and carefully buttoned the flap.

"Now what we should do," he said, "we should get a handle on the basic chronology. How things happened, more or less." He gave Vinny Pearson a cautionary glance. "Your wife apparently took off sometime yesterday?"

"That's right."

"Yesterday morning?"

"Right."

"And what time would that be?"

"I don't know," Wade said. "Early, I suppose. She was gone when I got up."

"Which was when?"

"Sorry?"

"When you woke up, sir—the time?"

"I just told you, I'm not sure. Maybe eleven, maybe noon."

"You're a late sleeper then?"

"Not usually," Wade said. "It's a vacation."

The sheriff nodded pleasantly. "Well, sure, I should've figured that. Terrific vacation country." He took a moment to consider this. "So if I understand right, your wife could've still been here up until noon or so. Yesterday's noon."

"She could've."

"And the last time you actually saw her?"

Wade thought about it. Recent events seemed fluid and insubstantial. "A little after midnight," he said. "I got up at one point, made myself some tea. She was still here."

"Asleep?"

"Sure. Asleep."

"Nothing unusual?"

"Not at all."

"All right then. But just so I'm clear, that gives us a twelve-hour time frame. Midnight to noon. Which is when she would've taken off?"

"Yes, I suppose so."

"And you didn't see—"

"I didn't *see* anything," Wade said sharply. "I woke up, she was gone. It's that simple."

"All this was yesterday?"

"Right. Yesterday."

Lux took notes in a slow, painstaking hand, underlining phrases here and there. He looked up. "Good, we're getting somewhere. And when did you first decide there might be a problem? Things out of the ordinary?"

"I'm not sure. Pretty quick, I guess."

"Quick?"

"Well, yes. Sort of." Wade was conscious of his own voice, the tone and language. "I mean it bothered me right away, but I didn't think—you know—I didn't think it was anything serious. She could've been anywhere. Out for a hike."

"Your wife's a hiker?"

"Sometimes."

"So you waited around?"

"Yes."

"Nothing else?"

"Nothing."

Vinny Pearson grunted under his breath. "Waited," he said, then took out a fingernail clipper and went to work peeling the grime from under a thumbnail. The man's skin had a smooth, almost colorless quality, pallid and sickly. Not an albino, Wade decided, but close enough. Like a huge white fetus. Wade made himself look away.

"So you waited," Lux said. "How long?"

"Quite a while, I guess. All day."

"Doing what?"

"Just things. Housework, cleaning up. I can't see how it matters."

"Oh, hell, it probably doesn't. Except you never know—it's a funny world—sometimes a stupid little detail can jump up and wiggle its ass and turn awful damn smart." The sheriff looked down at his notepad. "Anyhow, I guess you finally decided there was a problem."

Wade nodded. "It got dark, she wasn't back."

"So you went looking?"

"Yes."

"We're talking when? Pitch dark?"

"Not at first. Must've been around dusk, sometime after seven. I took a quick walk up the road—hoped I'd stumble into her, it was all I could think of. Then I walked on back and kept waiting."

"Just waited?"

"Naturally. What else?"

Lux smiled politely. "Maybe you needed to relax. Knocked back a drink or two. Nerves and all."

"Maybe. So what?"

"Nothing." The man's smile brightened. "Reason I ask, Mr. Rasmussen says you seemed a wee bit tipsy. Later on that night, I mean."

"Oh, Christ."

"He's mistaken, then?"

"No, I had a couple." Wade felt something sour rise up in his throat, a faint cabbage taste. "Kathy's lost out there, stranded probably, and we sit here talking about how many drinks I had."

"Which was how many?"

"The number?"

"Numbers help."

"Five or six," Wade said. "Not enough."

Vinny Pearson looked up from his fingernail clipper. "The boat," he said. "Ask how come he never once looked to see if—"

"Vin, clam up."

"But the man never—"

"Just ease off," Lux said, and turned toward Wade with an amused little grin. "No offense, that's Vinny's way. Swedish blood. What he's driving at, he's wondering why this whole time—while you're waiting for your wife—why you apparently didn't think to check out the boathouse. Most people, they'd say it's a logical place to start."

"No reason," Wade said. "It didn't occur to me. Not until later."

"At what point was that?"

"Late. Midnight or so."

"Which is when you finally went for help? After you found the boat was gone?"

"That's right."

"Twelve hours after you first missed her?"

"Correct."

Lux studied his notepad, the smile sliding away. He seemed displeased with his own handwriting.

"Well, see, here's the thing," he said. "This boat business doesn't quite figure. The whole problem with noise, for instance. An outboard kicks in, it's something you'd hear."

"Not necessarily. I was asleep."

Lux nodded thoughtfully. "I understand that. But those old Evinrudes, they make one bitch of a racket. Wake up the dead, so to speak." He paused and frowned. "Maybe you wear earplugs?"

"I don't."

"A deep sleeper, then?"

Vinny Pearson chuckled and said, "*Amazing* deep."

The air in the room had a tightly packed feel, dense and brittle. It was a welcome distraction when Ruth Rasmussen walked in with a pot of coffee and a large plate of muffins. She gave Wade an encouraging smile, filled their cups, and turned back to the kitchen. For a moment Wade felt himself tumbling through a crack in reality. Kathy's scent filled the cottage, a mix of perfumes and lotions; he could sense her passage through the air, the draw of her body.

"Mr. Wade?"

"Sorry, I wasn't—"

"No sweat. What I was wondering, sir, it's one of those questions I hate to ask." The sheriff tested another smile. "You and your wife. There wasn't any trouble?"

"I don't follow."

"Domestic problems. Disagreements or whatnot."

"No."

"Any stresses?"

"Well, come on, you read the papers, don't you?" Wade felt his face heat up. "Christ, yes, there was stress."

"The primary?"

"The primary."

Lux nodded. "Hard thing to deal with, I imagine. Losing like that, it can't be fun. And the Vietnam mess too. TV and newspapers, the media boys, I guess you could say they gave you a pretty firm going-over. Made for some rough sledding, I bet."

"We were handling it," Wade said.

"Even so. Not one of your polite elections." Lux paused. "Vinny here, he's another Nam type. Marines."

Pearson frowned without looking up. "Didn't kill no babies."

"Wonderful," Wade said. "Swell for you."

"Yeah, man, swell."

"So anyway," the sheriff said, "I figure there had to be some bad feeling. Tension or whatever."

"I don't get the point."

"No exact point," Lux said. "Background."

Vinny Pearson made a light scoffing noise. "Forget background. Ask about what Myra told us."

"Vin, I wish to fuck in heaven you'd *please* shut up."

"So ask."

Almost invisibly, the two men exchanged glances, then the sheriff's eyes swept across the living room floor. "The girl down at the Mini-Mart—Myra Shaw—you might remember her. Chubby thing, about eighteen."

"She ain't chubby," Vinny Pearson said. "She's my cousin, she's hog-fat."

"Right. So this girl says you and your wife stopped in the other day, had a little dispute at the counter. Pretty warm discussion, she says."

Wade shook his head. "It was nothing."

"You're saying it didn't happen?"

"No, I'm saying it's ridiculous. Couple of words, maybe, it barely lasted a minute." Wade pushed to his feet and crossed over to the living room window. A dazzling autumn day, almost too bright, and it was hard to fit the sunlight with what was happening inside him.

"There was no fight," he said quietly. "A disagreement, that's all it was."

"I understand completely."

"You make it sound—"

Lux wagged his head. "That wasn't my intention. You say it's nothing, it's nothing." Again there was sympathy in his eyes. He leaned back and crossed his legs. "All I meant was, the strain and so on, it might explain your wife's state of mind. Maybe she needed a breather, just went off by herself for a while."

"Went *where?*" Wade said.

"There's the question. She doesn't have friends in the area?"

"None."

"Relatives?"

"Not here. A sister down in Minneapolis."

The sheriff's smile returned. "Well, hey, it's worth a try. Get on the phone, see if your wife's been in touch with . . . I didn't catch the name. The sister."

"Pat. Patricia Hood."

"That's a married name?"

"Yes—divorced."

"And no other family to alert?"

Wade shook his head. "No one close. Both parents are dead."

"What I'd suggest then," Lux said, "I recommend you contact anybody you can think of. Acquaintances and so on. What happens sometimes, people get this hankering to take off—bang, they're gone—then after a week or two they'll show up again. I've seen it happen." He removed his glasses and looked up. "She ever run off before, sir?"

"Not like this."

"Like what?"

Wade felt a sudden deep fatigue. There were matters he did not want to discuss. "Like nothing. Now and then she'd pop away for a while. A few hours at most."

"Nobody else in the picture?"

"Sorry?"

"Another man."

"Not a chance," Wade said.

"You sound positive."

"I am. I'm positive." Briefly, the image of a dentist came to mind. "Forget it."

"All right, sure. Will do." The sheriff sighed and glanced down at his wristwatch. "One last item. Mr. Rasmussen says there was a problem with your phone last night. Apparently you had some trouble locating it?"

"Is that illegal?"

"No, sir. Except it was under the sink, I believe. Wrapped in a dish towel."

Wade's mouth filled with the sour cabbage taste. His own breathing seemed unfamiliar.

"Well, look, it's just one of those things people do. Like a symbol or something. The telephone, it hooks up with the outside world, all the crap out there—the election. I just unplugged the thing and put it away and forgot about it. A symbol, you know?"

"Symbol," Lux said. "I'll write that down."

"Do that."

"And the houseplants? Those were symbols too?"

There was a short silence. Vinny Pearson laughed.

"No, I didn't—" Wade stopped himself. "It's not all that complicated. Kathy's *out* there. Everything else is pure bullshit."

A small muscle moved at Lux's jaw.

"Bullshit," he murmured.

He closed his notebook, stood up, made a motion at Vinny Pearson.

His eyes shifted toward the window. "Mr. Wade, you're an important guy. Politics and all that, it's way out of my league, so you'll have to be tolerant. I'm just a hayseed cop. Vinny here, he's worse. Pumps gas for a living, pulls in some part-time deputy pay. Couple of rubes, for sure, but I'll tell you what, we'll do our best to find the lady. Drain the lake if we have to. Bulldoze those woods, pry up the floorboards." He smiled generously. "That's not bullshit, sir, that's a guarantee in gold."

The two men put on their hats and walked to the door.

"Give it a few hours," Lux said. "I'll be in touch. Don't forget those phone calls."

When they were gone, Wade stood for a few minutes at the living room window. What he needed was sleep. Something kept revolving behind his eyes, a shiny black stone. He could feel the weight in his forehead. It required some concentration to pick up the coffee cups and carry them out to the kitchen. Claude sat on a stool at the counter, Ruth was cracking eggs over a frypan.

"Three minutes," she said, "and we'll shovel this into your stomach." She used a wrist to sweep back her hair. "How'd it go out there?"

Wade put the cups in the sink. He wasn't sure what to do with himself. The fact of Kathy's absence would not settle inside him; it had no substance.

"I say how'd things *go?*"

He looked at the big iron teakettle. "Fine, I guess. Except for the part about my being a drunk."

Claude laughed. "Yeah?"

"A lot of other crap, too."

"Well, jeez." The old man grinned and tilted back on his

stool. "Tact's not my number one specialty. But I didn't say drunk, I said you seemed a little juiced up, and that's the plain nuts of it. Nobody blames you."

"Terrific."

"They don't."

"What about Pearson? The guy didn't seem—"

Ruth looked up from the frypan. "Vinny's just Vinny. Few more hours, I bet, Kathy'll come ambling right through that kitchen door, then we'll all get looped." She slid the eggs onto a plate, dropped on a muffin, brought the plate over to the table. "Eat," she said, "then hit the sack."

The eggs helped. When he was finished, Wade tried calling Kathy's sister in Minneapolis. There was no answer, and after a second he nodded at Ruth and moved unsteadily down the hallway to the bedroom.

Sleep was impossible. The fatigue had hardened inside that small black stone behind his eyes; his knees and elbows felt full of gravel. He lay face-up on the bed, eyes open, surveying his own state of being. The inner biology seemed impaired. Sparks of silvery white light jumped across the ceiling, and at the top of his head he noticed a sharp, tingling voltage, an irregular current, as if electrodes had been implanted just under his scalp.

Sorrow was also a problem. He couldn't feel much, just a shadowy uneasiness about his own conduct or misconduct. The interrogation bothered him. Important lines of inquiry, he realized, had not been pursued. Mental health, for one; memory, for another. Even now it was hard to come up with a neat chronology of those last hours together. The images did not connect—the darkness, the teakettle, the way he'd glided from spot to spot as if gravity were no longer a factor. He remembered the sound of mice beneath the porch. He remembered the rich forest smells and the fog and the curious motion Kathy sometimes made with her fingers, a slight fluttering, as if to dispel all the things that were wrong in their lives. Other things, though, he remembered only dimly. Getting out of bed that night. It had been late—that much he knew—but the wee-hour glide lifted him above ordinary time. He remembered the steam, the amps under his skin. He remembered a savage buzzing sound—"Kill Jesus," he was saying. He couldn't stop. And so he boiled a big green geranium near the fireplace, then a dwarf cactus, then several others he couldn't name. He was wearing undershorts, he remembered that. The night smelled of rot. He remembered refilling the teakettle, waiting for the water to boil, moving to the bedroom. His hands had no relation to his wrists. The mental scaffolding was gone, all the dreams for himself, all the fine illusions and ambitions. The world was electricity. He remembered watching Kathy sleep, admiring the tan at her neck and shoulders, the little wrinkles at her eyes, how in the dim light she seemed to be smiling at something, or half smiling, a thumb curled alongside her nose. At one point a great tenderness had seized him. Like a radio signal from another universe—it made his bowels go slack, it sucked his breath away—a high, shrill command to comfort and protect. Love, he thought. He remembered the weight of the teakettle. He remembered puffs of steam in the dark. A strange flapping sound, like wings, then a deep buzzing, and then later he'd found himself waist-deep in the lake. Naked now, and he felt the mushy bottom between his toes. He was examining the stars: hot white stars in a black sky. These were not memories. These were sub-memories. Images from a place beneath the waking world, deeper than dream, a place where logic dissolved. It was beyond remembering. It was knowing. The steady lap of waves against his chest, how cold he was, and how eventually he let himself go under —not a dive, just sinking—and how his mouth filled with the taste of fish and algae, how his legs scraped against something sharp—a terrible heaviness pressing through his lungs and arms—and how he was finally caught up in layers of forgetfulness. Later on, he sat trembling on the dock. He was naked. He was watching the stars.

Absurd, Wade thought.

He folded a pillow under his head and lay there inspecting the possibilities.

When he awakened, it was nearly dark, the trees webbed in gauzy purples. The clock on the nightstand showed 5:56.

Wade dressed, washed his face, and moved out to the living room.

"Sleeping Beauty," Claude said.

The old man sat playing solitaire at a card table in front of the stone fireplace. Even with a fire burning, the cottage seemed cold and drafty.

"Nothing yet, so don't ask," Claude said. "Your friend Lux checked in an hour ago, he's got extra boats lined up for tomorrow. Right now we just hang tight." The old man shuffled the cards and dealt himself a new game. "Ruth and me, we'll sack out in the spare bedroom. No sense stewing in your own juices."

"It's not necessary."

"Maybe not. But still."

Wade shrugged. "So you don't have me on trial?"

"For what?"

"Oh, please. Don't be coy."

The old man looked up and laughed. "Vinny spooked you, didn't he? The guy's made that way. Show him a full moon, he'll talk about the dark side."

"Then you don't think—"

"Hell, no, I don't. And not Ruth either. Except it might help to start acting like a husband. Some normal concern, it'll look real sweet to people."

The evening passed quietly. After supper Wade took a short walk along the shore, then showered and shaved, then fixed a pair of vodka tonics and carried them out to the porch. The dock and boathouse were already wrapped in fog. He leaned back against the stoop and worked on the drinks for almost an hour, listening to the woods, letting the small black stone revolve behind his eyes. Long ago, as a kid, he'd learned the secret of making his mind into a blackboard. Erase the bad stuff. Draw in pretty new pictures.

Around nine o'clock he put in another call to Kathy's sister. He tried several more times, on the hour, but didn't reach her until nearly midnight.

It was a difficult conversation. They had a history between them—distance and distrust. Her voice seemed blurry, almost deformed, as if she were holding a handkerchief over the mouthpiece. "Twenty minutes ago, I turned on the TV—" There was a crackling on the line. "What *happened?*"

"I'm not sure. She took a boat out. That's all anybody knows."

"God."

Again there was static, a warped sound. They spoke for another five minutes, mostly questions and answers, both of them careful to keep things civil. She hadn't heard from Kathy since the night of the primary; she couldn't imagine anything except the obvious, an accident of some sort. Her voice broke and for a moment there was silence.

"Look, I've already packed," she said. "I'll be there tomorrow. Early, I hope."

"I'm not sure that's—"

"Tomorrow," she said.

16

Evidence

Q: How do you evacuate someone with a hand grenade?
A: I don't have any idea, sir.
Q: Why did you make that statement?
A: It was a figure of speech, sir.
Q: What did you mean when you said it?
A: I meant just—I meant only that the only means I could
   evacuate the people would be a hand grenade. And that
   isn't exactly evacuating somebody.[1]
   —William Calley (Court-Martial Testimony)

Son My Village is located approximately 9 kilometers north-east of Quang Ngai City and fronts on the South China Sea. In March 1968, the village was composed of four hamlets, Tu Cung, My Lai, My Khe, and Co Luy, each of which contained several subhamlets . . . The Vietnamese knew many of these subhamlets by names different from those indicated on US topographic maps of the area . . . For example, the subhamlet

---

1. In Richard Hammer, *The Court-Martial of Lt. Calley* (New York: Coward, McCann & Geoghegan, 1971), p. 272.

identified on the topographic map as My Lai (4) is actually named Thuan Yen.[2]

— The Peers Commission

Q: What did you do?
A: I held my M-16 on them.
Q: Why?
A: Because they might attack.
Q: They were children and babies?
A: Yes.
Q: And they might attack? Children and babies?
A: They might've had a fully loaded grenade on them. The mothers might have throwed them at us.
Q: Babies?
A: Yes.
Q: Were the babies in their mothers' arms?
A: I guess so.
Q: And the babies moved to attack?
A: I expected at any moment they were about to make a counterbalance.[3]

— Paul Meadlo (Court-Martial Testimony)

I raised him up to be a good boy and I did everything I could. They come along and took him to the service. He fought for

2. *Report of the Department of the Army, Review of the Preliminary Investigations into the My Lai Incident,* Volume I, Department of the Army, March 14, 1970, p. 3–3. Hereafter referred to as The Peers Commission.

3. In Hammer, *The Court-Martial of Lt. Calley,* pp. 161–162.

his country and look what they done to him. Made a murderer out of him, to start with.[4]
> —Mrs. Myrtle Meadlo (Mother of Paul Meadlo)

. . . there is a line that a man dare not cross, deeds he dare
not commit, regardless of orders and the hopelessness of the
situation, for such deeds would destroy something in him that
he values more than life itself.[5]
> —J. Glenn Gray (*The Warriors*)

John had his own way of handling it all. It destroyed him,
you could say. But maybe in a lot of ways he was already destroyed.
> —Anthony L. (Tony) Carbo

I am struck by how little of these events I can or even wish
to remember . . .[6]
> —Colonel William V. Wilson (U.S. Army Investigator)

Look, I don't remember. It was three years ago.[7]
> —Ronald Grzesik (Court-Martial Testimony)

Q: Did you ever tell any officer about what you'd seen?
A: I can't specifically recall.[8]
> —Ronald Haeberle (Court-Martial Testimony)

---

4. CBS Evening News, Nov. 25, 1969, in Michael Bilton and Kevin
Sim, *Four Hours in My Lai* (New York: Viking, 1992), p. 263.

5. J. Glenn Gray, *The Warriors: Reflections on Men in Battle* (1959;
reprint, Harper Torchbooks, 1970), p. 186.

6. Colonel William V. Wilson, *American Heritage*, Feb. 1990, p. 53.

7. In Hammer, *The Court-Martial of Lt. Calley*, p. 151.

8. Ibid., p. 91.

Q: How many people were in the ditch?

A: I don't know, sir.

Q: Over how large an area were they in the ditch?

A: I don't know, sir.

Q: Could you give us an estimate as to how many people were in the ditch?

A: No, sir.[9]

   —William Calley (Court-Martial Testimony)

Q: What happened then?

A: He [Lieutenant Calley] started shoving them off and shooting them in the ravine.

Q: How many times did he shoot?

A: I can't remember.[10]

   —Paul Meadlo (Court-Martial Testimony)

All I remember now is flies. And the stink. Some of the guys made these gas masks—dunked their T-shirts in mosquito juice and Kool-Aid. That helped a little, but it didn't help with the flies. I can't stop dreaming about them. You think I'm crazy?

   —Richard Thinbill

The ordinary response to atrocities is to banish them from consciousness.[11]

   —Judith Herman (*Trauma and Recovery*)

John really suffered during the campaign. Those terrible things people said, it wasn't right. I don't believe a word.

   —Eleanor K. Wade

---

9. Ibid., p. 269.

10. Ibid., p. 155.

11. Herman, *Trauma and Recovery*, p. 1.

Q: Did you see any dead Vietnamese in the village?

A: Yes, sir.

Q: How many?

A: Most of them. All over.[12]

> —Gene Oliver (Court-Martial Testimony)

Persons taking no active part in the hostilities, including members of armed forces who have laid down their arms and those placed *hors de combat* by sickness, wounds, detention, or any other cause, shall in all circumstances be treated humanely . . .[13]

> —The Geneva Conventions on the Laws of War

Q: Can you describe what you saw?

A: There was a large mound of dead Vietnamese in the ditch.

Q: Can you estimate how many?

A: It's hard to say. I'd say forty to fifty.

Q: Can you describe the ditch?

A: It was seven to ten feet deep, maybe ten to fifteen feet across. The bodies were all across it. There was one group in the middle and more on the sides. The bodies were on top of each other.[14]

> —Richard Pendleton (Court-Martial Testimony)

Q: How did you know they were dead?

A: They weren't moving. There was a lot of blood coming

---

12. In Hammer, *The Court-Martial of Lt. Calley*, p. 101.

13. The Geneva Conventions on the Laws of War, 1949, article 3, section 1.

14. In Hammer, *The Court-Martial of Lt. Calley*, p. 104.

from all over them. They were in piles and scattered. There were very old people, very young people, and mothers. Blood was coming from everywhere. Everything was all blood.[15]

— Charles Hall (Court-Martial Testimony)

Q: Did you see any bodies shot?

A: Right, sir.

Q: Women and children?

A: Right, sir, women and children, about twenty-five of them in the northeastern part of My Lai (4).

Q: Did you see any other bodies?

A: Right, sir. About ten of them, in that place north of My Lai. They were all women and they were all nude.

Q: Were there any soldiers from your platoon there?

A: Right, sir. Roshevitz, he was there. He had an M-79. Those women, they died from a canister round from his M-79.[16]

— Leonard Gonzalez (Court-Martial Testimony)

Exhibit Eight: John Wade's Box of Tricks, Partial List

Deck of playing cards (all the jack of diamonds)

Thumb tip feke

Photographs (12) of father

Pack of chewing gum

Bronze Star with V-device

Purple Hearts (2)

Army Commendation Medal

Combat Infantryman's Badge

---

15. Ibid., p. 117.
16. Ibid., p. 193.

Waxed rope
Adhesive false mustache
Vodka bottle (empty)
Book: *Mental Magic*
Book: *Feats of Levitation*

Q: What were they firing at?
A: At the enemy, sir.
Q: At people?
A: At the enemy, sir.
Q: They weren't human beings?
A: Yes, sir.
Q: They were human beings?
A: Yes, sir.
Q: Were they men?
A: I don't know, sir. I would imagine they were, sir.
Q: Didn't you see?
A: Pardon, sir?
Q: Did you see them?
A: I wasn't discriminating.
Q: Did you see women?
A: I don't know, sir.
Q: What do you mean, you weren't discriminating?
A: I didn't discriminate between individuals in the village, sir.
   They were all the enemy, they were all to be destroyed,
   sir.[17]
   —William Calley (Court-Martial Testimony)

It is a crucial moment in a soldier's life when he is ordered to
perform a deed that he finds completely at variance with his

---

17. Ibid., p. 263.

own notions of right and good. Probably for the first time, he discovers that an act someone else thinks to be necessary is for him criminal . . . Suddenly the soldier feels himself abandoned and cast off from all security. Conscience has isolated him, and its voice is a warning. If you do this, you will not be at peace with me in the future. You can do it, but you ought not. You must act as a man and not as an instrument of another's will.[18]

—J. Glenn Gray (*The Warriors*)

The violation of human connection, and consequently the risk of a post-traumatic stress disorder, is highest of all when the survivor has been not merely a passive witness but also an active participant in violent death or atrocity.[19]

—Judith Herman (*Trauma and Recovery*)

Q: Did you receive any hostile fire at all any time that day?
A: No, sir.[20]

—Frank Beardslee (Court-Martial Testimony)

Q: Did you obey your orders?
A: Yes, sir.
Q: What were your orders?
A: Kill anything that breathed.[21]

—Salvatore LaMartina (Court-Martial Testimony)

18. Gray, *The Warriors: Reflections on Men in Battle*, pp. 184–185.
19. Herman, *Trauma and Recovery*, p. 54.
20. In Hammer, *The Court-Martial of Lt. Calley*, p. 93.
21. Ibid., p. 188.

John! John! Oh, John![22]
— George Armstrong Custer

Fucking flies!
— Richard Thinbill

I just went. My mind just went. And I wasn't the only one that did it. A lot of other people did it. I just killed. Once I started the . . . the training, the whole programming part of killing, it just came out . . . I just followed suit. I just lost all sense of direction, of purpose. I just started killing any kinda way I could kill. It just came. I didn't know I had it in me.[23]
— Varnado Simpson (Charlie Company, Second Platoon)

Q: Then what happened?
A: Lieutenant Calley came out and said take care of these people. So we said, okay, so we stood there and watched them. He went away, then he came back and said, "I thought I told you to take care of these people." We said, "We are." He said, "I mean kill them." I was a little stunned and I didn't know what to do . . . I stood behind them and they stood side by side. So they — Calley and Meadlo — got on line and fired directly into the people . . . It was automatic. The people screamed and yelled and

---

22. Evan S. Connell, *Son of the Morning Star* (San Francisco: North Point Press, 1984), p. 307. Connell writes that "John" was the name "ordinarily used by whites when addressing an Indian." At the Little Big Horn, on June 25, 1876, one terrified trooper "was heard sobbing this name, as though it might save his life. *John! John! Oh, John!* This plea echoes horribly down a hundred years."

23. In Bilton and Sim, *Four Hours in My Lai*, p. 7.

fell. I guess they tried to get up, too. They couldn't. That was it. The people were pretty well messed up. Lots of heads was shot off. Pieces of heads and pieces of flesh flew off the sides and arms.[24]

—Dennis Conti (Court-Martial Testimony)

The dismounted troopers then ran downhill and slid into the ravine where their bodies were found . . . [T]hey must have felt helplessly exposed and rushed toward the one place that might protect them. Yet the moment they skidded into the gully they were trapped. All they could do was hug the sides or crouch among the bushes, looking fearfully upward, and wait. A few tried to scramble up the south wall because the earth showed boot marks and furrows probably gouged by their fingers, but none of these tracks reached the surface.[25]

—Evan S. Connell (*Son of the Morning Star*)

Q: Can you describe them?
A: They was women and little kids.
Q: What were they doing?
A: They were lying on the ground, bleeding from all over. They was dead.[26]

—Rennard Doines (Court-Martial Testimony)

Q: Did you have any conversation with Lieutenant Calley at that ditch?
A: Yes.
Q: What did he say?

---

24. In Hammer, *The Court-Martial of Lt. Calley*, pp. 122–124.
25. Connell, *Son of the Morning Star*, p. 309.
26. In Hammer, *The Court-Martial of Lt. Calley*, p. 112.

A: He asked me to use my machine gun.

Q: At the ditch?

A: Yes.

Q: What did you say?

A: I refused.[27]

> —Robert Maples (Court-Martial Testimony)

Q: Did you ever open your pants in front of a woman in the village of My Lai?

A: No.

Q: Isn't it a fact that you were going through My Lai that day looking for women?

A: No.

Q: Didn't you carry a woman half-nude on your shoulders and throw her down and say that she was too dirty to rape? You did that, didn't you?

A: Oh, yeah, but it wasn't at My Lai.[28]

> —Dennis Conti (Court-Martial Testimony)

Every man has some reminiscences which he would not tell to everyone, but only to his friends. He has others which he would not reveal even to his friends, but only to himself, and that in secret. But finally there are still others which a man is even afraid to tell himself, and every decent man has a considerable number of such things stored away . . . Man is bound to lie about himself.[29]

> —Fyodor Dostoyevsky (*Notes from Underground*)

---

27. Ibid., p. 114.

28. Ibid., p. 127.

29. Fyodor Dostoyevsky, *Notes from Underground*, translated by Ralph E. Matlaw (New York: E. P. Dutton, 1960), p. 35.

Married veterans or guys who married when they got back had difficulties, too. Waking up with your hands around your wife's throat is frightening to the vet and to the wife. Is he crazy? Does he hate me? What the hell's going on?[30]

    —Patience H. C. Mason (*Recovering from the War*)

Like I told you, he used to yell things in his sleep. Bad things. Kathy thought he needed help.

    —Patricia S. Hood

Something was wrong with the guy. No shit, I could almost smell it.

    —Vincent R. (Vinny) Pearson

. . . the crimes visited on the inhabitants of Son My Village included individual and group acts of murder, rape, sodomy, maiming, assault on noncombatants, and the mistreatment and killing of detainees.[31]

    —Colonel William V. Wilson (U.S. Army Investigator)

---

30. Mason, *Recovering from the War: A Woman's Guide to Helping Your Vietnam Vet, Your Family, and Yourself*, p. 181.

31. Wilson, *American Heritage*, p. 53. The number of civilian casualties during operations in Son My village on March 16, 1968, is a matter of continuing dispute. The Peers Commission concluded that "at least 175–200 Vietnamese men, women and children" were killed in the course of the March 16th operation. The U.S. Army's Criminal Investigation Division (CID) estimated on the basis of census data that the casualties "may have exceeded 400." At the Son My Memorial, which I visited in the course of research for this book, the number is fixed at 504. An amazing experience, by the way. Thuan Yen is still a quiet little farming village, very poor, very remote, with dirt paths and cow dung and high bamboo hedgerows. Very friendly, all things considered: the old folks nod and smile; the children giggle at our white foreign faces. The ditch is still there. I found it easily. Just five or six feet deep, shallow and unimposing, yet it was as if I had been there before, in my dreams, or in some other life.

17

The Nature of Politics

In late November of 1968 John Wade extended his tour for an extra year. He had no meaningful choice. After what happened at Thuan Yen, he'd lost touch with some defining part of himself. He couldn't extricate himself from the slime. "It's a personal decision," he wrote Kathy. "Maybe someday I'll be able to explain it, but right now I can't leave this place. I have to take care of a few things, otherwise I won't *ever* get home. Not the right way."

Kathy's response, when it finally came, was enigmatic. She loved him. She hoped it wasn't a career move.

Over the next months John Wade did his best to apply the trick of forgetfulness. He paid attention to his soldiering. He was promoted twice, first to spec four, then to buck sergeant, and in time he learned to comport himself with modest dignity under fire. It wasn't valor, but it was a start. In the first week of December he received a nasty flesh wound in the mountains west of Chu Lai. A month later he took a half pound of shrapnel in the lower back and thighs. He needed the pain. He needed to reclaim his own virtue. At times he went out of his way to confront hazard, walking point or leading night patrols, which were acts of erasure, a means of burying one great horror under the weight of many smaller horrors.

Sometimes the trick almost worked. Sometimes he almost forgot.

In November of 1969 John Wade returned home with a great many decorations. Five months later he married Kathy in an outdoor ceremony, pink and white balloons bobbing from the trees, and just before Easter they moved into the apartment in Minneapolis. "We'll be happy," Kathy said, "I know it."

John laughed and carried her inside.

They decorated the place with hanging plants and printed fabrics stretched over wooden frames. They had fun shopping together, picking out cheap furniture and rugs and a portable television; they used the floor for lovemaking until Kathy found a decent secondhand bed.

"There, you see?" she said. "I was right."

John began law school that fall, which was part of the plan, and in late August of 1973 he passed the bar on his first try. A week later he went to work as an assistant legislative counsel with the Minnesota Democratic Farmer Labor Party. It was nuts-and-bolts work, with a salary next to nothing, but he was prepared to bear the sacrifices. For more than three years he herded legislation through the statehouse, where he discharged favors and tucked away IOUs for future redemption. The war seemed light-years away.

On the morning of their fifth anniversary, John carried Kathy's breakfast into the bedroom on a plastic tray. He caused five red roses to appear under cover of a dish towel.

"It's funny," she said, "you seem different somehow. More relaxed or content or something."

"You think so?"

"Yes. And I'm glad."

John nodded at her. He showed his empty hands, made a move, and displayed a pair of glass earrings. He caused a pair of new white tennis shoes to appear; on the insteps he had written JOHN + KATH, encircling this combination with hearts. All the tricks were working. In the early spring of 1976 he announced his candidacy for the Minnesota State Senate.

"You want to win?" Tony Carbo said.

"Obviously."

"I'm talking real wanting. Stomach-wanting."

"It's there," Wade said. "Exactly there, in the stomach."

Tony nodded and pinched a roll of flesh at his chin. They were not close friends, and never would be, but there was a compatibility between them, a precise matching of opposites. Lock and key, Tony called it. They'd met at a party fundraiser two years earlier. A few dinners, a few lunches, and afterward things were assumed.

"Well, beautiful," Tony said. "You're hungry, that's a start. Nothing beats a healthy appetite."

He stared dubiously at one of Kathy's wall hangings, then deposited himself on the couch and looked up at John with a pair of small slanted eyes. As a human specimen he wasn't much. Obese and jowly and yellow-skinned. Now, as always, he wore his standard green corduroy suit and stained red tie. His breath came in shallow gusts.

"So how about it?" John said. "On board?"

"Oh, sure." Tony grinned and glanced over at Kathy. He lit up a cigarette. "Handsome candidate. Spectacular wife."

"I'm not running on handsome."

"Oh, my," Tony said. "Woe is us."

Kathy looked at him with distaste. Tony beamed at her. "So what's the pitch? War hero?"

"No heroics," John said. "Straight issues."

"Oh, I see." Tony leaned back heavily and aimed a smile at Kathy through the smoke. "Well, listen, we've got a problem then, a big one, because you won't find this Mister Issue listed on the ballot. Other guys, sure, but not him." He chuckled. "Thought you wanted to win."

"Not like that," Kathy said.

"Beg pardon?"

"John wants to do things. Accomplish things. That's the point of it."

Tony was still grinning at her. "Spectacular. Didn't I say that? And I appreciate the input, except in the real world you don't accomplish zip without winning. Losers just lose." He rearranged his weight on the sofa. For a few seconds he seemed to be considering a number of amusing options. "This whole game—politics—it's like hustling a woman. Same principle more or less."

Kathy rolled her eyes but said nothing.

"Wrap your mind around it," Tony said. "You're at a party, say. You spot this hot looker across the room, this real babe, so you wander over and start politicking. Nice firm handshake, look her in the eye. Talk about every damn thing under the sun. Talk about Aristotle and Gandhi, how these guys affected you on a deep personal level, how they changed your life forever. Tell about your merit badges, that terrible experience you had with polio, what a sensitive human being you are, and then after a while, real polite, you invite this broad to dinner. Blow a month's pay, shovel out the oysters and caviar. Pretty soon she starts to owe you. It's never said like that, not direct, but this little pumpkin knows the rules, she knows how the deal works. Code of commerce, so to speak. Anyhow, the whole time you keep talking up your qualifications, how you're nuts about public TV, et cetera, ad shitum. The spiel's important, right? Wining and dining, all the courtship stuff, you got to do it. Because this girl's human just like you and me. She's got an ego. She's got her dignity. I mean, she's a living, breathing piece of ass and you got to respect that."

Tony's gaze slid along the floor toward Kathy.

"A metaphor," he said.

John Wade spent six years in the state senate. Tony ran the campaigns, which were slick and expensive, but the numbers increased nicely over the years, the margins almost tripling between 1976 and 1980.

Among his colleagues in the statehouse, John was regarded as a comer. He knew how to get along with people, how to twist arms without causing fractures. Compromise, he came to realize, was the motor that made government move, and while an idealist in many ways—a Humphrey progressive, a believer in the fundamental human equities—he found his greatest pleasure in the daily routine of legislative politics, the give and take, the maneuvering. Almost by instinct, he knew when to yield and what to require in return. He was smart and discreet. People liked him. Early on, with practice, he cultivated an aspect of shyness in his public demeanor, a boyish quality that inspired trust, and by the end of his first term, in 1980, this and numerous other virtues had been noted in important places. The papers rated him as one of the hot young stars; there was talk about a future at higher levels.

John's attitude toward all this was straightforward. He had humane instincts. He genuinely wanted to do good in the world. In certain private moments, without ever pondering it too deeply, he was struck by the dim notion of politics as a medium of apology, a way of salvaging something in himself and in the world.

Still, Tony Carbo was right. Politics was his profession, and there was nothing dishonorable about presenting himself as a winner. He wore expensive suits, watched his weight, nursed friendships where friendships mattered. Slender and sandy-haired, bony in the face, he photographed well, especially with Kathy at his side, and as a public figure he had the sort of presence that made people pay attention. On the dinner circuit he was modest and articulate, but it was never the sort of smoothness that could be mistaken for insincerity. This, too, was something he cultivated—sincerity. He worked on his posture, his gestures, his trademark style. Manipulation, that was still the fun of it.

The state senate ate up huge chunks of time, including weekends and most holidays, and as a consequence his life with Kathy sometimes suffered. They were happy, of course, but it was a happiness directed toward the future. They deferred things. Vacations and children and a house of their own. At night, sometimes, they would pore through a stack of travel brochures, making lists of resorts and fancy hotels, but in the end there was always the next campaign to pay for, the next election, and money was always a problem. They cut back on luxuries. They learned to be versatile with credit cards. In his off hours, and when the legislature was out of session, John supplemented his income with work for a St. Paul law firm, and in the autumn of 1981 Kathy took a full-time job in the admissions office at the University of Minnesota, which helped cover the bills. But even then they felt some strain. At times it seemed as if they were making their way up a huge white mountain, always struggling, sometimes just hanging on, and for both of them the trick was to remain patient, to keep their eyes fixed on the summit where all the prizes were. They tried to be optimistic, but on occasion it was hard to keep believing. They didn't go out much. They didn't have real friends. They rarely found the energy to make love.

"It's strange," Kathy said one evening. "Back in college, we'd just screw and screw, a couple of rabbits. Now it feels sort of—" She bit down as if to check herself. "I don't know. Sometimes it feels like I'm living with this *door*. I keep trying to get in, I keep pushing, but the damn thing's stuck shut and I just can't budge it."

"I'm not a door," John said. "And I'm not stuck."

"It feels that way."

"Then I'm sorry. We'll fix it."

She looked straight at him. Maybe it was the light, he thought, but her eyes had a strange silvery cast.

"John, listen. I don't know if anything's really sacred to you. Final and sacred."

"Us," he said. "Your tongue, my mouth. No one else's. Forever."

"You aren't keeping anything from me?"

"That's ridiculous."

"Is it?"

"Yes," he said. "Totally."

She glanced away for a second, then sighed and looked back at him. "Except you wouldn't ever tell, would you?

I mean, if there *were* secrets, you wouldn't ever let on?"

John took her in his arms. He feigned a teasing laugh, a clear conscience. He was terrified of losing her, and always had been, but he did not say that.

"Nonsense," he said. "I love you, Kath. We're aces."

"You *are* clean?" Tony Carbo said.

"I am."

"No ghosts?"

"None."

"But like if there's something in your closet, some deep dark shit with little girls . . ."

"Nothing."

"For sure?"

John smiled and said, "Positive."

"Well, let's hope so," Tony said, "because you damn well better be. There's any snot up your nose, somebody'll dig it out and squish the stuff right up against your forehead. Sooner or later, man, it's bound to happen. That means for sure. Small-time politics, you can hide the boogers. Not in the big leagues."

"I understand."

"So you're safe?"

John looked away for a moment. A red ditch flashed across his field of vision.

"Right," he said. "Safe."

Tony nodded and picked up a notepad. "What about religion? You've got religion, I hope to Christ."

"I'll find it."

"Lutheran."

"Fine with me."

"Terrific. Church once a week, ten o'clock sharp." Tony

flicked his eyebrows. "I got this feeling we're gonna have a genuine god-fearing Lutheran for lieutenant governor."

Again, John Wade won big, by more than 60,000 votes, then spent the next four years cutting ribbons. Predictably, the lieutenant governorship was a do-nothing job, worse than tedious, but from the beginning he viewed it as little more than a stop along the way. He ran errands, paid attention to his party work, kept his face in the papers. If a Kiwanis club up in Duluth needed a luncheon speaker, he'd make the drive and tell a few jokes over chicken fricassee and give off a winner's golden glow. Already he had his sights locked on the U.S. Senate.

In July of 1982 Kathy told him she was pregnant.

In bed that night John held her close. They were young, he told her. Plenty of time. They were near the top of that mountain they'd been climbing, almost there, one last push and then they'd rustle up a whole houseful of kids.

In the morning John made a phone call.

Forms were signed.

A freckled young doctor explained things, then sent them out to the waiting room. Kathy paged through magazines while John tried to concentrate on a framed print of grazing cattle.

When the nurse called her, Kathy smoothed out her skirt and stood up.

"Well," she said. "Keep an eye on my purse."

John watched a swinging door compress the air behind her. And then for an indeterminate period of time he sat appraising the grazing cattle. Curiously, he felt the beginnings of sorrow, which perplexed him, and it required effort to direct his thoughts elsewhere. A few phone calls, maybe. Check in with Tony. He looked around for a telephone, half rising, but then some strange force seemed to press him back into the chair. The room wasn't quite solid. Very wobbly, it seemed. And suddenly, as though caught in a box of mirrors, John looked up to see his own image reflected on the clinic's walls and ceiling. Fun-house reflections: deformations and odd angles. He saw a little boy doing magic. He saw a college spy, madly in love. He saw a soldier and a husband and a seeker of public office. He saw himself from inside out and upside down, the organic chemistry, the twisted chromosomes, and for a second it occurred to him that his own stability was at issue.

At supper that night he tried to describe the experience to Kathy. Except it was hopeless. He couldn't find the words. Kathy's eyes went skipping across the surfaces of things.

At one point he suggested taking a drive.

"Drive?" she said.

"If you're up to it."

Kathy regarded him without expression. Her hair was blond and curly, thinning slightly, the corners of her eyes worn by their years together.

"All right," he said, "no drive."

They sat in silence. It was mid-July, warm and humid, and for a long while there was only the sound of knives and forks.

"Kath," he finally said. Then he stopped and said, "We did the right thing."

"Did we?"

"Yes. Bad timing."

"Timing," she said.

"Next year we can always . . . You all right?"

She blinked and looked down at the table. "Am I all right?

Am I? God, I don't even know. What *is* all right?" She pushed her plate away. "A baby. It's all I wanted."

"I know that."

"What else did I ever ask for?"

"Nothing."

"Tell me. What else?"

"Nothing," he said.

They watched TV for an hour.

Afterward, Kathy did some ironing, then carried a book back to the bedroom.

John waited until well after midnight before turning off the television. He undressed, took a Seconal, and lay down on the couch. The apartment was full of odd noises. He loved her. More than anything. Drifting, feeling the drug, he closed his eyes and gave himself over to the mirrors in his head. He was awed and a little frightened by all the angles at play.

They never talked about it. Not directly, not obliquely. On those occasions when it rose up in their minds, or when they felt its presence between them, they would carefully funnel the conversation toward safer topics. They would speak in code or simply go quiet and wait for the mood to change. But for both of them, in different ways, there was now an enduring chill in their lives. Some nights Kathy would wake up crying. "So terrible," she'd say, and John would take her in his arms, doing what he could, and then for a long while they would lie silently in the dark and take guesses at each other's thoughts. They were not ashamed. They knew all the wonderful reasons. They knew it was an accident of nature. They knew that biology should not dictate, that their lives were already far too complicated, that they were not yet prepared for the responsibilities and burdens. They understood all this. But lying there in the dark, they also understood that they had sacrificed some essential part of themselves for the possibilities of an ambiguous future. It was the guilt of a bad wager. They understood this, too, and they felt the consequences.

On January 18, 1986, in a Hilton ballroom six blocks from Karra's Studio of Magic, John Wade announced his candidacy for the United States Senate. Kathy was there, and Tony Carbo, and a happy-looking assembly of dignitaries in pinstripes and starched blue shirts. There was enthusiasm and good humor. John had the streamlined look of a winner. There was still a primary to get through, which could be tricky, but the polls had him fifteen points up on an old warhorse named Ed Durkee, his closest rival. Not a lock, but close enough. For well over a year Tony had been fitting the pieces together, and in the ballroom that morning it was evident that his labors had paid off. People were smiling. The troops were in line, the appropriate blessings had been secured.

John kept his speech short. He talked about fresh air and fresh starts.

When it was over, the three of them took a cab across town to an expensive restaurant near the capitol. John and Kathy ordered salads and vodka tonics, Tony had the pot roast special with a pair of bourbons. When the drinks came, Tony stood and raised his glass. He wore his green corduroy suit, freshly dry-cleaned, tight at the shoulders. "To freshman senators," he said. "Fresh air and fresh starts. Fresh new blood."

"Amen," said Kathy, and laughed.

Beneath the table, she put a hand on John's knee. The restaurant was full of the usual noontime pack of watchful lobbyists and string-pullers. The background music was from Broadway.

"So I guess we're off," Kathy said. "The press conference, it went all right?"

Tony chuckled. "Pretty all right. Four TV crews, half the *Star-Trib*'s newsroom. Couldn't do better for Mr. Goulet."

"Who?"

"Camelot. You're listening to him." He sighed and cupped his hands at his belly. "Mister Who. Just proves you got to stay fresh."

Kathy smiled. "But everything clicked?"

"Oh, sure. Hubby's a star."

"Well, good. Except it seemed . . ." She hesitated and moved her hand along John's knee. "I don't know, it just seemed a little empty, that's all. I'm not sure what the message was."

Tony winked at her. "Win," he said.

"You aren't that cynical."

"No?"

"You're not."

"Well, gosh, you've got me semi-curious. What am I?" His eyes glittered. He finished off one of the bourbons and tucked a napkin under his collar. "Go on," he murmured. "Say nice things."

Kathy shrugged. "Nothing, really. You put up that ridiculous front of yours, the cynic act. Down below you're another poor sad dreamer like the rest of us."

"Ah, I see. And the rest of us? Who be they?"

"Everybody. John and me."

Tony's pot roast came. He made a may-I gesture, forked a potato, looked up at her with a half smile.

"John, you say? A dreamer?"

"Certainly."

"And where'd you dredge up this interesting theory?"

"Nowhere," Kathy said. "I married him."

Tony glanced over at John and chewed thoughtfully for a moment. "True enough, you married him, and what a happy stroke of fortune for the candidate. Mind-boggling, I might add. Did I ever mention how spectacular you are?"

"Not nearly enough," Kathy said. "I just wish you'd let him *say* things."

"Oh, really?"

"Yes."

"Which things are these? Which things would the candidate care to say?"

John smiled. He was conscious of Kathy's hand on his knee.

"Issues," he said. "No big deal."

"Explain," Tony said. "Honest, I'm dying to hear about these red-hot issues on your mind. Nuclear waste? Fresh plan for the isotopes?"

"Come on, man, don't start."

"The welfare state. I'll bet that one keeps you awake at night. Aid to dependent children."

John's necktie felt tight. He turned toward Kathy and tried to firm up his lips. "He's right, I guess. First the election, then worry about the rest."

"I see."

"That doesn't—"

"Win and win again," Kathy said. "And it won't ever stop, will it?"

"I didn't mean anything by that."

"Win and win."

Tony Carbo looked on with a lazy smile. "Spectacular. I'm in love with the boss's wife."

Kathy's hand slipped away.

For a while they sat listening to the noontime clatter, the dishes and deal-making.

Tony finally put his fork down.

"Maybe I'm wrong," he said merrily, "but it looks to me like this table could use a blow of fresh air. The lady's right, of course, it doesn't ever stop. Win and win and win. Very perceptive. On the other hand, there's this item called democracy, that's what all the nice patriotic folks call it. Count up the votes and deal out the power. The American way, tried and true. But, see, here's the bizarre part. Those same nice folks get awful upset when somebody goes out and jumps into the trenches and tries to make it work. People get nasty, start calling you names."

Tony was smiling, but his manner didn't carry it off. He drained the second bourbon, looked up for a waiter.

"The fact is, if you actually give a shit—if you bust your nuts and get involved and make it your life—well, fuck you, you're one more political dickhead. Gets to the edge of irony. All those holier-than-thou idiots out there. Fred Q. Public. Dumb bastard can't find his own statehouse without Rand McNally and Shep the Guide Dog. Watches a little TV news and calls himself a good citizen. Maybe votes once a year, probably doesn't. And guys like me, we're slick-dick pols. We're a pack of thieves."

The smile was gone now. Tiny beads of sweat coated his forehead.

"Anyhow, fuck that," he said. "They want better, they can unass themselves. They can *have* this fucking job."

Kathy looked at him thoughtfully. "Hooray for you. A dreamer. So why not give John a chance?"

"Me?"

"See what happens."

Tony studied her for several seconds. "Sweet Kathleen. You don't get it, do you?"

"Get it?"

"Hierarchy," he said, and smiled at John. "The sorry truth is I'm just one more hired gun. You want preacher politics, talk to the boss here."

"I don't see how that's—"

"Hubby's in charge. And I don't believe he's all that hot for issues right now. The man's got his priorities. Winning first, issues second. But go ahead and ask."

Kathy nodded.

She sipped her drink, closed her eyes for a second, then excused herself and moved off toward the ladies' room.

Tony watched until she was gone.

"Yummy specimen," he said.

"You didn't have to pull that stunt."

"Stunt?"

"It wasn't necessary."

Tony grinned and wiped his mouth. "My apologies. Thinks you're Mr. Clean, doesn't she?"

"I am clean."

"Of course and absolutely." Tony seemed amused as he took a bite of pot roast and scanned the room. It took him a long while to swallow. "However you want it. Just seems a trifle odd how you stay so quiet on certain unnamed subjects."

"Such as what?"

"Don't be a party pooper. If I named them, they wouldn't be unnamed, would they?"

"Bullshit," John said. "That's a reach."

"Probably so." Tony saluted and pulled an imaginary trigger. "Anyhow, don't pin that ruthless crap on me. Things go wrong, man, I pity the poor fucker gets in your way. Real honest-to-God pity." He wiggled his eyebrows. "Still the old magician, right? Fool all the assholes some of the time, some of the assholes all the time. Can't fool Tony Carbo none of the time."

He nudged his plate aside and waved across the room.

"And here she is, all freshly powdered. Weird thing, you know? Give me a shot, I'd drop fifty pounds for the lady. I do not joke."

18

Hypothesis

When she cleared Magnuson's Island, Kathy gave the Evinrude an extra shot of gas and continued north past American Point and Buckete Island, holding a course roughly west toward Angle Inlet. It was mostly open lake, wide and blue, and the boat planed along with a firm, rhythmic thump, the bow stiff against the waves. She felt better now. The morning sunshine helped. Here and there she passed little islands with forests pushing up flush against the shoreline, purely wild, too isolated for lumbering, everything thick and firm to her eye. The water itself seemed solid, and the sky, and the autumn air. Like flesh, she thought—like the tissue of some giant animal, a creature too massive for the compass of her city-block mind. All around her, things were dense with color. On occasion she spotted a deserted fishing cabin, or a broken-down dock, but after a time the wilderness thickened and deepened and became complete. She could hear her thoughts unwinding. No more politics, not ever again. All that was over. It was nothing. Less than nothing.

And so she leaned back and gave the throttle a quarter turn and allowed herself to open up to the sun and speed. A golden September day, fresh-feeling, crisp and new, and everything was part of everything else. It all blended into a smooth repetitive oneness, the trees and coves and water and sky, each piece of wilderness identical to every other piece. Kathy put a hand overboard, letting it trail through the water, watching its foamy imprint instantly close back on itself. Identical, which erased identity. Or it was all identity. An easy place, she thought, to lose yourself.

Which is what happened, maybe.

Maybe the singleness of things confused her. Maybe Buckete Island was not Buckete Island. Maybe she missed the channel into Angle Inlet by only a fraction of a mile, a miscalculation of gradient or degree. Daydreaming, maybe, or closing her eyes for an instant, or stretching out to absorb the fine morning sun. It was one possibility. No accident at all, just a banal human blunder, and she would've continued up the lake without worry, soon crossing into Canadian waters, into a great interior of islands and forests that reached northward over many hundred square miles.

For well over an hour she would've been lost without knowing how lost she was. Her eye was untrained. She had no instinct for the outdoors. She knew nothing about the sun's autumn angles, or how to judge true north, or where in nature to look for help. She was ignorant of even the most fundamental rule of the woods, which was to stop moving if ever in doubt, to take shelter and wait to be found.

Almost certainly she would've tried to work her way out; almost certainly she would've ended up hopelessly turned around.

And so at some point that morning she must've felt the first soft nudge of anxiety. Too much time, she thought. Twice before, with John, she had made the trip by water into Angle Inlet—barely forty minutes, dock to dock.

She looked at her wristwatch. The obvious thing was to start backtracking. Swing the boat south, keep her eyes open.

She was in a wide, gently curving channel flanked by four little islands, and for a few seconds she idled there, not sure about direction. She opened the red gas can, refueled, then turned the boat in a slow semicircle and took aim at a stand of pines a mile or so back down the channel. The breeze had picked up now. Not quite a wind, but the waves stood higher on the lake, and the air was taking sharp bites at her neck and shoulders. There was no sound except for the rusty old Evinrude.

Kathy buttoned up her sweater. No problem, she thought. Connect the dots.

And then for well over an hour she held a line toward the southeast. It was thick, gorgeous country, everything painted in blues and greens, and the engine gave off a steady burbling noise that reassured her. A good story for dinner. Danger and high adventure. It might give John a few things to think about. Like the priorities in his life, and where his marriage ranked, and how he was in jeopardy of losing something more than an election. You could get lost in all sorts of ways—ways he'd never considered—and she'd *tell* him that.

Humming to herself, Kathy adjusted the tiller and began planning a dinner menu, two big steaks and salad and cold beer, imagining how she'd describe everything that was happening out here. Get some sympathy for herself. Get his attention for a change.

The idea gave her comfort. She could almost picture a happy ending.

After twenty minutes the channel forked around a large rocky island, narrowing for a mile, then breaking off into three smaller channels that curled away into the trees. The place struck her as both familiar and foreign. On whim, she took the center channel and followed it through a funnel of pine and brush for what seemed far too long. Occasionally the channel widened out, opening into pretty little bays and then closing up tight again. Like a river, she thought, except it didn't flow. The water beneath her had the feel of something static and purposeless, like her marriage, with no reality beyond its own vague alliance with everything else.

Curiously, she felt no fear at all. It occurred to her that she was almost comfortable with the situation. She felt strong and capable, the same calm that came over her whenever she opened up a new crossword puzzle—all that stern geography to negotiate, a fixed grid full of hidden connections and hidden meanings. She liked unlocking things, finding solutions. For more than twenty years she'd started the day with a crossword and a cup of coffee, easing into the daylight, enjoying the soft flowering sensation that came into her bones as blocks of space suddenly took on clarity and design. It was more than habit; it was something in her genes. Even as a kid she'd lived in a puzzle world, where surfaces were like masks, where the most ordinary objects seemed fiercely alive with their own sorrows and desires. She remembered giving secret names to things, carrying on conversations with chairs and trees. Peculiar, yes, but she couldn't help herself. It had always seemed so implausible that the world could be indifferent to its own existence, and although she'd long ago given up on churches, Kathy couldn't help believing in some fundamental governing principle beneath things, an aspect of consciousness that could be approached through acts of human sympathy.

Like John, she thought. All that sadness under the flat gray surface of his eyes. A good feeling to be away from it.

Ahead, the channel widened out into a stretch of open water, deep blue and icy looking. She squinted up at the sun to calculate the remaining daylight. Maybe five hours until dark. Angle Inlet had to be somewhere off to the south, probably a shade to the west.

She nodded to herself and said, "All right, fine," and fixed the boat on a southerly course, or what she took to be south, now and then checking her direction against the sun. The day was bright and windy, a string of filmy white clouds scudding eastward. She eased back on the throttle and for more than two hours moved through a chain of silvery bays and lakes that unfolded without stop to the horizon. There were no cabins, no other boats. Along the shoreline, thick growths of cattails bent sideways in the wind, and there were occasional flights of ducks and loons, but mostly it was a dull succession of woods and water. After a time she felt a detached laziness come over her, a shutting-down sensation. At one point she found herself singing old nursery songs; later on she laughed at the memory of one of Harmon's filthy jokes—a chipmunk, a deaf rhinoceros. A spasm of guilt went through her. Not that she'd ever loved the man, not even close, but there was still the shame of what had happened back then. She pictured his bare white chest, the fingers so thick and stubby for someone who made a living at dentistry. Hard to believe she'd felt things for him.

Enough, she thought. Leave it alone.

Still, it was hard to keep her mind on the boat. Hard to sustain much resolve. Overhead, a big pale sun burned without heat. The day was slowly tilting toward shadow.

Her mind, too.

"Harmon, Harmon," she said.

Five minutes later she ran out of gas. The abrupt quiet

surprised her. Even with the wind, the afternoon seemed hugely empty. She was bobbing thirty yards off the shore of another small wooded island.

For a few minutes Kathy sat still. What she needed, really, was a nap. Curl up and let the waves rock her to sleep. Instead, she got to her knees, opened the red gas can, and carefully refilled the Evinrude's tank. At least she'd had enough foresight to stow the extra fuel. And the thing now was not to waste any. A good steady speed, straight lines from point to point. She closed her eyes and jiggled the can, estimated another four gallons or so. Which was plenty. She said it aloud—"Plenty"—then bent forward and yanked on the starter cord. The Evinrude gave off a weak whine. She tried again, twice more, but there was nothing.

Good thoughts, Kathy told herself. Good thoughts for good girls. She gripped the cord with both hands, braced herself and pulled back hard.

There was a short coughing sound. The Evinrude sputtered, then caught.

Kathy gave it some throttle. *Good thoughts for good girls.* It was one of those proverbs her Girl Scout leader used to clip out of Methodist magazines and recite to the troops as a way of bludgeoning them toward rectitude. The old lady—Mrs. Brandt—she had banality to burn. A jingle for every occasion: birthdays, menstruation, first love.

Kathy couldn't help smiling as she turned the boat back into open lake.

Never pout, never doubt, that's our famous Girl Scout.

Right now, though, it was hard to push away the apprehension. The shadows were rapidly lengthening, and in the air there was the crisp, metallic scent of winter. A shift in the ozone, maybe. Mrs. Brandt would've been ready with all the technical details. *When you're lost, look for the moss. It's on the north, so sally forth.*

It took almost twenty minutes to cross the open water. This time there were no channels south. Directly ahead, the shoreline loomed up as a blunt, gently curving mass of rock and pines, a long green wall arcing out in front of her as far as she could see. Kathy cut back on the power, idling offshore, trying to settle on a proper course of action. Nothing sensible revealed itself. She gazed at the dense forest, then up at the sky. The facts seemed obvious. Lost and totally alone. And the physical universe had no opinion. Trees did not talk. No face behind the clouds. No natural laws, only nature. Which was the truth, she told herself, so she might as well get on with it.

She brought the boat around and followed the shoreline in what she took to be a generally westward direction, looking for a channel south. The afternoon had passed to a ghostly gray. She was struck by the immensity of things, so much water and sky and forest, and after a time it occurred to her that she'd lived a life almost entirely indoors. Her memories were indoor memories, fixed by ceilings and plastered white walls. Her whole life had been locked to geometries. Suburban rectangles, city squares. First the house she'd grown up in, then dorms and apartments. The open air had been nothing but a medium of transit, a place for rooms to exist.

Very briefly, closing her eyes, Kathy felt the need to cry. Her throat tightened up. "Don't be an idiot," she said. "Just find a goddamned *way*." And then for a long while she followed the curving shoreline, moving at low throttle, watching the sun sink toward the trees straight ahead. The wind was colder now. She passed between a pair of tiny islands, veered north to skirt a spit of rocks and sand, then aimed the boat west into a wide stretch of choppy water. After more than an hour nothing much had changed. The purest wilderness, everything tangled up with everything else. At best, she decided, the day contained another half hour of useful light, twenty minutes to be safe. She hesitated, then turned in toward a small dome-shaped island off to her left. No choice, she thought. Get some sleep. Start fresh.

Thirty yards offshore she cut the power. Already dusk was coming down hard.

The little island seemed to float before her in the purply twilight, partly masked by a stand of reeds and cattails. She unlashed the oars, set them in their locks, and began pulling in toward what appeared to be a narrow strip of beach beyond the reeds. It was harder work than she would've guessed. The waves kept turning her, and after only a few strokes she felt a dull ache settle into her neck and shoulders. Twice she got caught in the reeds and had to back off and pick out a new angle of approach. On the third try she stopped and pulled up the oars. "For Pete's sake," she said, "you're not a child."

She stripped off her sneakers and jeans, moved to the stern, hopped out into thigh-deep water. The quick cold made her skin tighten. Partly wading, partly swimming, she got behind the boat and wrestled it through the cattails and up onto the narrow beach. She used the bow line to secure the boat to a big birch and then lay back on the sand to let herself breathe. It felt good to have ground beneath her.

The darkness now was almost complete. Six o'clock, she guessed.

For a few minutes she lay listening to things, the waves and nighttime insects, then she got up and took off her underpants and wrung them out. In the boat she found an oilcloth to dry herself. She put on her jeans, slicked her hair back, used the last slivers of dusk to do an inventory. There wasn't much. No matches or lighter. Nothing to eat. She had the life vest, which she now slipped on for warmth, and she had her wallet and a pack of Life Savers and a tackle box and some Kleenex and the gasoline and the two oars and the boat. In her pockets she found a comb and a few coins.

She dragged the boat higher up onto the beach, wedged a couple of rocks under the stern.

It wasn't a beach, really. Just a ledge of sand jutting out from the main body of the island. It was shaped something like an arrowhead, forty or fifty feet wide at the base, narrowing toward the tip. Behind her, where the ledge hooked up with the rest of the island, she could make out a long dark smudge of heavy forest.

Kathy spanked her hands together. "Well, let's *go*" she said, which gave her confidence. Quickly, she moved to the tree line and collected an armful of pine boughs and carried them over to a level spot beside the boat; in five minutes she had a mattress. She covered it with the oilcloth and sat down. Good enough, she decided. And nothing more could be done until morning. She took out a Life Saver, leaned back against the boat, and looked up at a bright yellow moon rising over the pines to the north. She wouldn't starve. Plenty of fish in the lake. Mushrooms and berries, all kinds of things.

Right now, she thought, John would be getting a search organized. Helicopters and floodlights. A whole army of Girl Scouts out beating the bush.

Things would work out.

She was strong. Good health, good brains.

Yes, and in the morning she'd get out the tackle box and do some trolling, pull in a nice big breakfast. Find a way to make a fire. Then look for a channel south. Keep going until somebody found her, or until she ran dead-on into the Minnesota mainland.

Easy, she thought. Like one-two-three.

Kathy pulled her arms inside the life vest. For a while she listened to the waves, the swishings in the trees, then later she found herself thinking about John. A New Year's Eve back in college when they'd gone dancing at The Bottle Top over on Hennepin Avenue. The way he'd looked at her, no tricks at all. Just young and in love. Sentimental, maybe, but it was one of those times when all the mysteries of the world seemed to condense into something solid. People all around them, drums and guitars, but even so, they were all alone in their own little bubble, not really dancing, just moving, smiling from inside themselves. At one point he'd taken her face in his hands. He'd put his thumbs against her eyelids. "Boy, do I *love* you," he'd said, and then he'd made a small turning motion with his hand, as if to drop something, and whispered, "Girl of my dreams."

She'd never figured out what he'd dropped that night. Himself, maybe. Or a part of himself.

But it didn't matter. Because in the morning he was stationed outside her dorm again, the same old games, and after all these years nothing had really changed. The secrecy and spying, it never stopped, not for long, and at times she'd felt an overwhelming need to remove herself from him, to make herself vanish.

Which was what happened finally.

The thing with Harmon—it wasn't love.

Not infatuation, either, and not romance, just the need to break away. Someone kind and decent.

Kathy tucked her chin into the life vest, closed her eyes.

Love wasn't enough. Which was the truth. The saddest thing of all.

She curled up against the boat.

In the morning she'd start fresh. Find something to eat and fill up the gas tank and see what the day brought. Fresh, she thought.

19

What Was Found

By early morning of the second day, September 21, the organized search force included close to a hundred volunteers, three State Police aircraft, two patrol boats from the Ontario Provincial Police, and a U.S. Border Patrol plane equipped with air-to-ground optical mappers and a General Electric infrared heat scope. More than thirty private boats were out; others were on the way from Warroad and Baudette. The search zone encompassed more than six hundred square miles of lake and woods.

Nothing at all was found.

No boat, no body.

John Wade spent most of the morning on the telephone. Claude and Ruth Rasmussen took turns playing secretary, filtering out the news rats, but still Wade found himself mumbling things to people whose faces he couldn't summon up. He felt tired and helpless. Just before noon Kathy's sister called from International Falls to say she'd be coming in by float plane at one o'clock.

Her tone was brusque, almost rude. "I'll need to get picked up," she said. "I mean, if it's no problem."

"One o'clock," Wade said.

"Any word?"

"Nothing. They keep saying to be patient."

There was a buzz on the line before Pat said, "Unreal," and broke the connection.

Wade showered, put on clean clothes, and made the twenty-minute drive into town. Another bright day, almost hot, and the trees along the road flamed up in brilliant reds and golds. Now and then he'd catch a glimpse of the lake off to his right, which brought Kathy's face to mind, but he told himself to cut it out. Thinking wouldn't help. Not him, not anyone. As the road flattened out into open country, Wade tried to prepare himself for what was coming with Pat. There was a tension between them that never seemed to unwind. Cold civility at best. Right from the start, way back in the college years, Pat had always appraised him with a frosty, calculating stare, searching for the flaws, beaming in on him. Partly it was a distrust of men in general. Two divorces, a long string of live-in boyfriends. Four years ago she'd taken up with a weight trainer at a fancy health club over in St. Paul. The trainer was long gone, but Pat now owned the club and three more out in the suburbs. It was the only relationship that had ever worked out for her: a thriving business and the sort of body you didn't insult. A hard case, he thought. And the trick now would be to keep a buffer between them, polite but plenty of distance.

He pulled into the gravel lot behind Pearson's Texaco station. He parked and went inside. Art Lux was sitting at a pair of marine-band radios.

The sheriff got up, poured coffee into a styrofoam cup, passed it over to Wade. "Not a whole lot to report," he said. "Still at it, lots of lake to check out." Behind him, the two radios made sharp crackling noises. "Got yourself some rest, sir?"

"A little. What's the plan?"

"Nothing fancy. Keep at it." Lux pointed up at a large survey map tacked to a wall. "That whole area there, we got it covered solid. Checked out the resorts. All closed up for the season, no signs of nothing. Right now the wild card's gasoline. How much she's got, how she uses it. Those little Evinrudes, they go forever on a lousy tablespoon."

Wade nodded. He watched Lux pour himself a half cup of coffee and sit down in front of the radios. The man was wearing his dairy farmer outfit, gray on gray, a green Cargill cap perched up top.

"So you're hanging tough, sir?"

"Well enough. Kathy's sister comes in at one."

Lux offered an approving smile. "Glad to hear that. A person needs company."

"True, but it doesn't help—"

"If you don't mind my saying so, a thing like this, it tends to put everything else in perspective. What's important, what's not. Politics and all that." Lux glanced at the radios, then at the concrete floor. "Not that it matters, I guess, but I voted for you. Great big X next to your name."

Wade rolled his shoulders. "That's two of us."

"You deserved better."

They looked at each other with a kind of curiosity. Not friendly, not hostile either. Lux locked his hands behind his head, tilted back in his chair. "I should be totally straight. Vinny Pearson, he thinks you're—what's the right way to say this? He thinks you're not quite explaining everything."

"Vinny's wrong."

"Is he?"

"Yes," Wade said. "I love my wife."

"Well, absolutely. I can tell. Thing is, though, Vinny says you should be out looking. That's what he keeps blabbing about—'The man ain't even *looking*.' Exact words."

"No kidding?"

"Yes, sir."

"In that case," Wade said, "tell him to fuck himself. Exact words."

The sheriff grinned. "Right *there*, that's how come I voted for you. Spit and vinegar. All the same, a piece of advice, you might want to think about getting some fresh lake air."

"Fine then. I'll do that."

Wade looked at his wristwatch and turned toward the door.

"One other thing," Lux said. "You get a chance, bring the sister by. A couple simple questions."

It was a little before one o'clock when Wade stepped outside. He walked up past the post office and turned into the boatyard behind Amdahl's Mini-Mart. The place was littered with barbed wire and rotting lumber and a dozen old boats in various stages of decay. Near the water a hand-lettered yellow sign said TOWN LANDING. The place seemed inanimate, no cars or people.

Wade made his way out onto one of the wooden docks and looked across the inlet to where the horizon was almost black with forest. His headache was back. Too much booze, obviously. It was time, he decided, for some reforms. The positive approach. Dispense with the liquor, get himself together.

Tomorrow, he thought. No doubt about it.

At one-fifteen the float plane splashed down, settled onto its pontoons, and turned in toward the docks. Pat was first off. No mistaking her—a taller, more muscular version of Kathy.

She wore a red tank top, black jeans, high white sneakers. Even from a distance her arms had the gloss of new copper piping.

Wade felt a curious shyness as they touched cheeks.

"Still nothing," he said. "Let me help with that."

He took her suitcase and led her up to the car, talking fast, feeling clumsy and thick-tongued as he tried to summarize the steps Lux had taken.

Pat seemed distracted. "No sign at all?"

"Not yet. No."

"How long has it been?"

"Two days. A little more." He tried out a smile. "The weather's decent, we don't have to worry about that part. She's probably all right."

"Shit."

"Almost for sure."

Pat got into the car, buckled the seat belt, folded her arms tight to her chest. For the first mile or two she kept her eyes straight ahead.

"Two days," she finally said. "You could've called a little sooner. No big joy to hear about it on TV."

"I didn't know if . . . I kept thinking she'd be back."

"She's my *sister*."

"Sorry. You're right."

"Right I'm right."

Pat shifted uncomfortably in her seat. For the rest of the ride nothing much was said.

When they reached the cottage, Wade parked near the porch and carried her suitcase inside. The place had a musty, unlived-in smell, dank and oppressive. On the kitchen table was a note from Claude and Ruth saying they'd gone off to pick up a few things, they'd be back in an hour.

Pat sniffed the air and kicked off her sneakers.

"I'll shower," she said, "then we'll talk."

"Hungry?"

"Maybe a little."

Wade led her down the hall to the spare bedroom, dug out a clean towel, then returned to the kitchen and opened up a can of minestrone. He tried to imagine a decent conclusion to things. A call from Lux. Kathy walking in the door. Grinning at him, asking what was for lunch.

The fantasies didn't help.

He dumped the soup in a pan, got out the bread and butter. He could hear the shower going down the hall.

Right now, he told himself, caution was the key. Almost certainly Kathy had confided in Pat about certain things. Which could cause difficulties. And there was also that resentment in her eyes, the suspicion, whatever it was.

He gave the soup a stir.

For a few minutes he stood very still, gliding here and there. Too many discontinuities, too many mind-shadows. His eye fell on the iron teakettle. On impulse he picked it up, took it outside and dumped it in the trash.

When he came back in, Pat was sitting at the kitchen table. She wore a pair of baggy blue shorts and a U of M sweatshirt. Her hair was slicked straight back.

Wade dished up two bowls of soup.

"All right," she said. "So talk."

She was mostly interested in practical matters—Kathy's health, the search, the condition of the boat—and over the next half hour Wade did his best to give short, practical answers.

The boat, he said, was perfectly serviceable. No health problems. A good professional search.

Not too bad, he thought, but not easy either.

On occasion he could see doubt forming in her eyes, all the personal issues, and it was a relief when she stood up and asked to see the boathouse. He led her down the slope, opened up the double doors, and stood to one side as she stared down at the dirt floor. For a while she was quiet.

"Doesn't make sense," she said. "I don't get it."

"Get it?"

"That day. Where was she *going?*"

Wade looked away. "Hard to tell. Into town, I guess. Or maybe—I don't know—maybe for a ride."

"A ride?"

"Maybe."

"For no reason?"

Wade shrugged. "She didn't need reasons. Sometimes she'd take off without ever . . . Just pick up and go."

"Not exactly. She had reasons and more reasons. Way too *many* reasons."

Pat turned and went outside and stood hugging herself at the edge of the lake. After a few minutes Wade followed. "She'll be fine," he said. "It'll work out."

"I just feel—"

"What we'll do, I'll arrange for a boat tomorrow. Get out there and give a hand. At least it's something."

"Right, something," she said.

They stood looking out at the lake. Pat reached down and splashed a handful of water against her face.

"God," she said. "I'm afraid."

"Yes."

"The last time I talked to her . . . I don't know, she seemed so happy, like she could finally relax and get on with her life."

"Happy?" Wade said.

"The fact that it was all over. The politics."

"I didn't know."

"You should have."

Pat waited a moment, then sighed and hooked his arm. The gesture startled him—he almost backed off.

"Bother you?" she said. "Body contact?"

"Just the surprise."

"Oh, I'll bet. Let's walk."

They followed the dirt road for a quarter mile, then turned south on a path that curled through deep forest toward the fire tower. The scent of leafy autumn filled the air, yet the afternoon had the temperate, silky feel of mid-summer. They crossed an old footbridge and followed a stream that bubbled along off to their left. Despite himself, Wade couldn't help scanning the brush. Kathy had walked this trail almost every day since they'd taken the cottage, the same spongy earth, and now he was struck by the sensation that she was somewhere close by, watching from behind the pines, maybe.

After twenty minutes they reached the fire tower. A green and white Forest Service sign warned against trespassing.

"Nice spot," Pat said. "Very outdoorsy."

She sat down in a patch of sunlight, studied him for a moment, then yawned and tilted her face up to the sky. "So tired," she said, "so dead, dead tired."

"We can head back."

"Soon. Not yet."

Wade lay back in the shade. The forest seemed to wash up against him, lush and supple, and presently he shut his eyes and let the glide carry him away. Maybe it was the mild autumn air, or the scent of pine, but something about the afternoon made his breathing easier. Pleasant memories came to mind. Kathy's laughter. The way she slept on her side, thumb up against her nose. The way she'd go through five or six packs of Life Savers a day. Lots of things. Lots of good things. He remembered the times back in college when they'd gone dancing, how she'd look at him in a way that made him queasy with joy, totally full, totally empty.

Joy. That was the truth.

And now it was something else. Ambition and wasted time. Everything good had gotten lost.

For a while he let the guilt take him, then later he heard Pat sit up and clear her throat. A woodpecker was rapping in the woods behind them.

"John?"

"Yes."

"Nothing. Forget it." A few minutes passed. "You know what I keep thinking? I keep thinking what a good person she is. Just so good."

"I know."

"In love, too. Crazy about you."

"It went both ways."

Pat shook her head. "Like a little girl or something, all tied up in knots. Couldn't even think for herself—John this, John that. Drove me up the wall."

"I can understand that."

"Can you?"

"Sure. I think so."

Pat brushed a clump of pine needles from her arm. In the streaky sunlight her hair took on a color that was only a tone or two away from gray. "What I mean," she said, "I mean Kathy sort of—you know—she almost *lost* herself in you. Your career, your problems."

"Except for the dentist," Wade said.

"That was nothing."

"So I'm told. It didn't feel like nothing."

"Knock it off. The guy was just a walking panic button, something to wake you up. That's what the whole stupid fling was all *about*—to make you see what you were losing. Besides, it's not like you didn't have some private crud of your own."

"Not that kind. I've been faithful."

"Faithful," Pat muttered. She waved a hand. "And what about Little Miss Politics? Wooing the bitch day and night. That's faithful, I'm the rosy red virgin."

Wade looked straight at her. "I had my dreams," he said. "So did Kathy. It was something we shared."

"You're not serious."

"I am."

"Man, you really *didn't* know her, did you? Kathy despised it all, every crummy minute. The political wifey routine—paste on the smiles and act devoted. It gets pretty demeaning."

"But we had this—"

"John, listen to me. Just *listen*. Hate, that's a polite way of saying it. She used to get the shakes out in public, you could actually see it, like she was packed in ice or something. Completely obvious. All you had to do was look."

"I did look."

"All the wrong places. Which is something we haven't touched on yet. The great spy."

Wade shook his head. "There were problems, maybe, but it's not like we were on different tracks. I wanted things, she wanted things."

"Wanted?"

"Want. Still want."

"I won't argue."

"Pat, there's nothing to argue about."

She sat rocking for a time, toying with a heavy silver bracelet on her wrist, then made a small, dismissive motion with her shoulders.

"We should go."

"Right, fine," Wade said. "Just to be clear, though, Kathy and I had something together. It wasn't so terrible."

"That's not quite the point."

"Which is what?"

Pat seemed to flinch. "We shouldn't talk about it."

"*What* point?"

They looked at each other with the knowledge that they had come up against the edge of the permissible. Pat stood and brushed herself off. "All right, if you want the truth," she said, "Kathy got scared sometimes. The detective act. The stuff you'd yell in your sleep. It gave her the heebie-jeebies."

"She told you that?"

"She didn't have to. And then the headlines. One day she wakes up, sees all that creepiness splashed across the front page. Finds out she's hooked up with a war criminal."

"It wasn't that simple," Wade said.

"No?"

"Not by half."

"Well, whatever. She's your wife. You could've opened up, tried to explain."

Wade looked down at the palms of his hands. He wondered if there was anything of consequence that could be said.

"Very noble, but it's not something you sit down and explain. What could I *tell* her? It looks black and white now—very clear—but back then everything came at you in these bright colors. No sharp edges. Lots of glare. A nightmare like that, all you want is to forget. None of it ever seemed real in the first place."

"What about the dead folks?"

"Look, I can't—"

"Awfully real to them." Pat swung around and looked at him hard. "You didn't do something?"

"Do?"

"Don't fake it. You know what I mean."

She watched him closely for a few seconds. There were birds in the trees, ripples of sunlight.

"No," Wade said, "I didn't *do* something."

"I just—"

"Sure. You had to ask."

Ruth and Claude were waiting for them back at the cottage. Wade made the introductions, excused himself, and went to the phone to put in a call to Lux. The sheriff's voice seemed hollow and very distant. "No dice," he said, "I'm sorry," and after a short silence the man made a clucking sound that could've meant anything, maybe sympathy, maybe exasperation.

When he hung up, Wade looked at the clock over the kitchen stove. The cocktail hour. Reformation could wait. He fixed four stiff screwdrivers, got out a box of crackers, and carried everything on a tray to the living room. Claude and Ruth were talking quietly with Pat, who sat cross-legged on the sofa.

The old man lifted his eyebrows.

"Nothing," Wade said. He passed out the drinks. "I'll want a boat tomorrow. Probably all day."

Claude nodded. "Six-thirty sharp. Just be ready."

"Fine, but there's no need to tag along."

"Hell there isn't. Last thing I need, it's two more customers out there. Public relations, all that."

Wade shrugged. "Fine, then. Thanks."

"Nothing to thank. Six-thirty."

After fifteen minutes Pat went back to the spare bedroom. Claude and Ruth stayed for another drink, then Wade walked them out to the old man's pickup. When they were gone, he went back inside, built a fire in the stone fireplace, freshened his drink, and sat down with a *Star-Tribune* that Claude had picked up in town. Kathy was page-two news. He skimmed through the piece quickly, barely concentrating. There were quotes from Tony Carbo, who expressed his concern, and from the governor and the party chairman and a couple of Kathy's colleagues at the university. Below the fold was a grainy photograph taken on primary night. Kathy stood with one arm hooked around Wade's waist, the other raised in a shielding motion. Her eyes were slightly out of focus, but there was no mistaking the radiance in her face, the purest elation.

Wade put the paper down. For several minutes he sat watching the fire, then he finished his drink and went out to the kitchen for replenishment.

———

It was a bad night. He kept tumbling inside himself, half asleep, half awake, his dreams folding around the theme of depravity—things he remembered and things he could not remember.

Around midnight he got up.

He put on jeans and a sweatshirt, found a flashlight, and made his way down to the boathouse.

He wasn't certain what was drawing him out. Maybe the dreams, maybe the need to know.

He opened up the doors and stepped inside, using the flashlight to pluck random objects from the dark: an anchor, a rusty tackle box, a stack of decoys. A sense of pre-memory washed over him. Things had happened here. Things said, things done. He squatted down, brushed a hand across the dirt floor, and put the hand to his nose. The smell gave him pause. He had a momentary glimpse of himself from above, as if through a camera lens. Ex-sorcerer. Ex-candidate for the United States Senate. Now a poor hung-over putz without a trick in his bag.

He sniffed his hand again, then shook his head. The dank odor revived facts he did not wish to revive.

There was the fact of an iron teakettle. Kill Jesus, that also was a fact. Defeat was a fact. Rage was a fact. And there were the facts of steam and a dead geranium. Other things were less firm. It was almost a fact, but not quite, that he had moved down the hallway to their bedroom that night, where for a period of time he had watched Kathy sleep, admiring the tan at her neck and shoulders, her fleshy lips, the way her thumb lay curled along the side of her nose. At one point, he remembered, her eyelids had snapped open.

He stood still for a moment. The wind seemed to lift up the boathouse roof, holding it briefly, then letting it slap down hard. Even in the weak light Wade could make out a number of grooves and scratchings where the boat had been dragged out to the beach. He tried to imagine Kathy handling it alone, and the Evinrude too, but he couldn't come up with a convincing flow of images. Not impossible, but not likely either, which left room for speculation.

The thing about facts, he decided, was that they came in sizes. You had to try them on for proper fit. A case in point: his own responsibility. Right now he couldn't help feeling the burn of guilt. All that empty time. The convenience of a faulty memory.

He stepped outside, closed the doors, switched off the flashlight and walked back up the slope to the cottage.

Pat sat waiting for him on the porch.

"Out for a stroll?" she said.

20

Evidence

The man was like one of them famous onions. Keep peeling back the layers, there's always more. But I liked him. Her, too. In some ways they was a lot alike, more than you'd figure. Two peas in a pod, Claude used to say, but I always claimed onions.

—Ruth Rasmussen

There was plenty he wasn't saying. Plenty. One of these days I'd like to go out and do some more digging around that old cottage, or dredge the lake. I bet bones would come up.

—Vincent R. (Vinny) Pearson

We live in our own souls as in an unmapped region, a few acres of which we have cleared for our habitation; while of the nature of those nearest us we know but the boundaries that march with ours.[1]

—Edith Wharton (*The Touchstone*)

---

1. Edith Wharton, *The Touchstone* (1900; reprint, New York: Harper Perennial, 1991), p. 102.

He was constantly doing weird things, like he'd trail her around campus like one of those private eyes or something, except he was a klutz and Kathy always knew about it. I can't see how she tolerated him, but she did. Head over heels, you could say.[2]

> —Deborah Lindquist (Classmate of Kathleen Wade, University of Minnesota)

Johnny had slick hands. With magicians that's a compliment. Ten, eleven years old, he could work freestyle, no apparatus, just those beautiful little hands of his. And he knew how to keep his mouth shut.

> —Sandra Karra (Karra's Studio of Magic)

You will never explain your tricks [to an audience], for no matter how clever the means, the explanation disappoints the desire to believe in something beyond natural causes, and admiration for cleverness is a poor substitute for the delight of wonderment.[3]

> —Robert Parrish (*The Magician's Handbook*)

Forget the dentist! She was my *sister*—why can't you just leave her alone? It's like you're obsessed.[4]

> —Patricia S. Hood

GLOSSARY

Effect: The professional term for a magician's illusion.

Stripper deck: A deck of cards whose sides or ends have been

---

2. Interview, Worthington, Minnesota, April 2, 1993.

3. Parrish, *The Magician's Handbook*, p. 16.

4. Obsessed? See footnote 21 on page 199.

planed on a taper so that if a card is reversed, it can be located by feeling the protruding edges.

Vanish (noun): A technical term for an effect in which an object or person is made to disappear.

Transposition: A magic trick in which two or more objects or persons mysteriously change places.

Causal transportation: A technical term for an effect in which the causal agent is itself made to vanish; i.e., the magician performs a vanish on himself.

Double consummation: A way of fooling the audience by making it believe a trick is over before it really is.[5]

He had two lives: one, open, seen and known by all who cared to know . . . and another life running its course in secret.[6]

    —Anton Chekhov ("The Lady with the Dog")

Q: How many people did you gather up?

A: Between thirty and fifty. Men, women, and children.

Q: What kind of children?

A: They was just children.

Q: Where did you get these people?

A: Some of them was in hootches and some was in rice paddies when we gathered them up.

Q: Why did you gather them up?

A: We suspected them of being Viet Cong. And as far as I'm concerned, they're still Viet Cong.[7]

    —Paul Meadlo (Court-Martial Testimony)

---

5. Kaye, *The Stein and Day Handbook of Magic*, pp. 304–307.

6. Anton Chekhov, "The Lady with the Dog," in *The Lady with the Dog and Other Stories*, translated by Constance Garnett (New York: The Macmillan Company, 1917), pp. 24–25.

7. In Hammer, *The Court-Martial of Lt. Calley*, pp. 153–154.

I didn't shoot nobody. I shot some cows.
—Richard Thinbill

Love and War are the same thing, and stratagems and policy are as allowable in one as in the other.[8]
—Miguel de Cervantes

I found his father in the garage. I knew. I really did. Even before I went in.
—Eleanor K. Wade

[Houdini's father] took the young Houdini to a stage performance by a traveling magician named Dr. Lynn. Dr. Lynn's magic act featured an illusion called "Palegenisia." In this illusion, he pretended to administer chloroform to a man, and then, after tying him in place inside a cabinet, Dr. Lynn proceeded to dismember the man with a huge butcher knife, cutting off legs and arms, and finally (discreetly covered with a black cloth) the man's head. The pieces were then thrown into the cabinet and the curtain was pulled. Moments later, the victim appeared from the cabinet restored to one living piece, and seemingly none the worse for the ordeal. Many years later Houdini purchased this illusion . . . It is significant that, at an early age, Houdini had been fascinated by this particular illusion literally embodying the theme of death and resurrection, for this was a motif that reoccurred in all of Houdini's performances throughout his career.[9]
—Doug Henning (*Houdini: His Legend and His Magic*)

---

8. Miguel de Cervantes, *Don Quixote* (reprint, New York: Modern Library, 1955), p. 580.

9. Doug Henning, *Houdini: His Legend and His Magic* (New York: Times Books, 1977), p. 26.

I told you how secretive he was—you never knew what he was thinking—and it just got worse after his father hanged himself.

—Eleanor K. Wade

[Woodrow] Wilson's own recollections of his youth furnish ample indication of his early fears that he was stupid, ugly, worthless, and unlovable . . . It is perhaps to this core feeling of inadequacy, of a fundamental worthlessness which must ever be disproved, that the unappeasable quality of his need for affection, power, and achievement, and the compulsive quality of his striving for perfection, may be traced. For one of the ways in which human beings troubled with low estimates of themselves seek to obliterate their inner pain is through high achievement and the acquisition of power.[10]

—Alexander and Juliette George (*Woodrow Wilson and Colonel House*)

We'd just started gym class. I had the kids shooting baskets and after five or ten minutes the school principal came in and called me over and gave me the news. Then she walked away—a pure coward. I wasn't much better. I told John to hit the showers, his mom was waiting. A kid that age, it breaks your heart.[11]

—Lawrence Ehlers (Phys-Ed Teacher)

Another cousin, Jessie Bones, recalled a typical instance of Dr. Wilson's "teasing." The family was assembled at a wed-

---

10. Alexander L. George and Juliette L. George, *Woodrow Wilson and Colonel House: A Personality Study* (New York: The John Day Company, 1956), p. 8.

11. Interview, St. Paul, Minnesota, March 1, 1994.

ding breakfast. Tommy [Woodrow] arrived at the table late. His father apologized on behalf of his son and explained that Tommy had been so greatly excited at the discovery of another hair in his mustache that morning that it had taken him longer to wash and dress. "I remember very distinctly the painful flush that came over the boy's face," Mrs. Brower said.[12]

> —Alexander and Juliette George (*Woodrow Wilson and Colonel House*)

His father was never physically abusive. When he wasn't on the bottle, Paul could be very attentive to the boy, extremely caring. John loved him like crazy. Everybody did. My husband had this wonderful magnetic quality—this glow—he'd just point those incredible blue eyes at you and you'd feel like you were under a big hot sun or something . . . Except then he'd go back to the booze and it was like the sun burned itself out. He was a sad person underneath. I wish I knew what he was so sad about. I keep wondering.

> —Eleanor K. Wade

When he was a college student, [Lyndon Johnson's] fellow students . . . believed not only that he lied to them constantly, lied about big matters and small, lied so incessantly that he was, in a widely used phrase, "the biggest liar on campus"—but also that some psychological element *impelled* him to lie.[13]

> —Robert A. Caro (*The Years of Lyndon Johnson*)

---

12. George and George, *Woodrow Wilson and Colonel House*, p. 8.
13. Caro, *The Years of Lyndon Johnson: The Path to Power*, p. xx.

He was ambitious, no doubt about it, but that's not a black mark in my book. No ambition, no politics—it's that simple. But John also had ideals. A good progressive Democrat. Very dedicated. Help the needy, et cetera, ad weirdum. In retrospect, knowing what I know now, I guess he wanted to make up for what happened during the war. The way I see it, he came back pretty shattered, pretty fucked up, then he got married to Kathy and they had this really great love thing going. Never saw two people so feelie-grabbie. So he gets his life back together. Doesn't say anything about the Vietnam shit—not to his wife or me or anybody. And then after a while he *can't* say anything. Sort of trapped, you know? That's my theory. I don't think it started out as an intentional lie, he just kept mum about it—who the hell wouldn't?—and pretty soon he probably talked himself into believing it never happened at all. The guy was a magic man. He could fool people. Sure as fuck fooled me . . . Anyhow, I think the lies were sort of built into this whole repair-your-life thing of his—the ambitions, the big Washington dreams—and I guess it basically boils down to a case of colossal self-deception. State office, that's one thing, but this was a run for the United States Senate. The shit *had* to come out: a principle of politics. And so we get pulverized and he's right back to square one. Shattered again. That blank deadman look I told you about.

—Anthony L. (Tony) Carbo

I didn't know what to do. At his dad's funeral. The way he was yelling—he wouldn't stop. It was embarrassing.

—Eleanor K. Wade

Kill Jesus![14]
> —John Wade

I took down a single-barreled gun which belonged to my father, and which had often been promised me when I grew up. Then, armed with the gun, I went upstairs. On the first floor landing I met my mother. She was coming out of the death-chamber . . . she was in tears. "Where are you going?" she asked . . . "I'm going to the sky!" I answered. "What? You're going to the sky?" "Yes, don't stop me." "And what are you going to do in the sky, my poor child?" "I'm going to kill God, who killed Father."[15]
> —Alexandre Dumas (*My Memoirs*)

John never accepted it. I'd hear him in his room at night, he'd be having these make-believe conversations with his dad. Just like me, he wanted explanations—he wanted to know *why*—but I guess we both finally had to come up with our own pathetic answers.
> —Eleanor K. Wade

Indeed, many young children express anger because they believe the death of a parent is deliberate abandonment . . . [T]here are negative consequences for those who carry unresolved childhood grief into adulthood.[16]
> —Richard R. Ellis ("Young Children: Disenfranchised
> Grievers")

---

14. Reported by Patricia S. Hood, from a conversation with Kathleen Wade.

15. Alexandre Dumas, *My Memoirs*, in D. J. Enright, ed., *The Oxford Book of Death* (New York: Oxford University Press, 1983), p. 275.

16. Richard R. Ellis, "Young Children: Disenfranchised Grievers," in Kenneth J. Doka, ed., *Disenfranchised Grief: Recognizing Hidden Sorrow* (Lexington, Mass.: Lexington Books, 1989), pp. 202, 206.

Shame . . . can be understood as a wound in the self. It is frequently instilled at a delicate age, as a result of the internalization of a contemptuous voice, usually parental. Rebukes, warnings, teasing, ridicule, ostracism, and other forms of neglect or abuse can play a part.[17]

   —Robert Karen ("Shame")

I came to a hootch and a lady jumped out. I shot and wounded her, and she jumped in again and then came out with a baby and some others . . . There was a man, a woman, and two girls . . . [A] guy from the Second Platoon came up and grabbed my rifle and said, "Kill them all!" He shot them.[18]

   —Roy Wood (Court-Martial Testimony)

Q: Who did the shooting?

A: Almost everybody. Some of it was just by accident. My buddy Sorcerer, he just . . .

Q: Who?

A: Sorcerer. He shot this old guy by accident, that's what he told me. Like a reflex, I guess.

Q: Who's Sorcerer?

A: A guy. I can't remember his actual name.

Q: Could you try?

A: I *could*.[19]

   —Richard Thinbill (Court-Martial Testimony)

---

17. Robert Karen, "Shame," *The Atlantic Monthly*, February 1992, p. 42.

18. In Hammer, *The Court-Martial of Lt. Calley*, p. 110.

19. Richard Thinbill, transcript, Court-Martial of Lieutenant William Calley, U.S. National Archives, box 4, folder 8, p. 1734.

John! John! Oh, John!
  —George Armstrong Custer

Q: Well, what did you see in that ditch?
 A: Inside the ditch there were bodies.
Q: Do you know how many?
 A: Thirty-five to fifty.
Q: What were they doing?
 A: They appeared to be dead.[20]
  —Ronald Grzesik (Court-Martial Testimony)

The place stunk, especially that ditch. Flies everywhere. They glowed in the dark. It was like the spirit world or something.[21]

—Richard Thinbill

---

20. In Hammer, *The Court-Martial of Lt. Calley*, p. 150.

21. It *was* the spirit world. Vietnam. Ghosts and graveyards. I arrived in-country a year after John Wade, in 1969, and walked exactly the ground he walked, in and around Pinkville, through the villages of Thuan Yen and My Khe and Co Luy. I know what happened that day. I know how it happened. I know why. It was the sunlight. It was the wickedness that soaks into your blood and slowly heats up and begins to boil. Frustration, partly. Rage, partly. The enemy was invisible. They were ghosts. They killed us with land mines and booby traps; they disappeared into the night, or into tunnels, or into the deep misted-over paddies and bamboo and elephant grass. But it went beyond that. Something more mysterious. The smell of incense, maybe. The unknown, the unknowable. The blank faces. The overwhelming otherness. This is not to justify what occurred on March 16, 1968, for in my view such justifications are both futile and outrageous. Rather, it's to bear witness to the mystery of evil. Twenty-five years ago, as a terrified young PFC, I too could taste the sunlight. I could smell the sin. I could feel the butchery sizzling like grease just under my eyeballs.

21

The Nature of the Spirit

The killing went on for four hours. It was thorough and systematic. In the morning sunlight, which shifted from pink to purple, people were shot dead and carved up with knives and raped and sodomized and bayoneted and blown into scraps. The bodies lay in piles. Around eleven, when Charlie Company broke for chow, PFC Richard Thinbill sat down with Sorcerer along a paddy dike just outside Thuan Yen. He opened a can of peaches, cocked his head. "That sound," he said, "you *hear* that?"

Sorcerer nodded. It wasn't one sound. It was many thousand sounds.

After a while Thinbill said, "Oh, man."

Later he said, "They told us there wouldn't be no civilians. Didn't they say that? No civilians?" He finished his peaches, tossed the can away, unwrapped a chocolate bar. "I guess they was Communists."

"Probably."

"How many you get?"

"Two," Sorcerer said.

Thinbill licked his lips. He was a young, good-looking kid, a full-blooded Chippewa with nervous eyes and gentle moves.

For a few seconds he looked down at his chocolate bar. "That *sound*, man."

"It'll go away."

"Bullshit it will. At least I didn't kill nobody."

"Good. That's good."

"Yeah, but . . . What *happened* here?"

"The sunlight," Sorcerer said.

"Say again?"

"Eat your chocolate."

Thinbill started to say something, then stopped and pressed the palms of his hands to his ears. "Jesus, man. What I'd give for earplugs."

The polls had gone from bad to depressing, then to impossible, and the landslide on September 9 came as no surprise. Around nine in the evening Tony Carbo turned off the TV set. "Why wait?" he said.

John Wade went to the telephone and put in the call to Ed Durkee. It was easy. All he could feel was the cool shadow of emotion. At one point, still on the phone, he nodded at Kathy and lifted a thumb.

Ten minutes later they took an elevator down to the hotel's ballroom, where John delivered a brisk concession speech. His career was over, he knew that, but he talked about politics as a grand human experiment. He thanked Kathy and Tony and others. He waved at the crowd and took Kathy's hand, and they kissed and walked off the platform and went back up to the room and got undressed and took the phone off its cradle and turned out the lights and lay in bed and listened to the flow of traffic below their window.

After an hour they got dressed again.

John made a few calls, and took a few, then they ordered

a late dinner. Around midnight Tony Carbo knocked on the door. He had a bottle under his arm; his plump white face was beaded with sweat. "One for the road," he said.

He rinsed out a pair of glasses and sat on the bed next to Kathy.

"She's a trooper," he said to John. "I love your wife. Dearly, dearly."

Kathy smiled. She'd never looked happier.

Tony filled the two glasses, passed them out, kept the bottle for himself. The lapels of his corduroy jacket were stained with something yellow. "My God, look at me," he said, "I'm a pig." He took a swallow and wiped his mouth. "I've talked with your pal Durkee. Man signed me up—lousy hours, lousy pay."

"That was quick," John said.

"Quick and the dead."

"You're a bastard."

"It's a job. Keeps a pig busy." He glanced up at Kathy and tried to smile. "Anyhow, I'm not impressed by the guilty-Tony stuff. I asked a million times about skeletons."

"That's not what—"

"All you had to do was *say* something. Could've made it work for us. Whole different spiel." He clamped a hand to his chest. "A village is a terrible thing to waste."

"I should throw you out the window."

"Yeah, you should. Way too chubby."

For a while they were silent. Very carefully, Kathy put her glass down, went into the bathroom, and locked the door.

"Ah, well," Tony said.

He studied his hands, grunted, and stood up. He didn't look well.

"There's the tough part. Your wife and me—no more

dreams. *C'est la politique.* Pity, pity. Tell her it's how the game gets played."

"Fuck you."

"Right. Fuck me." He crossed over to the bathroom door, kissed it lightly, and turned around to face John. "Breaks my heart, you know? She's a sweetheart."

"You can leave."

"In a jiff. Need a belt?"

"No."

"Old times. One belt."

"If it helps you leave."

"Oh, sure. Bingo-zingo." Tony swayed sideways, caught himself, and spilled some Scotch into John's glass. "You look like a dead man."

"Thanks."

"To dead men. Long may they live."

They drank and looked at each other. There was the sound of running water in the bathroom.

"Lady's pissed," Tony said. "That's what I presume. I do presume it. Hope you'll explain that a guy has to work. Can't live on fat alone."

"You could've waited."

"I could've. And you could've mentioned a certain fucked-up body count. Saved me some calories. Lots of could'ves zipping through the cool night air. One last nip?"

"No."

"Good for heartburn. Wakes up the dead."

"No."

Tony walked over and put his ear against the bathroom door. He listened for a moment, then sighed. "Alas, we all got peccadilloes. Indeed we do. Dirty laundry, et cetera and so on. You want to hear about mine?"

"I want you to leave."

"Sweet, sweet Kathleen. Embarrassing to admit, but I used to lie in bed at night and squish the blubber and say her name right out loud. Sad case. Lovesick. Kept thinking all I had to do was shape up, she'd run away with me. Actually went over to this gym on Lake Street. Big plans, real torture. Sweated like crazy. Eighty bucks a sit-up, didn't drop a pound."

John felt a sudden crushing fatigue. "Fine. You can take off now."

"Dreamy dreams."

"Go," John said.

Tony tucked his bottle into a side pocket and moved unsteadily toward the door. After a couple of steps he stopped. "For what it's worth, I could've jumped ship a month ago. Hung around just for the love rays. Sad situation." He wagged his head and smiled. "Poor me, poor you. All those skeletons—what a madhouse."

"Have fun with Durkee," John said.

Tony laughed lightly. "I'm a pig. It's all I know."

In mid-afternoon Charlie Company saddled up and headed east toward the sea.

Sorcerer kept to himself near the rear of the column. Head down, shoulders stooped, he counted his steps and tried to push away the evil. It wasn't easy. The buzz had gone into his head. Flies, he thought, but other things too. The earth and the sky and the sunlight. It all joined together.

Late in the afternoon they set up a perimeter near the coast. Off to the west, where the mountains were, the sky went to waxy red, then to violet, and soon the twilight was animated by curious shapes and silhouettes. "The spirit world," Thinbill said, and there was a short quiet before someone said, "Fuckers just don't *die*."

They sat in ragged groups at their foxholes, some of them silent, others putting moral spin on the day. Rusty Calley was among the talkers. Gooks were gooks, he said. They had been told to waste the place, and wasted it was, and who on God's scorched green earth could possibly give a shit? Boyce and Conti laughed at this. Thinbill glared at the lieutenant and got up and moved away.

Calley glanced over at Sorcerer. "What's Apache's problem? Not some weenie roast."

"Chippewa," Sorcerer said. "Thinbill is."

"Is he now?"

"Yes, sir."

Calley looked off into dead space. There was a conspicuous blood stench coming from his clothes and skin. "Not up on my tribes, I reckon, but you can tell him it was a slick operation. Lock an' load and do our chores."

"Yes, sir," Sorcerer said.

"Search and waste."

"Except there weren't any weapons to speak of. No incoming. Women and babies."

Calley brushed a fly off his sleeve. "Now which babies are these?"

"The ones . . . You know."

"Hey, *which* babies?" Calley lifted his eyebrows at Boyce and Mitchell. "You troopers notice any VC babies back there?"

"No way," said Boyce. "Not the breathing kind."

Calley nodded. "There we are, then. Anyhow, if you ask

me, the guilty shouldn't cast no stones. Another famous Bible regulation."

In the dark someone chuckled.

Somebody else said, "Roger-dodger."

The night had come down dark and solid. Sorcerer sat listening for a while longer, then stood up and crossed the perimeter to Thinbill's foxhole. The kid was sitting alone, staring out at the paddies.

Ten or fifteen minutes went by before Thinbill said, "Lieutenant Stupid. Blow snot in his face, he'll say it's the monsoons. A killer, too."

"Not just him."

Thinbill let out a shallow, helpless sigh. "Man, I close my eyes, I can't stop seeing . . . Like a butcher shop. How many you think got—?"

"I didn't count."

"Three hundred. Three hundred easy."

"Probably."

"For sure. Not probably." Thinbill lay back and looked up at the stars. After a time he made a soft noise in his throat. "And that stink, man. I can't shake it."

"We'll find a river. Wash it off."

"It's not the washable kind. I mean, how do you live with it? What the fuck do you put in your letters home?"

"I don't know," Sorcerer said. "Try to forget."

"Like how?"

"Concentrate. Think about other things."

Once again they fell silent, listening to the flies, the deep droning buzz all around them.

"Oh, wow," Thinbill said.

———

In the morning Charlie Company headed south toward a river called the Song Tra Khuc. The day was hot and empty. After a half hour the First Platoon veered off to the west and began moving up a low, gently sloping hill that rose from the paddies like some weary old beast pushing to its knees. An elephant, Maples said, but somebody else shook his head and said, No way, it was more like a mangy water buffalo, and then the argument went back and forth as they climbed the hill.

Sorcerer could not see how any of it mattered. He kept picturing an old man with a hoe, how the poor guy went skidding through the powdery red dust, how his hoe sailed up high like a baton and twinkled in the morning sunlight and came down uncaught. Forget it, he thought, but the pictures wouldn't go away.

Halfway up the hill, the column took a break while Calley and Meadlo went ahead with the mine detector. It was a dangerous piece of ground, heavily mined and booby-trapped, and the men were careful to pick out harmless-looking spots to sit or kneel. A few lit up cigarettes. Most just sat and waited. The blood smell had soaked into their skin. "Grave robbers," Conti said. He giggled and made ghost sounds until Thinbill told him to zip up.

Sorcerer tried not to listen. He rubbed his eyes and gazed out on the flat green countryside below. To the north, maybe a klick away, the village of Thuan Yen was a darkly wooded smudge against the paddies. A half-dozen hootches were still sending up smoke.

"Zombie patrol," Conti said, "that's us," and he let out a ghoulish howl, and an instant later a land mine tore off Paul Meadlo's left foot.

The explosion wasn't much. A quick, dull thud.

Sorcerer looked over his shoulder. There was a moment of indecisive silence, then rising voices, then the flies again.

Jiggling John, his father used to call him, even though he wasn't fat. It was the booze talking, John understood that, but he still felt baffled and ashamed.

Sometimes he wanted to cry. Sometimes he wondered why his father hated him.

More than anything else John Wade wanted to be loved, and to make his father proud, and so one day in sixth grade he secretly wrote away for a special diet he'd seen advertised in a magazine. When it arrived in the mail a few weeks later, along with a bill for thirty-eight dollars, his father brought the envelope up to John's room and dropped it in his lap. He didn't smile. He didn't act proud. "Thirty-eight bucks," he said. "That's a whole lot of bacon fat."

It was a relief when John finally started growing. By eighth grade he'd gone tall and slender, almost skinny, which looked good in the mirrors.

"Javelin John," his father said, chuckling a little, slapping him on the back.

The mirrors helped him get by. They were like a glass box in his head, a place to hide, and all through junior high, whenever things got bad, John would slip into the box of mirrors and disappear there. He was a daydreamer. He had few friends, none close. After school, and on most weekends, he spent his free time down in the basement, all alone, no teasing or distractions, just perfecting his magic. There was something peaceful about it, something firm and orderly; it gave him some small authority over his own life. Now and then he'd put on fifteen-minute magic shows at school assemblies, or at birthday parties, and it was a surprise to find that the applause seemed to fill up the empty spaces inside him. People looked at him in new ways. It wasn't affection, not quite, but it was the next closest thing. He liked being up on stage. All those eyes on him, everybody paying close attention. Down inside, of course, he was still a loner, still empty, but at least the magic made it a respectable sort of emptiness.

By eighth grade John had come to realize that secrecy carried its own special entitlements. Which was how the spying started. Another survival trick. At home, just for practice, he'd sometimes tail his father out to the garage and stand listening by the door. Later, when the coast was clear, he'd slip inside and dig around until he found the bottles. Sometimes he'd just stand looking at them. Other times he'd perform another little trick: carry the bottles outside, turn on a spigot, transform the vodka into cold water.

Later, in the house, it was hard not to laugh. He'd sit grinning at the TV set.

Sometimes his father would glance up.

"What's wrong with *you?*" he'd say, but John would shrug and say, "Nothing."

"Well, cut it out. You look ridiculous."

Everybody had secrets, obviously, including his father, and for John Wade the spying was like an elaborate detective game, a way of crawling into his father's mind and spending some time there. He'd inspect the scenery, poke around for clues. Where did the anger come from? What *was* it exactly? And why didn't anything ever please him, or make him smile, or stop the drinking? Nothing ever got solved—no answers at all—but still the spying made things better. It brought him close to his father. It was a bond. It was something they shared, something intimate and loving.

In the late morning of March 17, 1968, after Meadlo was taken away, the platoon received orders to head back to the village of Thuan Yen. It was an easy twenty-minute march. They crossed two broad paddies and followed their noses through the morning heat. After ten minutes they began to tie towels and T-shirts around their faces.

They entered the village's northern outskirts just before noon. The place was dead—a loud, living deadness. Along the main east-west trail they found a few fresh graves, a few white marking stones, but most of the bodies still lay in the sunlight, badly bloated, their clothing stretched tight like rubber skins. The wounds bubbled with flies. There were horseflies and blackflies and small iridescent blue flies, millions of them, and the corpses seemed to wiggle under the bright tropical sunlight. An illusion, Sorcerer knew.

Deeper into the village, just off the trail, they came across a young female with both breasts gone. Someone had carved a C in her stomach.

Boyce and Maples went off to be sick. Sorcerer took refuge behind the mirrors. He watched Rusty Calley stroll over to the body and stoop down, hands on his knees, examining things with an eye for detail. The man seemed genuinely curious. "Messy, messy," he said.

He scooped up a handful of flies and held them to his ear. After a second he smiled.

"You *hear* this? Fuckin' flies, they're claiming something criminal happened here. Big noisy rumor. Anybody else hear it?"

No one spoke. Some of them looked at their boots, others at the woman's body.

Calley walked over to Thinbill. "You hear that rumor, man?"

"I don't know, sir."

"You don't know."

"No, sir."

"Well, gosh." Calley grinned and pressed the flies up against Thinbill's ear. "That better?"

"I guess so."

"You hear any murder talk?"

Thinbill took a step backward. He was taller than Calley, and stronger, but he was young.

"No, sir," he said.

"Listen close."

"I don't hear it, sir. Nothing."

"Positive?"

"Yes, sir."

Calley's lips tightened. He turned to Sorcerer and lifted up the fistful of flies. "What about you, Magic Maker? How's the hearing?"

"Not so good," said Sorcerer.

"Take your time."

"Deaf, sir."

"Deaf?"

"It's a trick."

Somebody laughed. Boyce and Maples were back now, wiping their mouths. Mitchell stood gazing wistfully at the dead woman's carved-up chest.

"Well, good," Calley said softly. "What about the eyesight?"

"Sir?"

"The eyes. Notice any atrocities lately?"

"Not a thing, sir. Blind too."

The little lieutenant pushed up on his toes, arranging his shoulders in an authentic command posture. He looked briskly from man to man. "Here's the program. No more flappin' lips. Higher-higher's already got a big old cactus up its ass, people blabbing about a bunch of dead civilians. Personally, I don't understand it." He smiled at Sorcerer. "These folks here, they look like civilians?"

"No, sir."

"Course not." Calley crushed the flies in his fist, put the hand to his nose and sniffed it. "Tear this place apart. See if we can find us some VC weapons."

They broke up into two-man teams. There was nothing to find, they all knew that, but the search went on all afternoon. At dusk they established a perimeter along the irrigation ditch just outside Thuan Yen. The stench was deeper now. It was something physical, an oily substance that coated their lungs and skin. A steady buzzing sound came from the ditch to their front. There were fireflies and dragonflies and huge blackflies with electric wings. The ditch seemed to glow in the dark.

"Trip," someone whispered.

After an hour the same voice said, "Turn it *off*."

Restless and wide awake, Sorcerer did mind-cleansing tricks. He thought about Kathy, her curly hair and green eyes, the way she smiled, the good life they would someday have together. He thought about the difference between murder and war. Obvious, he decided. He was a decent person. No bad intentions. Yes, and what had happened here was not the product of his own heart. He hadn't wanted any of it, and he hated it, and he wished it would all go away.

He closed his eyes. He leaned back and punched an erase button at the center of his thoughts.

And then late in the night Thinbill came to sit at Sorcerer's foxhole. Together, they watched the flies.

At one point Thinbill seemed to be asleep.

Later he said, "Don't you think we should . . . We should *do* something."

"Do what?"

"You know. Tell somebody. Talk."

"And then?"

Thinbill made a vague motion with his shoulders. His face was slick with moisture. "You and me, we could report it and . . . Wouldn't be so bad, would it? Do it like a team."

"What about Calley?"

"Little turd."

"And the others?"

"I didn't sign up for the Mafia. Wasn't any code of silence."

Sorcerer looked out at the night. Everything moved. Directly in front of him, thick swarms of flies swirled just over the lip of the ditch, a wild neon fury in the dark. The buzz made it hard to think straight. There was his future to take into account, all the dreams for himself; there was the problem of an old man with a hoe. And PFC Weatherby. He didn't blame himself—reflex, nothing else—but still the notion of confession felt odd. No trapdoors, no secret wires.

Thinbill nudged his arm. "What do you think?" he said. "At least we'll sleep at night."

"I don't know."

"We *have* to."

Sorcerer nodded. An important moment had arrived and he could feel the inconvenient squeeze of moral choice. It made him laugh.

"Hey, come on," Thinbill whispered, "you can't—"

Sorcerer couldn't help it. He covered his face and lay back and let the giggles take him. He was shaking. In the dark someone hissed at him to shut up, but he couldn't quit, he couldn't catch his breath, he couldn't make the nighttime buzz go away. The horror was in his head. He remembered how he'd turned and squealed and shot down an old man with a hoe—automatic, no thinking—and how afterward he'd crawled through a hedgerow and out into a wide, dry paddy full of sunlight and colored smoke. He remembered the sunlight. He remembered a long, bleached-out emptiness, and how later he'd found himself standing at the lip of an irrigation ditch packed tight with women and kids and old men.

The pictures turned him upside down.

"Man, you all right?" Thinbill said, but Sorcerer wasn't Sorcerer anymore, he was just a helpless kid who couldn't shut down the giggles.

He rolled sideways and pressed his nose into the grass, but even then it wouldn't go away. He saw mothers huddled over their children, all the frazzled brown faces. Rusty Calley was firing from the shoulder. Meadlo was firing from the hip. Impossible, Sorcerer told himself, but the colors were very bright and real. Mitchell was doing trick shots over his shoulder. PFC Weatherby rattled off twenty rounds and wiped his rifle and reloaded and leaned over the ditch and shook his head and stood straight and kept firing. It went on and on. Sorcerer watched a red tracer round burn through a child's butt. He watched a woman's head open up. He watched a little boy climb out of the ditch and start to run, and he watched Calley grab the kid and give him a good talking to and then toss him back and draw down and shoot the kid dead. The bodies did twitching things. There were gases. There were splatterings and bits of bone. Overhead, the pastel sunlight pressed down bright and warm, hardly a cloud, and for a long time people died in piles and layers. Ammunition was a problem. Weatherby's weapon kept jamming. He flung the rifle away and borrowed somebody else's and wiped the barrel and thumped in a fresh magazine and knelt down and shot necks and stomachs. Kids were bawling. There were shit smells. Something moist and yellow dangled from Calley's forehead, but Calley didn't seem to mind, he wiped it off and kept firing. The bodies were all one body. They were mush. "You ask me," Calley said, "these personnel got definite health problems," and Weatherby said, "Roger that," and then they both reloaded and fired into the mush. Paul Meadlo was crying. He sobbed and shot at the ditch with his eyes closed. Mitchell had gone off to have some lunch. More elastic time went by, sunlight and screams, then later Sorcerer felt something slip inside him, a falling sensation, and after a moment he found himself at the bottom of the irrigation ditch. He was in the slime. He couldn't move, he couldn't get traction.

The giggles seemed to lift him up.

"Easy," Thinbill was saying, "take it slow."

Sorcerer bit down on his hand. A half moon was up now, pale and cool, and the flies made an electric blue glow over the ditch to his front.

Thinbill clucked his tongue. "Deep breaths," he said. "Drink the wind, man, suck it in."

"I'm all right."

"Sure you are. A-okay."

Sorcerer composed himself.

The giggles were mostly gone. He folded his arms tight and swayed in the dark and tried not to remember the things he was remembering. He tried not to remember the ditch, how slippery it was, and how, much later, PFC Weatherby had found him there. "Hey, Sorcerer," Weatherby said. He started to smile, but Sorcerer shot him.

"That's the ticket," Thinbill said. "Looking good. Whole lot better."

"I'm fine."

"Absolutely."

They stared out at the ditch. Nearby, someone was weeping. There were other sounds, too. A canteen, a rifle bolt.

"You okay now?"

"Sure. Perfect."

Thinbill sighed. "I guess that's the right attitude. Laugh it off. Fuck the spirit world."

22

Hypothesis

Maybe this.

Maybe in the bleak light of dawn Kathy arranged a pile of twigs on the beach. A shrewd, resourceful woman. She would've pried off the Evinrude's steel hood. She would've held a wad of Kleenex over the spark plugs, yanked on the starter cord, whispered prayers until the tissues flared up.

"Genius," she would've said. And maybe then she smiled to herself. Maybe she pictured the proud face of her Girl Scout leader.

Carefully then, guarding against the breeze, she would've transferred the burning tissues to her pile of twigs and watched the wood smolder and rise up into a compact fire. She would've dropped on a few more twigs, then the thicker stuff, and when the fire was solid she would've pulled off her sweater and shirt, draping them over a couple of rocks to take the heat.

Breakfast was a Life Saver.

The hunger, she decided, wasn't all that bad yet. Certainly nothing painful. Right now the only requirement was warmth. Squatting down, she opened her arms to the fire, bent forward, and drew in the heat through her nose and mouth. A dismal night, now a dismal morning. Sheets of fog still hovered over the lake, wet and durable. The cold air seemed to punch tiny holes in her skin.

She placed another branch on the fire and tried to conceive a sensible agenda for the day.

Dry clothing, that was first. Then fill up the gas tank. Then point the boat south and keep going until she struck the Minnesota mainland. Just go. No matter what. Later in the morning, if the hunger got worse, she could try her hand at some fishing, but for now the imperative was to lay a mental ruler across the wilderness and follow it home. Straight south and nothing else.

She pressed her lips together. It was decided. There was no reason to think about it any longer.

When her clothes were dry, she got dressed and replaced the Evinrude's hood and poured the last of her gasoline into the tank. The morning had turned even colder. Like winter almost, except for the heavy fog. The wilderness seemed to bend low under its own weight, and the day was soggy and oppressive, and for an instant she felt her resolve vanish altogether. Impossible, she thought. Completely lost, that was the fact, and it was silly to pretend otherwise. Her ignorance of the natural world was vast. North, south, it was all the same, and either someone found her or she was dead.

Still, there was also the need to move. She could at least choose the circumstances.

"So stop diddling," she told herself.

Quickly, before she could undo the decision, Kathy stowed her tackle box and oilcloth. She pushed the boat out into the shallows and got in, slipped on her life vest, started up the Evinrude, and turned out into the empty lake. When she looked back, the fire was a soft discoloration in the fog; a minute later it was gone entirely. She tucked one arm inside the life vest, steering with the other. Already a murderous chill was in her bones. The sun was somewhere behind the clouds off to her left, which had to be east, and in her head she conjured up an imaginary map and a steel ruler to put herself on course. The map was large and blank. She penciled in North at the top and then lay the ruler down and pictured the boat moving along its edge from top to bottom.

The exercise gave her encouragement. Simple, really. Follow the geometry.

Slowly, over the next hour, the fog thinned out into smudgy patches. The sky remained overcast, but at least she could make out the somber forests ahead. Everywhere, the wilderness seemed desolate beyond reason. All the color had been washed out of things, pale grays blending into deep iron grays; there was the feel of rain without rain, everything wet, everything sad and dreary and obscure. Even the birds looked grim—a few geese, a few lonely loons. The country had a dense, voluptuous sameness that made her wish for a billboard or a skyscraper or a giant glass hotel, anything glitzy and man-made.

The thought carried a certain comfort.

Maybe someday she'd build a casino up here. Blackjack under a plastic dome. Lots of neon. Outdoor escalators. She recalled a trip to Las Vegas several years ago. One of those do-nothing political conferences—the party was paying—and John and Tony had talked her into tagging along. Ridiculous, she'd thought, but after the first two hours she'd been hooked hard. She loved the flash. She loved the sound of dice and slot machines, the clatter of mathematics. It wasn't the money that had kept her up all night; rather, in ways she didn't care to fathom, it had to do with the possibility of a prodigious jackpot just out of reach. Possibility itself. The golden future. Everything was *next*—the next roll, the next card, the next hour, the next lucky table. Gaudy and artificial, cheap in the most fundamental sense, the place represented everything she found disgusting in the world, but still she couldn't deny the thrill of a black ace descending like a spaceship on a smiling red queen. It did not matter that her wager was only five dollars. What mattered was the rush in her veins. The pursuit of miracles, the rapture of happy endings.

Kathy smiled out at the thick morning.

"Go ahead," she said. "Hit me."

After ten minutes a low wooded island materialized directly ahead. Ideal for a casino. Something sleek and glittery. Designed in the shape of a spaceship or maybe a fine young penis.

She passed along the island's eastern shore, adjusted the ruler in her head.

And then later, when the lake opened up again, she let herself slide back to that last extraordinary night in Vegas. A sizzling hot blackjack table, she and Tony camped out there, all the pretty chips piled up in front of them, lots of greens and blacks. She remembered a giddiness blowing through her. All evening the table had been under a cone of supple white light—hot light—a soft shimmering incandescent glow. Anything was possible. Luxury and bliss. Neither of them had budged in well over two hours.

Around midnight John had come up behind her. He'd rested his hands on her shoulders and stood quietly for a while. His grip seemed stiff.

"Profitable," he'd finally said. "Lots of plunder. Maybe it's time to pack it up."

She remembered laughing. "You're kidding," she'd said.

"But we shouldn't be—"

"*Watch* this."

She remembered looking over at Tony, smiling, then pushing out four green chips. Her skin felt hot. She was only vaguely aware of John's fingertips digging into her shoulders. When the dealer busted, she yelped and slapped the table. John squeezed harder.

"Very nice," he said.

"Very! Very better than very!"

"And late."

"Late?"

"It's getting there."

"It *isn't*. My God, they'd have to bomb the place."

"All right, fine. Just doesn't seem like you."

Tony looked up with a rubbery sallow smile. "And which *you* is that? Seems to me she's got yous galore. Yous here, yous there."

"Does she?"

"Yes, indeed. She does."

There was a hesitation before John forced an equivocal little laugh.

"I don't get the point."

"Well, no," Tony said.

She remembered John's hands slipping off her shoulders. He made the stale laughing sound again and moved off into the crowd.

"Forget it," Tony said.

"I will. I have."

"Doesn't mean anything."

"Of course not."

They played another few minutes, watching their chips flow back across the table, then they cashed in and moved into a noisy leather-cushioned bar and ordered drinks. Even with the cold streak, she was more than eight hundred dollars ahead, yet all she could feel was the hurt in her stomach. The casino was just a casino again.

"Cards come, cards go," Tony said. He looked at her attentively. "That's the world. It wasn't his fault."

"Bastard."

"He's not."

"It's still rotten," she said. "Like he can't tolerate things going right."

"There's that wad in your purse."

"It isn't money."

"No?"

"Not at all. Something better." She was conscious of the resentment in her voice, a sticky bitterness that clung to the roof of her mouth. "I mean, the whole feeling was incredible, wasn't it? Awesome and perfect. Like we had this—I don't know—like there was this spell or something."

"It wasn't a spell. It was luck."

"Either way. We made a wonderful team."

Tony looked down into his drink, stirred it with the tip of a thumb. "Right," he said, "but I wouldn't knock the money."

"It just *felt* good, that's all. Then he ruins everything, just breaks the spell."

"Not intentionally."

"Who knows?"

"It's who he is," Tony said. "His character."

"Let's not talk about it."

"What then?"

"Something good. The glow."

"We could try again."

"In a while. I like sitting here."

She remembered Tony making a short humming sound like a computer processing a new piece of data. His quick little eyes flicked out across the casino. Nervous, she thought, or apprehensive about something, the way his gaze never quite settled on any one object. An odd creature. Coarse and shy and cynical and vain and rude and insecure to the point of self-hatred. The elements didn't coordinate. Like the way he was dressed now, the corduroy suit pants and pink sport shirt and scuffed-up black shoes. Funny, but mostly sad. The shirt seemed to add another twenty pounds to his belly. His hair had been slicked straight back, thin and colorless.

Bizarre, that was the word. Especially the eyes. Always darting here and there, seeking out the angles.

When he spoke, though, his voice was mild and thoughtful. He didn't look at her.

"I guess the thing to bear in mind," he said, "is that your significant other doesn't place a whole lot of faith in lady luck. Doesn't believe in risk. The magician in him. Likes to rig up the cards. Luck's irrelevant."

"You're defending him?"

"No. I wouldn't put it that way."

"How would you put it? I'm interested."

"Just his mode," Tony said. He finished his drink. "You're married to the guy."

"Well, yes. That's another thought." She looked across the casino to where John stood with a group of young legislators, all of them fresh-faced, all very spiffy and cologned and neatly barbered.

"Anyway," she said, "he's not a card rigger."

"Whatever you wish."

"He's not."

"Another drink?"

"Sure, a big one. He's not a cheat."

Tony looked up and smiled, but his gaze seemed to slip off her forehead. He chuckled.

"No, I suppose not. Slay the dragons, feed the poor. And I admire that. Thing is, he doesn't care much for losing." He leaned back heavily in his chair. "Like with his hobby. The man yanks a rabbit out of a hat, you don't yell cheater, do you? You *know* it's a trick. It's *supposed* to be a trick. All you do is clap like crazy and think, Hey, what a clever fucker. Same with politics. Bunch of tricksters, they're all making moves." He paused and grinned at her. "Dirty isn't operative. Nature of the show."

"And you too?"

He smiled. "The trusty assistant. Help with the props. Load him up with bunnies."

"But you adore it. The intrigue."

"Sadly, sadly. I do adore it."

"And John?"

"My lord and master." Tony sighed. He waved at a waiter and turned his glass upside down on the table. "My David Copperfield. Maybe someday he'll whisk me off to Washington, we'll play the big show together."

"Go solo," Kathy said. "Be a star."

"Yeah, right."

"Seriously."

Tony rolled his eyes. "Very astute. I'd look real super-svelte in Copperfield's duds. Tight pants, spangled vest."

"That's ridiculous."

"What is?"

"Nobody cares."

He made a short, almost angry sound. "If *what?* If I need a periscope to find my own dick? Guys like me — the waddlers — we know our place. And don't give me any crap about losing weight."

"I won't."

"It was halfway out your mouth."

She nodded at him. "You're right."

"Okay. I'm right."

"So?"

"So nothing."

"Time out," she said, and covered his hand with hers. "I'm sorry. Let's just be nice to each other. Where's that waiter?"

"Right. The waiter."

"I am sorry."

"Elegant astute Kathleen."

For the next hour they did what they could to retrieve the glow. She remembered curious little details. His pink shirt clinging to the curve of his belly. How he couldn't keep his hands still. How he kept stirring his drinks and letting his eyes skate across her face and down the slope of her shoulders and then off into the dark behind her.

Even now, looking out across the flat gray lake, she could feel the discomfort behind his gestures, the way he'd covered himself up with banter and cynicism.

Odd creature, she thought again.

Adjusting the tiller slightly, Kathy nudged the boat up against the ruler in her head. The fog now had mostly lifted. A shapeless white sun hung behind clouds to the east, hazy and without heat. Here and there patches of metallic blue glinted among the waves. No rain, she thought. At least there was that. But the morning seemed even colder now, a ragged cutting cold like barbed wire. She felt some fleeting nostalgia for her morning fire. A mistake to have left it behind. Probably a bad mistake.

Then she told herself not to think about it.

Anything else.

What day was it?

September something—the 20th probably. Or the 21st. Which meant it was still summer by the calendar. She wouldn't freeze. The odds could be beaten. And she would do it—she'd feel that glow again. Yes, she would. With John, too. She loved him so much, despite everything, just so much. She always had. But they used to have that astonishing glow all around them, which was where they lived, inside a brilliant white light that seemed to suck them up and carry them beyond all the ordinary limits, suspended there. Other marriages might go stale, but not theirs, because the law of averages had been suspended, or they were suspended above the averages. A few elections to win, then a few more, and then they'd have the beautiful lives they wanted and deserved—they had wagered on it, they had bet the baby in her stomach—but then the glow had gone away and they had lost very badly and apparently they were still losing.

She wanted the feeling back. She wanted to believe again, just to hope and keep hoping.

Kathy closed her eyes briefly. When she looked up, a cluster of starkly silhouetted islands lay a quarter mile off the bow, the lake breaking into six narrow channels that arrowed off into the wilderness like spokes on a wheel.

She checked her direction against the sun and chose a passage that seemed to run south.

Go with the glow.

Flow with the glow.

And then she permitted herself a little smile. She recalled

how in Vegas that night, after three or four drinks, Tony had explained in great drunken detail how luck wasn't something you could force. All you could do, he'd said, was open yourself up like a window and wait for fortune to blow in. And then they'd talked about stuck windows. Tony suggested she unstick herself. So she'd shrugged and said she had tried it once, but the unsticking hadn't gone well. Very badly, she told him. She did not utter Harmon's name, nor anything about what had happened at Loon Point, but she explained that in the end the unsticking got awfully sticky. Unpleasant outcome, she said. Thoroughly busted. No glow at all. Tony had listened to this with his eyes off elsewhere, and when she was finished he nodded and said, "I get the point," and she said, "No point, I'm afraid." She asked if he wanted to know more. He said no thanks. Maybe he knew anyway. Probably so. But he didn't know about the pain and misery, so she told him that part. She told him how she couldn't sleep for many months afterward. She told him that it was a very terrible unsticking thing she had done, and that after it was over, all she'd wanted was to keep it secret, but the secret had soon become worse than the terrible thing itself.

"So he found out?" Tony said.

"Some. Not all."

"And then?"

"Weeping, horror. I was holy, he said. My tongue, my insides. Our us. He'd be gone forever if it happened again."

"Will it? Again?"

"Well, there's a question." She remembered shaking her head, then standing up. "I shouldn't be bothering you. Stupid of me."

"No bother."

"But still stupid. Come on, let's try our luck."

They played for another hour, mostly losing, then took the elevator up to the eighth floor. At her door Tony said, "I'd kiss you if I weren't such a pork chop," and she'd laughed and said, "Good thing," and kissed his cheek, and Tony said, "I'll live forever."

"Good night," she said.

"Oh, yes."

She opened the door and watched him move off down the corridor.

Inside, John lay cradling a pillow in the dark. His breathing was the forced, wakeful kind. Pretending to sleep—it was something he would do. She remembered undressing and pulling the blankets back and lying down beside him without touching his skin. Tired of trying. All that trying. Not now. He could touch himself. She rolled onto her side and lay there for a long while listening to the afterhum of the casino, watching the bright chips accumulate in front of her. She'd won close to seven hundred dollars. A week's pay. But truly it was not the money that mattered. It was the distant glitter of everything that was possible in the world, the things she had always wanted for herself and could not name and called happiness because there was no other word. Maybe she'd counted too much on John to help name the things. Maybe so. It didn't feel that way. It felt like something else, like climbing a mountain that rose into the clouds and had no top and no end. It felt like work. The playfulness wasn't there, the fun they used to have. She thought about the way they had once played Dare You in the corner booth of that cozy bar back in college, how they had risked things and challenged each other and made good on the challenges. There was a glow then. They couldn't lose.

She remembered swinging out of bed. John was mumbling in his sleep—angry things.

Even then she didn't touch him.

It would not help. Nothing would.

In the dark she put on a fresh silk dress and brushed her hair. She found her purse, went out into the corridor, locked the door behind her, and took the elevator down to the casino. Three A.M., but the place was loud and alive. She found a lucky-looking table and squeezed in between a pair of Asian gentlemen. Already she felt better. The light was promising. She ordered coffee and orange juice, bought seven hundred dollars' worth of green chips, smiled at the dealer, asked him for a nice fat blackjack and hit it on the second run.

Verona, she thought. She'd win herself a future.

Flow with the glow.

She took the boat along the edge of the ruler in her head, utterly lost, low on gas, low on odds, looking out on the impossible gray reaches of sky and timber and water. So deal the cards, she thought. Always a chance. No play, no pay.

23

Where They Looked

At six-thirty on the morning of September 22 Claude Rasmussen nudged his eighteen-foot Chris-Craft up against the dock below the yellow cottage on Lake of the Woods. John Wade helped the old man tie up, steadied Pat's arm as she stepped in, then trotted back up to the porch for a styrofoam cooler that Ruth had loaded with soft drinks and sandwiches. He felt a rising freshness inside him. Not quite optimism, but a kind of health, a clarity that had not been there for a very long while.

When he returned to the boat, Claude was bent over a ragged chart book. "What we could use," he was explaining, "is a divining rod. Pure crapshoot unless somebody's got a piece of razzle-dazzle intuition."

Wade stowed the cooler and took a seat next to Pat. She did not look at him. She studied the lake briefly, then motioned at a string of islands a mile or two offshore.

"There," she said. "Close to home."

Claude nodded. He gave a little shove to the dock, letting the big boat nose out into the waves. "Sit tight," he said. "This mama moves."

For ten minutes he held a course straight east toward the islands, the throttle wide open. It was a raw, foggy morning, like early winter, and in the brittle light Wade could see his own breath snatched away by the wind, little gusts of silver vanishing into deeper silver. The sky was dull and opaque. As they approached the first little island, Claude cut down on the power and turned north along the shoreline. The solitude was startling—rocks and forest and nothing else. They circled the island and then cruised east past a half dozen smaller islands. There was no sign of human presence, not now, not ever, and after an hour Wade felt himself sliding off into reverie. He had nothing to say, no desire to speak. Sitting back, humming under his breath, he scanned the waters for anything that might present itself. A piece of the boat or an oar or a white tennis shoe: Did tennis shoes float? Would the hearts survive? JOHN + KATH? And what about the human body? What was the float quotient? How long did the gases last?

It was hard to sustain concentration. He tried dividing the lake into quadrants, carefully inspecting each quadrant. He was humming an old army marching tune. The lyric, he realized, had been spinning through his head all morning—*I know a girl, name is Jill!* He couldn't push it away; the tune dipped and curled . . . *I know a girl, name is Jill—babe, babe!* . . . And he remembered sloshing through the monsoons, everything wet and filthy, the war like fluid in his lungs, the whole company laughing and singing and marching through the rain. Other songs, too; other ghosts; odd flashes of this and that—the way Kathy used to chase him around the apartment with a squirt gun—an old man with a hoe—PFC Weatherby starting to smile—Kathy's skin going slick and

231

moist as they made love in the heat of July, the suction at their bellies, the traffic outside, her eyes softening and losing focus and rolling high in their sockets—the way she sometimes mumbled in her sleep—yes, and other happy times—the time he was Frank Sinatra—how he stripped down and pranced across the bedroom and sang *The record shows I took the blows*, buck naked, high-stepping, wiggling his ass, and how Kathy squealed and laughed and told him to put his flopper away and then lay back on the bed and grabbed her feet like a baby and rocked back and forth and kept laughing and squealing and couldn't stop.

"Senator, you *with* us?"

Wade looked up. The old man was reaching back for a can of soda, squinting at him. They were moving along an island identical to all the other islands.

"Sorry. I was off somewhere."

"Noticed that."

Wade tried to frame some appropriate remark. There was the pressure of oblique scrutiny.

"Green in the gills," Claude said. "For a second there, I thought you was ready to lose breakfast. Say the word, we'll take a breather, find some place to pull in for a while."

"Not a chance," Pat said.

"But if he's—"

Pat made a hard twisting motion. "We just got started, for God's sake. You'd think he'd want to *try*."

"I do," Wade said, "I'm not—"

"Such crap."

"Pat, cut it out."

"More of the same. Crap, crap." Her gaze skipped across the surface of the lake. The sound of the wind was conspicuous.

"Hey, both of you," Claude said, "let's try for some politeness. Mouths shut, eyes open. That's another real good rule out here."

"But he doesn't even . . . Just sits there half asleep."

"Enough," Claude said. "*Too* much."

Wade looked out at the water. It occurred to him that he might seize the chance to declare his own innocence. Something indignant. A loud, angry oration. Explain that it was all a mystery and that he loved his wife and wanted her back and that everything else was nothing.

He squeezed his hands together. "Pat, listen," he said, "I'm not sure what you think. Whatever it is, I'm sorry."

"Wonderful."

"That's not an apology."

"No," she said, "I'm sure it's not."

Twice they spotted other search boats moving silently in the distance. Later, as they approached Magnuson's Island, a small red pontoon plane banked low overhead, close enough to make out the pilot's beard and straw hat. Mostly, though, things were flat and empty. At Buckete Island they turned west, crossing over to American Point, where for well over an hour they moved along at half speed just off the shoreline.

By late morning the sky had cleared a little. There was still a wind, which kept the chop high, but to the west a spray of sunlight fell across the lake's horizon. Pat took off her jacket and hunched forward. She was wearing a yellow basketball jersey, a size too small, and it was clear that all the weight training had produced results. An imposing creature, Wade thought. Her whole posture. The way she attacked the world. He sat up straight, aware of the soft double fold at his own belly.

No more booze, he decided. Not a drop.

At noon they ate the sandwiches and then continued north through mostly open water. Wade kept to himself. There was still that sense of being watched—the elaborate way Pat had of turning her head, how her eyes always settled on things in the middle distance. He told himself to ignore it. Nothing he could do. A prime suspect. Not just with Pat—everyone. Art Lux and Vinny Pearson, the newspapers, the party bigwigs, the whole prissy state of Minnesota. He couldn't blame them. He'd tried to pull off a trick that couldn't be done, which was to remake himself, to vanish what was past and replace it with things good and new. He should have known better. Should've lifted it out of the act. Never given the fucking show in the first place. Pitiful, he thought. And no one gave a damn about the pressure of it all. Twenty years' worth. Smiling and making love and eating breakfast and keeping up the patter and pushing away the nightmares and trying to invent a respectable little life for himself. The intent was never evil. Deceit, maybe, but the intent was purely virtuous.

No one knew. Obviously no one cared.

A liar and a cheat.

Which was the risk. You had to live inside your tricks. You had to be Sorcerer. Believe or fail. And for twenty years he had believed.

Now it ends, he thought.

One more loser with no cards up his sleeve.

It was almost twilight when they tied up at the Angle Inlet boatyard. The mood of the place was somber. More than a dozen boats bobbed against the docks, their hulls restless in the approaching dusk. A bonfire was burning on the beach, and groups of dark-faced men stood around it, smoking and drinking beer. Even from a distance, Wade decided, there was something distinctly mournful in their voices. Now and then a note of laughter rose up, but even the laughter seemed part of a deeper and more permanent gloom. It reminded him of the way men talked in the hours after a firefight. After Weber died, or Reinhart, or PFC Weatherby. That same melancholy. The same musical rise and fall.

Claude stood surveying things for a few seconds. His face looked gaunt in the dimming light. "I'll say this," he muttered, "it ain't no celebration."

"I keep hoping—"

"We all do."

The old man hitched up his trousers, took Pat's arm, and led her down to the beach. Wade followed a few steps behind. A peculiar frothiness had come into his stomach. Bubble-gut, Kathy used to call it. The tension of the public eye. He could feel heads turning, the air going dead behind him. He moved straight ahead, toward the fire, trying for the correct balance of poise and husbandly concern. Here and there voices rose up in encouragement—dark beards, hooded stares—and as he made his way forward, the whisperings seemed to gust up and push him along.

Ahead, near the fire, Art Lux and Vinny Pearson were shaking hands with Pat. Wade stopped and waited, not sure what to do with himself.

Someone clapped his shoulder. Someone else pushed a can of beer at him. "Tomorrow's tomorrow," Lux was saying, then for a second his voice was lost under the sound of a big double-engined boat approaching the docks. He turned and nodded at Wade. "No luck, I'm afraid. In the morning we'll be out there again. Nobody's got the quits."

The big boat's engines went dead. The running lights flashed off and a thick silence filled up the dark.

Lux took a step forward. His eyes were mild and solicitous in the firelight. "Glad you're up and about, sir. Looking fit."

Vinny Pearson laughed. "Like a fiddle," he said. "Fit to fart. Three *days* it takes."

The sheriff waved a hand. He looked at Wade as if anticipating a joke. "Just tune it out, sir. What we'll do, Miss Hood and I'll go find a place for a chat. Maybe you two boys can figure a way to patch things up."

"No thanks," Wade said.

"Just a thought."

Wade tried to smile but couldn't manage it. "Christ," he said. "What's the point?"

"Sir?"

"Everybody thinks—" He made himself turn away. "I've had it. A bellyful."

"Poor man," Vinny Pearson said.

"Especially from this one. The great albino detective."

Vinny lowered his shoulders. His eyes were a smooth, lustrous yellow. "Ain't albino," he said. "Swedish."

"Good for you."

"A fact."

They stood at angles, not quite facing each other. Claude maneuvered between them. "Hey, back off. We don't need this."

Vinny snorted. "Ain't no albino."

"A fetus," Wade said. "Our great white albino deputy fetus."

Vinny's fingers twitched. The thought came to Wade's mind that the two of them shared some intuitive understanding about the nature of the human animal. Things that were possible, things that were not.

He felt relaxed and dangerous. That gliding sensation.

"Well, I'll tell you this," Vinny said slowly. "Albino or no albino, I never mass murdered nobody."

"Here's your chance."

"Fuck you."

"Sure. Both of us."

Vinny waited a moment, turned away, then stopped in the shadows beyond the fire. "Truth serum," he snarled. "That's what we need, a nice big *bellyful!*" He cackled and walked off.

Wade was aware of voices behind him. When he looked up, Lux was guiding Pat to a wooden bench across the beach. Claude clamped a hand on Wade's shoulder. "Don't pay it mind. The albino stuff tickled me. Come on, let's park ourselves."

They moved up closer to the fire. Six or seven dusky faces nodded beneath their caps as Claude made the introductions, and then for a long while Wade sat listening to a conversation that seemed to transpire in another language. Impossibly abstract: tides and winds and channel currents. It was hard to achieve focus. Partly it was Vinny, partly the glide. Once or twice he found himself tugged away on the backwash of voices, drifting here and there. Another universe, he thought. Everyday logic had gone inside out; the essential substances that had once constituted his daily being had been transformed into something vaporous and infinitely mutable.

What was real? What wasn't? Kathy, for instance. No firmness. It was difficult to imagine her out there right now, at this instant, looking up at this same starry sky.

He took a slug of beer and tried to brace himself.

"These boys here," Claude was saying, "they're water-smart. Real pros. They'll dig her out for you."

Positive murmurs came from the dark.

Across the beach Lux and Pat were huddled in conversation. Wade watched them for a few seconds, wondering if he should walk over and demand the handcuffs. Blurt out a few secrets. The teakettle and the boathouse. Tell them he wasn't sure. Just once in his life: tell everything. Talk about his father. Explain how his whole life had been managed with mirrors and that he was now totally baffled and totally turned around and had no idea how to work his way out. Which was the truth. He didn't know shit. He didn't know where he was or how he'd gotten there or where to go next.

Much later, it seemed, Claude clapped his arm. They stood up and walked over to where Pat and Art Lux were conversing in the dark. Vinny Pearson had disappeared.

Wade zipped up his jacket.

"Convicted?" he said pleasantly.

They went out again in the morning, and every morning for the next two weeks. The lake was huge and empty.

On October 8 the Minnesota State Police recalled its three search aircraft. Four days later the U.S. Border Patrol downgraded its operations to routine, and by October 17 only three private boats still remained on active search.

The weather mostly held—crisp days, cold nights. There was a snowfall on the morning of October 19, a light frost two days later, but then the skies cleared and a warming wind came up from the south and the autumn sunlight remained bright and steady.

The routine kept Wade going.

In the mornings Ruth Rasmussen would be ready with a cooler of sandwiches and soft drinks. Claude and Pat would look over the chart book, marking it up with a red pencil, then they would troop down to the boat and spend the day cruising back and forth in long silvery sweeps. The wilderness was massive. It was a place, Wade came to understand, where lost was a rule of thumb. The water here was the water there. Nothing in particular, all in general. Forests folded into forests, sky swallowed sky. The solitude bent back on itself. Everywhere was nowhere. It was perfect unity, perfect oneness, the flat mirroring waters giving off exact copies of other copies, everything in multiples, everything hypnotic and blue and meaningless, always the same. Here, Wade decided, was where the vanished things go. The dropped nickels. The needles in haystacks.

There was nothing to find—he knew that—but he felt a curious peace looking out on the endless woods and water. Like the box of mirrors in his head, the way he used to slip inside and just disappear for a while.

"No can do," Claude said.

"We'd cover more country."

"No."

"But it wouldn't be . . . I'd have maps."

"Maps my ass. No means no."

"I could do it anyway."

"You could."

"So why not?"

The old man sighed. "Just no."

At dinner that night Wade brought it up again. It wasn't a question of practicalities. It was something he should be doing.

The old man stared at him. "Agreed," he said. "You're already doing it."

"Alone, I mean."

"Don't con me."

"I'm not conning."

"Either way. Still no."

Wade looked over at Ruth, who shook her head, then at Pat, who rolled her shoulders in a gesture that suggested something close to ridicule. "Seriously, I'd be fine," he said. "A compass and maps, no problem. Maybe a radio."

"So?" Claude said. "And then what?"

"Just look."

"Right. End up same place as your wife."

"It's something I have to try."

Pat lifted her gaze. "God, such chivalry. I love it. I bet Kathy would too."

"I don't mean—"

"The Lone Ranger."

Claude glared across the table. He pulled out his upper denture, dipped it in his cup of coffee, and slipped it back in. "Whatever your personal problems, let's be real extra-clear. There's this word *no*, it means not a chance. It means forget it."

"He's good at that," Pat said. "A good chivalrous forgetter."

"Quiet," said Claude.

"I'm just commenting."

"Oh, yeah."

"All that gallantry," Pat said. "Hi ho Silver."

There was snow the next morning, which turned to heavy rain, and at noon Claude swung the boat back toward the cottage. They spent the day waiting. By midafternoon it was snowing again, with a hard slanting wind, and from the cottage windows there was nothing to be seen of the dock or the boathouse or the lake beyond. For a couple of hours they played a listless game of Scrabble in front of the fireplace. Around five, Wade went outside with a shovel, slowly working his way from the porch to the driveway. His thoughts were mostly on magic. He scooped up the heavy wet snow, digging hard, his mind ticking through the mechanics of a last nifty illusion. A piece of causal transportation. It could be done. Like those two crazy snakes in Pinkville.

Curiously, as he worked out the details, Wade found himself experiencing a new sympathy for his father. This was how it was. You go about your business. You carry the burdens, entomb yourself in silence, conceal demon-history from all others and most times from yourself. Nothing theatrical. Shovel snow; diddle at politics or run a jewelry store; seek periodic forgetfulness; betray the present with every breath drawn from the bubble of a rotted past. And then one day you discover a length of clothesline. You amaze yourself. You pull over a garbage can and hop aboard and hook yourself up to forever. No notes, no diagrams. You don't explain a thing. Which was the art of it—his father's art, Kathy's art—that magnificent giving over to pure and absolute Mystery. It was the difference, he thought, between evil and a bad childhood. To know is to be disappointed. To understand is to be betrayed. All the petty hows and whys, the unseemly motives, the abscesses of character, the sordid little uglinesses of self and history—these were the gimmicks you kept under wraps to the end. Better to leave your audience wailing in the dark, shaking their fists, some crying *How?*, others *Why?*

When dusk had come, Wade put his shovel aside and moved down the slope to the dock. The snow had let up.

He didn't think about it. Quickly, he stripped naked and filled his lungs and dove to the bottom where Kathy was.

To his bemusement there was no chill, or else the chill was lost on him. He did not open his eyes. He located a piling at the point where it had been driven into the gravel, took hold and propelled himself beneath the dock, belly-down, feeling only the discomfort of his own vague intentions. There was the quality of a rehearsal. Like a test run. Maybe his father had once done things very much like this in the musty stillness of the garage, emboldening himself, examining the rafters with an eye for levitation.

For a few moments Wade considered opening his eyes, just to know, but in the dark it wouldn't have mattered.

He came to the surface and went down again.

The possibilities were finite. She was there or she wasn't. And if she wasn't, she was elsewhere.

And even that didn't matter.

Guilt had no such solution. It was false-bottomed. It was the trapdoor he'd been performing on all these years, the love he'd withheld, the poisons he'd kept inside. For his entire life, it seemed, there had been the terror of discovery. A fat little kid doing magic in front of a stand-up mirror. "Hey, kiddo, that's a good one," his father could've said, but for reasons unknown, reasons mysterious, the words never got spoken. He had wanted to be loved. And to be loved he had practiced deception. He had hidden the bad things. He had tricked up his own life. Only for love. Only to be loved.

The cold pressed into his rib cage. He could taste the lake.

Eyes closed, deep, he glided by feel along the water-polished pilings beneath the dock. He could sense her presence. Yes, he could. The touch of her flesh. Her wide-open eyes. Her bare feet, her empty womb, her hair like wet weeds.

Amazing, he thought, what love could do.

He let out the last of his air, pushed to the surface, hoisted himself onto the dock, dressed quickly, and trotted through the snow to the cottage.

Shortly after eight Art Lux called. He spoke first to Pat, then to Wade. The man's dairy-farmer voice rode the scales of apology as he explained that the official search was being discontinued. Purely a formality, he said. Paperwork to file. Red tape and so on.

Wade shifted the receiver to his other hand. He glanced over at Pat, who was crying. "Give it up?" he said. "Just like that?"

"Not exactly."

"It sounds—"

"No, sir, we're not quitting. Still places to look, if you know what I mean."

"I don't," Wade said.

"Sir?"

"I don't know."

Lux paused. "Well. Places."

There was a sound on the line that Wade took to be someone else's voice. After a second Lux asked if he could speak with Claude.

243

Wade handed the phone over. He stood awkwardly at the center of the kitchen, off balance, wondering if there was something he should be doing or saying. Some overlooked gesture. Tears, maybe, except he was tired of pretending. He went to the refrigerator, took out a tray of ice cubes, built himself a vodka tonic. Pat's low crying irritated him. It seemed profoundly wrong. When all was lost, he thought, the thing to do was grab a hammer or mix a drink. Like father, like son.

In a few minutes Claude hung up and motioned at Wade. They went out to the living room.

The old man looked very tired. "Whole thing's ridiculous," he said, "but I guess you know what's gonna happen."

"Pretty much."

"I can't say no."

"That's fine."

Claude slumped on the couch, massaged the pouches under his eyes. "Wouldn't help none anyway. Either way, they'll rip this place apart. They got this idea—you know—they figure probably she's around here somewhere. The boathouse. On the grounds."

"She's not," Wade said, "but it doesn't matter."

"Fucking *does* matter. I just wish—"

The old man closed his eyes. Watching him, Wade was struck by the notion that he had a genuine friend in the world. Unique development, he thought.

Claude blinked and looked up pensively from the couch.

"A situation, isn't it?"

"That's what it is," Wade said.

"No win, no tie. They don't find anything, you're still a sinner. After what happened with the election, all the garbage that leaked out—" The old man looked at Wade's drink. "You mind?"

Wade gave him the glass. They were quiet for a time, passing the drink, then Claude reached out and put a hand on Wade's knee.

"I don't want to be sappy. She was all you had, right?"

"Yes."

"And you didn't do zilch."

"I did things. Not that."

"Right." Claude took his hand away. "And there ain't nothing else—you know—nothing else you can say?"

"There never was."

"Naturally. That's what I keep telling people. Guy yells wolf, he gets stuck with the mistake, can't say a goddamn thing to change anybody's mind." The old man sighed and finished off the drink. "Same with how you been acting, right? No use blubbering. Wouldn't help a bit."

"Maybe that's it," Wade said. "You get tired of the politics."

Claude nodded. "Which is how I'd handle it. The same. Let the bastards think what they want."

The old man got up and went to the kitchen and came back with two tall drinks. He switched on a lamp, but even so, the cottage had the feel of a funeral home. They didn't speak. Outside in the woods, a pair of owls were having their own conversation.

Claude finally sighed. "Well, anyhow, I guess you won't want to be here for the festivities. When they tear things up. There's the car. You could head back to the Cities, just sit tight. Right now you're still free to go."

"You know I can't do that. I'll want a boat, Claude."

"Sure you will."

"Gasoline. A full tank."

"Not from me. We been all through that. I don't need two good clients out there."

"And the chart book."

"I'm sorry."

"I'll find a way."

"Yeah, no doubt." Claude looked up with his tired old-crow eyes. It occurred to Wade that the man was not well. "No lie, Senator, I *am* sorry. Conscience and all that. Get to be my age, a guy needs his sleep at night." He took out a red hankie and ran it across his forehead. "You understand?"

"Yes, of course. How much time do I have?"

"Day after tomorrow. Or the day after that. Lux's got the State Police coming up, criminal-investigator types. Couple sniffer dogs."

"Lovely," Wade said.

"It had to happen."

"Sure it did." Wade winked. "Senator. I like that."

By morning the snow had mostly melted and the temperature was up in the high forties. They spent the day out on the lake, searching north and northeast of Magnuson's Island. There were no other boats out, no aircraft, no motion at all. On occasion the sun appeared low over the horizon, yet even then the sky had a dull grayish cast that seemed to take its color from their mood. The tensions were beyond coping. No one bothered. Pat sat like a rock at the rear of the boat. She wouldn't look at him, or even through him; when necessary, she addressed her remarks to the lake.

Wade preferred it that way. His own thoughts had mellowed. Certain burdens had already been put down. Others soon would be.

He regarded the lake without terror. One thing he'd learned: the world had its own sneaky little tricks. Over the past days, despite everything, the lost election had come to seem almost a windfall. He felt lighter inside, nothing left to hide. Thuan Yen was still there, of course, and always would be, but the horror was now outside him. Ugly and pitiful and public. No less evil, he thought, but at least the demands of secrecy were gone. Which was another of nature's sly tricks. Once you're found out, you don't tremble at being found out. The trapdoor drops open. All you can do is fall gracefully and far and deep.

And soon other issues would be settled. Sanity, for instance. Courage, for another. Love, for a last.

He gazed out at a pair of small islands passing by. For the first time in many years, maybe ever, he felt a sense of sureness about himself.

At three o'clock Claude pulled up to the docks in Angle Inlet to take on fuel. They walked up to Pearson's Texaco station, where Wade excused himself and crossed the street.

In the Mini-Mart he purchased two loaves of bread, sandwich meats, a fifth of vodka, a large tourist map, three cans of Sterno, and a small plastic compass endorsed by the Boy Scouts of America. The plump girl behind the counter gave him a long look as he paid. Myra Something. Albino blood —very nosy. The idea came to him that he should bare his teeth, but instead he wished her a pleasant day and walked out with the goods.

His dreams that night, as he would remember them, were situated inside a chrome computer. He'd crawled in through a manhole. He was demanding a recount—"Arithmetic!" he was yelling—but the computer made a coughing noise that turned into a deep mocking purr. All the wires were tangled. The circuitry was composed of electric eels, and there were colorful fish and liquid poisons and numerous examples of evil.

When he awoke, the hour was approaching dawn. He dressed in clean corduroys, cotton socks, a white flannel shirt, a finely woven cashmere sweater that Kathy had presented to him on a Christmas Eve not so long ago.

He rolled up a pair of blankets.

An old sheet, too.

There were traces of early light as he moved down the hallway to the kitchen. It was no great surprise to find the boat key lying squarely at the center of the Formica table. Alongside was an envelope. He pocketed these items, put on a pair of rubber boots, picked up his provisions, and walked down the slope to the dock. He felt no special sentiment. A misled life, nothing else.

Kath, oh, Kath, he thought. It was impossible to conceive of her as dead. Simply lost. Among the missing.

In the frail dark he stepped into the Chris-Craft and secured his things. A little dazed, a little dreamy. After all the lies, a couple of minor truths had now appeared, or whatever the certainty was that held his heart when he thought, Kath, my Kath. He untied the mooring ropes. He started up the engine, felt the boat rise and take to the water. A hundred yards out, he looked back at the small yellow cottage on the slope above the lake.

Love, he thought. Which was one truth. You couldn't lose it even if you tried.

He took out his new compass and swung the boat north.

Later, when he looked back, the yellow cabin was gone. But even then, in his mind's eye, he could see a man and a woman lying quietly on a porch in the dense night fog, wrapped in blankets, holding each other, pretending things were not so bad. He could hear their voices as they took turns thinking up names for the children they wanted—funny names, sometimes, so they could laugh—and he could hear them planning the furnishings for their new house, the fine rugs they would buy, the antique brass lamps, the exact colors of the wallpaper, all the details. "Verona," Kathy said, and then they talked about Verona, the things they would see and do, and soon the fog was all around them and inside them and they were swallowed up and gone. Not a footprint, not a single clue. All woods and water. A place where one plus one always came to zero.

24

Hypothesis

Or maybe she'd left him long ago, in the summer of 1983, when she flew off to meet Harmon in Boston. In the years that followed she had mostly kept the secret inside, where it was like a weight that had to be carried through her life and marriage, and maybe one day it became too much for her. Not just the affair. Everything. A decayed marriage. Deferred dreams, withheld intimacies. For all these years, even before the fling with Harmon, there had been an ever-widening distance between the life she wanted and the life she had.

Suicide?

Impossible to know.

Certainly the pressures were enormous. She was on Valium and Restoril. The ruins were everywhere. Her husband, the election, the unborn child in her heart. So maybe she'd planned it, or half planned it, taking the boat out and aiming it straight north and losing herself forever in Lake of the Woods. At some point—on a rocky beach, perhaps, in the dark—she might've found herself cataloging the events that had conspired to bring her here. The disappointments. The slow strangulation by politics. How the affair with Harmon had started almost by accident, a chance meeting, a few casual letters, and how after four months it had ended the same way, without choice or volition, as if she were strapped into the back seat of her own life.

And what had changed? Still out of control. Still at the whim of a world that seemed aligned against her. The sadness was crushing. How things were. How things could've been.

Maybe she had already swallowed the medications. Or maybe she did it now, with plenty of lake water, then sat down again and let her thoughts skip back to the Boston airport. Harmon meeting her there. The drive north along the coast of Maine to a resort called Loon Point, where they'd spent four days and three nights, and where on the morning of the fourth day, after breakfast, she had informed him that it was over. A mistake, she'd said. She loved her husband.

She remembered Harmon's round white face. A dentist's face—concentrating. "Well," he'd said.

Nothing else.

And now it was all a mystery. She couldn't recall the color of the man's eyes, or how she had come to care about him, or what had happened to wake her up. The whole affair struck her as something quaint and foreign. She remembered how they'd gone dancing one night at Loon Point, how adventurous it had seemed, how the music and starlight and danger had stirred her to feel close to him, almost giddy with pleasure, but how in a curious way it was not really Harmon in her arms, it was the idea of happiness, the possibility, the temptation, a slow, tantalizing waltz with some handsome future.

For a few minutes, maybe, Kathy looked out across the lake and allowed herself to cry. Or maybe the drugs were at work, a nice dark calm tugging her down.

The flight back to Minneapolis was a blur now. A mostly empty jet. A couple of martinis. It had been late afternoon when she carried her suitcase into the apartment and put it down and stood listening to the quiet. She remembered pouring herself a glass of wine. She remembered filling the bathtub, slipping in, soaking there for a long while. At six o'clock she'd moved out to the kitchen to start supper. A half hour later, when John walked in, she'd fixed her eyes elsewhere, adjusting the heat on her electric skillet, using a spatula to drop on three pork chops. John had come up behind her. "The globetrotter," he'd said, and kissed her neck, his fingers briefly squeezing the inch or two of loose flesh at her waist. It was a habit she disliked—it made her feel fat—but she remembered a quick rush of gratitude. Immediately, by the pressure of his fingers, she knew he had no inkling.

They'd eaten supper in front of the TV. During the commercials, in a voice she recognized as politely forced, he'd asked a few vague questions about the trip. He was interested in the airline food, the weather, the high school friend she'd been visiting. She had kept her answers short. The friend was a bore, the weather hot, the food poisonous. John had nodded at the TV. It was all too easy. At one point she'd apologized to him about the foul-up.

"Foul-up?" he'd said.

"You know. The flight."

"No kidding?"

She'd glanced over at him. "I was due in *tomorrow*. I explained how . . . You didn't get the message?"

"Whoops," he'd said, and grinned at her. "Never checked the machine."

She remembered staring at her plate. The pork chops had left a fleshy, rancid taste on her tongue. Stupidly, without calculation, she was seized by the need to retaliate. What she should've done, she thought, was to call in a message describing the dance floor at Loon Point. The cozy hotel room. The wallpaper, the bedspread. All the details.

She remembered carrying her plate into the kitchen, rinsing it off, moving out to the tiny back patio and just standing there in the leaden twilight.

He would never know. Not the specifics. The secret was safe.

Yet in the evening air, like a blank tape, there was the hum of a terrifying question—Does any of it really matter?—which then deepened into the sound of an imperfect, infinitely approximate answer—Who knows?

She remembered opening her robe to the humid night air. There was a huge and desperate wanting in her heart, wanting without object, pure wanting.

Later John had come out.

"Hey, gorgeous," he'd said, and stood beside her in the heavy twilight. "So you had fun? A good trip?"

She remembered pulling her robe tight, turning toward him without contrition or clues.

"Fine," she'd said.

Maybe, in the end, she blamed herself. Not for the affair so much, but for the waning of energy, the slow year-by-year fatigue that had finally worn her down. She had stopped trying. She had given up on squirt guns, she had forfeited her dreams, and the fling with Harmon was just an emblem of all the unhappiness in her life. Maybe there were secret forces she could not tolerate. Maybe memory, maybe drugs. Maybe in Lake of the Woods, where all is repetition, she whispered, "Why?" and then closed her eyes and sank into the sound of the endless answer—Who knows? Who ever knows?

25

Evidence

Reminds me of those three monkeys. The man didn't hear nothing, didn't smell nothing, didn't see nothing. He sure as shit *did* something.
> —Vincent R. (Vinny) Pearson

Ridiculous. Mr. Wade loved his wife, anybody could see that. Just like Claude and me.
> —Ruth Rasmussen

All I know is they come into the Mini-Mart awful unhappy. They sat there unhappy. They left unhappy. That's all I know.
> —Myra Shaw (Waitress)

I don't make guesses.
> —Arthur J. Lux (Sheriff, Lake of the Woods County)

I had prayed to God that this thing was fiction.[1]
> —Colonel William V. Wilson (U.S. Army Investigator)

_____
1. Wilson, *American Heritage*, p. 53.

Exhibit Ten: Photographs (12) of Victims at Thuan Yen
Date: 16 March 1968
Photographer: Ronald Haeberle

. . . the attitude of all the men, the majority, I would say, was a revengeful attitude.[2]
> —Gregory T. Olson (First Platoon,
> Charlie Company)

People were talking about killing everything that moved. Everyone knew what we were going to do.[3]
> —Robert W. Pendleton (Third Platoon,
> Charlie Company)

Vice never sees its own ugliness—if it did, it would be frightened by its own image. Shakespeare's Iago, who *behaves* in a way that's true to his nature, sounds false because he is forced by our dramatic conventions to unmask himself, to himself be the one to lay bare the secrets of his complex and crooked heart. In reality, man seldom tramples his conscience underfoot so casually.[4]
> —George Sand (*Indiana*)

. . . we were all psyched up because we wanted revenge for some of our fallen comrades that had been killed prior to this operation in the general area of Pinkville.[5]
> —Allen J. Boyce (First Platoon, Charlie Company)

---

2. The Peers Commission, p. 5-14.
3. Ibid.
4. George Sand, *Indiana* (1832; reprint, New York: Penguin Books, 1993), p. 232.
5. The Peers Commission, p. 5-14.

We were breathing flies when it was over. They crawled up into our noses.
  —Richard Thinbill

We must act with vindictive earnestness against the Sioux, even to their extermination, men, women, and children.[6]
  —General William Tecumseh Sherman

Exterminate the whole fraternity of redskins.[7]
  —*Nebraska City Press*

That day in My Lai, I was personally responsible for killing about 25 people. Personally. Men, women. From shooting them, to cutting their throats, scalping them, to . . . cutting off their hands and cutting out their tongues. I did it.[8]
  —Varnado Simpson (Second Platoon, Charlie
    Company)

No prisoners were being taken, and no one was allowed to escape if escape could be prevented. A child of about three years, perfectly naked, was toddling along over the trail where the Indians had fled. A soldier saw it, fired at about seventy-five yards distance, and missed it. Another dismounted and said: "Let me try the little—; I can hit him." He missed, too, but a third dismounted, with a similar remark, and at his shot the child fell . . . The Indians lost three hundred, all killed, of

---

6. General William Tecumseh Sherman, in Connell, *Son of the Morning Star*, p. 132.

7. *Nebraska City Press*, in Connell, *Son of the Morning Star*, p. 127.

8. Varnado Simpson, in Bilton and Sim, *Four Hours in My Lai*, p. 7.

whom about one half were warriors and the remainder women and children.[9]

> —J. P. Dunn, Jr. (*Massacres of the Mountains*)

Kathy tried, I'll say that. Way too hard. Personally, I guess, I never gave him much of a chance.

> —Patricia S. Hood

She wanted to travel. See the world. I remember she used to talk about Verona all the time, but I don't think she knew much about it except for Romeo and Juliet.

> —Bethany Kee (Associate Admissions Director, University of Minnesota)

You get involved, try to help, put your own needs aside. Then it's twelve years later and you don't know how to have fun anymore. You're exhausted, pissed off, anxious, profoundly depressed, guilty because you can't fix it. As a matter of fact, overfunctioning to hide your partner's problems from others is defined as normal in this society.[10]

> —Patience H. C. Mason (*Recovering from the War*)

It stays with me even after all these years. I guess it probably haunted John too, except he tried to do something about it. Erase it, you know? Literally.

> —Richard Thinbill

---

9. J. P. Dunn, Jr., *Massacres of the Mountains* (New York: Archer House, 1886), pp. 343–345. This passage describes, in part, the "battle" of Sand Creek, an attack by two regiments of Colorado militia on a Cheyenne village in present-day Oklahoma on November 29, 1864.

10. Mason, *Recovering from the War: A Woman's Guide to Helping Your Vietnam Veteran, Your Family, and Yourself*, pp. 278–279.

They did not fight us like a regular army, only like savages, behind trees and stone walls, and out of the woods and houses . . . [The colonists are] as bad as the Indians for scalping and cutting the dead men's ears and noses off.[11]

> —Anonymous British infantryman, 1775 (After the battles at Lexington and Concord)

When we first started losing members of the company, it was mostly through booby-traps and snipers . . . You didn't trust anybody . . . [I]n the end, anybody that was still in the country was the enemy.[12]

> —Fred Widmer (Member of Charlie Company)

[Our British troops] were so enraged at suffering from an unseen enemy that they forced open many of the houses . . . and put to death all those found in them.[13]

> —Lieutenant Frederick Mackenzie, 1775 (After the battles at Lexington and Concord)

Q: You killed men, women, and children?
A: Yes.
Q: You were ordered to do so?
A: Yes.
Q: Why did you carry out that order?
A: I was ordered to. And I was emotionally upset . . . And we were supposed to get satisfaction from this village for

---

11. Anonymous personal letter, in Vincent J-R Kehoe, *We Were There*, privately printed, p. 169. Available at Minuteman National Park, Concord, Massachusetts, *We Were There* is a compilation of British and American accounts of the running battle on April 19, 1775.

12. Fred Widmer, in Bilton and Sim, *Four Hours in My Lai*, p. 74.

13. Lieutenant Frederick Mackenzie, in Kehoe, *We Were There*, p. 128.

the men we'd lost. They was all VC and VC sympathizers and I still believe they was all Viet Cong and Viet Cong sympathizers.[14]
— Paul Meadlo (Court-Martial Testimony)

On the road, in our route home, we found every house full of people, and the fences lined as before. Every house from which they fired was immediately forced, and EVERY SOUL IN THEM PUT TO DEATH. Horrible carnage! O Englishmen, to what depth of brutal degeneracy are ye fallen![15]
— Anonymous British officer, 1775 (After the battles at Lexington and Concord)

Q: This Sorcerer, you can't recall his name?
A: Not right at this exact minute.
Q: And he giggled?
A: That was afterward. He was upset.[16]
— Richard Thinbill (Court-Martial Testimony)

I have encouraged the troops to capture and root out the Apache by every means, and to hunt them as they would wild animals. This they have done with unrelenting vigor. Since my last report over two hundred have been killed.[17]
— General Edward O. Ord

---

14. In Hammer, *The Court-Martial of Lt. Calley*, pp. 158–159.

15. In Kehoe, *We Were There*, p. 113.

16. Richard Thinbill, transcript, Court-Martial of Lieutenant William Calley, U.S. National Archives, box 4, folder 8, p. 1735.

17. General Edward O. Ord, in Dunn, *Massacres of the Mountains*, p. 617.

Kathy was no angel. That dentist . . . I shouldn't say his name. Anyway, I don't think there *are* any angels. I guess it hurt him pretty bad—John, I mean.
> —Patricia S. Hood

[The British troops] committed every wanton wickedness that a brutal revenge could stimulate.[18]
> —Anonymous observer, 1775 (After the battles at
> Lexington and Concord)

My conscience seems to become little by little sooted . . . If I can soon get out of this war and back on the soil where the clean earth will wash away these stains![19]
> —J. Glenn Gray (*The Warriors*)

HOMELESS MY LAI VET KILLED IN BOOZE FIGHT
Pittsburgh—A Vietnam veteran who participated in the My Lai massacre and later became a homeless alcoholic who lived under a bridge was shot to death in an argument over a bottle of vodka. Police have charged a female drinking companion with shooting Robert W. T'Souvas once in the head in the altercation earlier this month . . . "He had problems with Vietnam over and over. He didn't talk about it much," said his father, William T'Souvas . . . The Army charged T'Souvas with premeditated murder of two unidentified Vietnamese children with a machine gun, but he testified the children

---

18. In Kehoe, *We Were There*, p. 184.

19. Gray, *The Warriors: Reflections on Men in Battle*, p. 175. Gray, a professor of philosophy, served with the U.S. Army as a counterintelligence agent during World War II.

were bleeding, mutilated, and dying, and he killed them to put them out of their misery. [Lieutenant William] Calley was the only one convicted of the My Lai killings.[20]

— *Boston Herald*

Twenty years later, when you look back at things that happened, things that transpired, things you did, you say: Why? Why did I do that? That is not me. Something happened to me.[21]

— Fred Widmer (Member of Charlie Company)

Exhibit Eight: John Wade's Box of Tricks, Partial List
Invisible ink
Coin pull
Servante
The Floating Glass Vase
Book: *A Magi's Gift*
Book: The Peers Commission Report

After his father died, he spent a lot of time down here at the store . . . I think probably he had a little crush on me. The way he called me Carrot Lady, like I was something special.

— Sandra Karra (Karra's Studio of Magic)

I guess you could say John ran out of magic. Once the media jumped on him, it was all over. He knew that. Those ugly

---

20. *Boston Herald*, September 14, 1988.
21. Fred Widmer, in Bilton and Sim, *Four Hours in My Lai*, p. 80.

headlines, they would've knocked Saint Peter out of politics. Minnesota isn't the kind of place where you say you're sorry and expect people to forget. Lots of Lutherans here.
—Anthony L. (Tony) Carbo

Always John! You're driving me nuts! I mean, wake up. I get tired of saying it—*Kathy* had troubles, too, her own history, her own damn life!
—Patricia S. Hood

A lot [of political wives] are unhappy here [in Washington]. They have no life of their own and wonder, who am I? Am I just somebody's wife? Or is there something more?[22]
—Arvonne Fraser (Wife of former congressman Don Fraser)

Pat [Nixon] fooled everybody who did not know her intimately, never letting on that most of the time she hated the whole thing . . . [P]olitics was anathema to Pat . . . she made this luminously clear to persons she knew and trusted.[23]
—Lester David (*The Lonely Lady of San Clemente*)

[After his resignation] Nixon was gripped by deep melancholia. He would sit for hours in his study, unable or unwilling

22. Arvonne Fraser, in Abigail McCarthy, *Private Faces/Public Places* (Garden City, N.Y.: Doubleday, 1972), p. 202.
23. Lester David, *The Lonely Lady of San Clemente* (New York: Thomas Y. Crowell, 1978), pp. 73–74.

to move, eating little. He suffered from severe insomnia . . . There is reason to speculate that if it were not for Pat Nixon's constant attention and encouragement during the low points in his life from August until past Thanksgiving, Richard Nixon might have gone over the brink into total mental breakdown. He had come close. He admits that he had been in "the depths."[24]

—Lester David (*The Lonely Lady of San Clemente*)

Think about Waterloo. Think how Napoleon felt. Life's over, you're a dead man.

—Anthony L. (Tony) Carbo

[M]uch of the shame that therapists treat is repressed, defended against, *unfelt* . . . But the potential to feel the shame is nevertheless there, often so heightened that it has become like a deformed body part that we organize our lives to keep ourselves and others from seeing.[25]

—Robert Karen ("Shame")

It is a harsh question, yet is it possible that Nixon lied to his wife and to his family, as well as to the country, about the full scope of his involvement in the cover-up of the Watergate affair?[26]

—Lester David (*The Lonely Lady of San Clemente*)

---

24. Ibid., pp. 202–204.
25. Karen, "Shame," p. 42.
26. David, *The Lonely Lady of San Clemente*, p. 180.

That Sorcerer crap. Anybody makes up names for himself, you have to wonder. Like he didn't even know who the hell he was.
—Vincent R. (Vinny) Pearson

John had all kinds of extra names. I remember his father used to call him Little Merlin, or Little Houdini, and that Jiggling John one. Maybe he got used to it. Maybe he felt—maybe it sort of helped to call himself Sorcerer. I hope so.
—Eleanor K. Wade

By taking a new name . . . an unfinished person may hope to enter into more dynamic—but not necessarily more intimate—transactions, both with the world outside and with his or her "true soul," the naked self.[27]
—Justin Kaplan ("The Naked Self and Other
Problems")

[B. Traven's] longing to vanish, in death, without a trace and to return to the elements from which he came echoes his lifelong hunger for anonymity, for disappearing without a name, or with a fictitious name, so that his true identity would be lost forever. The life of a pseudonym is the life of a dead man, of one who does not exist.[28]
—Karl S. Guthke (*B. Traven*)

---

27. Justin Kaplan, "The Naked Self and Other Problems," in Marc Pachter, ed., *Telling Lives: The Biographer's Art* (Washington, D.C.: New Republic Books, 1979), p. 37.

28. Karl S. Guthke, *B. Traven: The Life Behind the Legends* (Brooklyn: Lawrence Hill Books, 1987), pp. 8–9.

Give it up. Totally hopeless. Nobody will ever *know*.
　　—Patricia S. Hood

I've said everything I can think of. Can't we just stop now? I'm an old lady. Why keep *asking* me these things?[29]
　　—Eleanor K. Wade

29. Why do we care about Lizzie Borden, or Judge Crater, or Lee Harvey Oswald, or the Little Big Horn? *Mystery!* Because of all that cannot be known. And what if we did know? What if it were proved —absolutely and purely—that Lizzie Borden took an ax? That Oswald acted alone? That Judge Crater fell into Sicilian hands? Nothing more would beckon, nothing would tantalize. The thing about Custer is this: no survivors. Hence, eternal doubt, which both frustrates and fascinates. It's a standoff. The human desire for certainty collides with our love of enigma. And so I lose sleep over mute facts and frayed ends and missing witnesses. God knows I've tried. Reams of data, miles of magnetic tape, but none of it satisfies even my own primitive appetite for answers. So I toss and turn. I eat pints of ice cream at two in the morning. Would it help to announce the problem early on? To plead for understanding? To argue that solutions only demean the grandeur of human ignorance? To point out that absolute knowledge is absolute closure? To issue a reminder that death itself dissolves into uncertainty, and that out of such uncertainty arise great temples and tales of salvation? I prowl and smoke cigarettes. I review my notes. The truth is at once simple and baffling: John Wade was a pro. He did his magic, then walked away. Everything else is conjecture. No answers, yet mystery itself carries me on.

26

The Nature of the Dark

They were young, all of them. Calley was twenty-four, T'Souvas was nineteen, Thinbill was eighteen, Sorcerer was twenty-three, Conti was twenty-one — young and scared and almost always lost. The war was a maze. In the months after Thuan Yen they wandered here and there, no aim or direction, searching villes and setting up ambushes and taking casualties and doing what they had to do because nothing else could be done. The days were difficult, the nights were impossible. At dusk, after their holes were dug, they would sit in small groups and look out across the paddies and wait for darkness to settle in around them. The dark was their shame. It was also their future. They tried not to talk about it, but sometimes they couldn't help themselves. Thinbill talked about the flies. T'Souvas talked about the smell. Their voices would seem to flow away for a time and then return to them from somewhere beyond the swaying fields of rice. It was an echo, partly. But inside the echo were sounds not quite their own — a kind of threnody, a weeping, something melodic and sad. They would sometimes stop to listen, but the sound was never there when listened for. It mixed with the night. There were stirrings all around them, things seen, things not seen, which was in the nature of the dark.

Charlie Company never returned to Thuan Yen. There were rumors of an investigation, nervous jokes and nervous laughter, but in the end nothing came of it. The war went on. More villages and patrols and random terror. On occasion, late at night, Sorcerer would find himself sliding back into wickedness, trapped at the bottom of a bubbling ditch, but over time the whole incident took on a dreamlike quality, only half remembered, half believed. He tried to lose himself in the war. He took uncommon risks, performed unlikely deeds. He was wounded twice, once badly, but in a peculiar way the pain was all that kept body and soul together.

In late November of 1968 he extended his tour for an extra year.

"It's a personal decision," he wrote Kathy. "Maybe someday I'll be able to explain it. Right now I can't leave this place."

On ambush sometimes, in the paddies outside a sleeping village, Sorcerer would crouch low and watch the moon and listen to the many voices of the dark, the ghosts and gremlins, his father, all the late-night visitors. The trees talked. The bamboo, and the rocks. He heard people pleading for their lives. He heard things breathing, things not breathing. It was entirely in his head, like midnight telepathy, but now and then he'd look up to see a procession of corpses bearing lighted candles through the dark—women and children, PFC Weatherby, an old man with bony shins and a small wooden hoe.

"Go away," he'd murmur, and sometimes they would.

Other times, though, he would have to call in artillery. He would fire up the jungles. He would make the rivers burn.

Two months before his tour was up, Sorcerer found a desk job in the battalion adjutant's office. It was easy duty: all paperwork, no humping, a tin roof over his head. The real war had ended. The trick now was to devise a future for himself.

He thought about it for several weeks, weighing the possibilities. Late one evening he locked himself in the office, took out the battalion muster roll, hesitated briefly and then slipped it into his typewriter. After ten minutes he smiled. Not foolproof, but it could be done. He went to the files and dug out a thick folder of morning reports for Charlie Company. Over the next two hours he made the necessary changes, mostly retyping, some scissors work, removing his name from each document and carefully tidying up the numbers. In a way it helped ease the guilt. A nice buoyant feeling. At higher levels, he reasoned, other such documents were being redrafted, other such facts neatly doctored. Around midnight he began the more difficult task of reassigning himself to Alpha Company. He went back to the day of his arrival in-country, doing the math in reverse, adding his name to the muster rolls, promoting himself, awarding the appropriate medals on the appropriate dates. The illusion, he realized, would not be perfect. None ever was. But still it seemed a nifty piece of work. Logical and smooth. Among the men in Charlie Company he was known only as Sorcerer. Very few had ever heard his real name; fewer still would recall it. And over time, he trusted, memory itself would be erased.

He completed his paperwork just before dawn on November 6, 1969. A week later he rotated back to the States.

At the airport in Seattle he put in a long-distance call to

Kathy, then chuckled and hung up on the second ring. The flight to Minneapolis was lost time. Jet lag, maybe, but something else too. He felt dangerous. In the skies over North Dakota he went back into the lavatory, where he took off his uniform and put on a sweater and slacks, quietly appraising himself in the mirror. After a moment he winked. "Hey, Sorcerer," he said. "How's tricks?"

27

Hypothesis

Maybe twice that night John Wade woke up sweating. The first time, near midnight, he would've turned and coiled up against Kathy, brain-sick, a little feverish, his thoughts wired to the nighttime hum of lake and woods.

Later he kicked back the sheets and whispered, "Kill Jesus."

Quietly then, he swung out of bed and moved down the hallway to the kitchen and ran water into an old iron teakettle and put it on the stove to boil. As he waited—naked, maybe, watching the ceiling—he would've felt the full crush of defeat, the horror and humiliation, the end of everything he'd ever wanted for himself. It was more than a lost election. It was disgrace. The secret was out and he was pinwheeling freestyle through the void. No pity in the world. All arithmetic—a clean, tidy sweep. St. Paul had been lost early. Duluth was lost four to one. The unions were lost, and the German Catholics, and the rank-and-file nobodies. A winner, he thought, until he became a loser. That quick.

The teakettle made a brisk whistling sound, but he could not bring himself to move.

Ambush politics. He could see it happening exactly as it

happened. Front-page photographs of dead human beings in awkward poses. Names and dates. Eyewitness testimony. He could still see Kathy's face turning toward him on the morning when it all came undone. Now she knew. She would always know. The horror was partly Thuan Yen, partly secrecy itself, the silence and betrayal. Her expression was empty. Not shocked, just dark and vacant, twenty years of love dissolving into the certainty that nothing at all was certain.

He felt electricity in his blood.

Maybe then, when the water was at full boil, he pushed himself up and went to the stove.

Maybe he used a towel to pick up the iron teakettle.

Stupidly, he was smiling, but the smile was meaningless. He would not remember it. He would remember only the steam and the heat and the electricity in his fists and forearms. He carried the teakettle out to the living room and switched on a lamp and poured the boiling water over a big flowering geranium near the fireplace. "Jesus, Jesus," he was saying. There was a tropical stink. "Well now," he said, and nodded pleasantly.

He heard himself chuckle.

"Oh, my," he said.

He moved to the far end of the living room and boiled a small young spider plant. It wasn't rage. It was necessity. He emptied the teakettle on a dwarf cactus and a philodendron and a caladium and several others. Then he returned to the kitchen. He refilled the teakettle, watched the water come to a boil, smiled and squared his shoulders and moved down the hallway to their bedroom. A prickly heat pressed against his face; the teakettle made hissing sounds in the night. He felt himself glide away. Some time went by, which he would not remember, then later he found himself crouched at the side of the bed. He was rocking on his heels, watching Kathy sleep. Amazing, he thought. Because he loved her. Because he couldn't stop the teakettle from tipping itself forward. Kathy's face shifted on the pillow. Her eyelids snapped open. She looked up at him, puzzled, almost smiling, as if some magnificent new question were forming. Puffs of steam rose from the sockets of her eyes. The veins at her throat stiffened. She jerked sideways. There were noises in the night—screechings—his own name, perhaps—but then the steam was in her throat. She coiled and uncoiled and coiled up again. Unreal, John decided. A dank odor filled the room, a fleshy scalding smell, and Kathy's knuckles were doing a strange trick on the headboard—a quick rapping, then clenching up, then rapping again like a transmission in code. Bits of fat bubbled at her cheeks. He would remember thinking how impossible it was. He would remember the heat, the voltage in his arms and wrists. Why? he thought, but he didn't know. All he knew was fury. The blankets were wet. Her teeth were clicking. She twisted away, pushing with her elbows, sliding off toward the foot of the bed. A purply stain spilled out across her neck and shoulders. Her face seemed to fold up. Why? he kept thinking, except there were no answers and never would be. Maybe sunlight. Maybe the absence of sunlight. Maybe electricity. Maybe a vanishing act. Maybe a pair of snakes swallowing each other along a trail in Pinkville. Maybe his father. Maybe secrecy. Maybe humiliation and loss. Maybe madness. Maybe evil. He was aware of voices in the dark—women and children, slaughterhouse sounds—but the voices were not part of what he would remember. He would remember darkness. The skin at her forehead blistered up, peeling off in long ragged strips. Her lips were purplish blue. She jerked once and shuddered and curled up and hugged herself and lay still. She looked cold. There was a faint trembling at her fingers.

Maybe he kissed her.

Maybe he wrapped her in a sheet.

Maybe some black time went by before he carried her down the slope to the dock, gliding, full of love, laying her down and then moving to the boathouse and opening up the double doors.

"Kath, my Kath," he would've whispered.

He would've dragged the boat out into shallow water, letting it fishtail there while he went back for the engine. The fog had lifted. There was a moon and many stars. For a few seconds he was aware of certain sounds in the dark, the nighttime murmur of lake and woods, his own breathing as he locked in the engine and waded back to the boathouse for the oars and gas can and life vest. He was Sorcerer now. He was inside the mirrors. He would've used the oars to pull over to the dock, tying up there, feeling the waves beneath him and lifting her up and thinking Kath, my Kath, placing her in the boat and then returning to the cottage for her sneakers and jeans and white cotton sweater. Maybe he whispered magic words. Maybe he felt something beyond the glide. Remorse, perhaps, or grief. But there were no certainties now, no facts, and like a sleepwalker he would've made his way back to the boat and started the engine and turned out into the big silent lake. He did not go far. Maybe two hundred yards. In the dark, the boat shifting beneath him, he caused her sneakers to vanish in deep water. Then her jeans and sweater. He weighted her with polished gray rocks from the slope below the cottage. "Kath, Kath," he must've said, and maybe other things, and then dispatched her to the bottom. Later, he would've eased himself into the lake. He would've tipped the boat and held it firm against the waves and let it fill and sink away from him.

Maybe he joined her for a while. Maybe he didn't. At one point he felt an underwater rush in his ears. At another point he found himself alone on the dock, cold and naked, watching the stars.

And then later still he woke up in bed. A soft pinkish light played against the curtains. For a few seconds he studied the effects of dawn, the pale ripplings and gleamings. He reached out for Kathy, who wasn't there, then hugged his pillow and returned to the bottoms.

28

How He Went Away

Three miles out, in open lake, Wade turned straight north. Dawn came up thin and cold.

By seven in the morning he was well beyond Buckete Island, moving at fifteen knots, nothing ahead but the wilds. On occasion he found himself scanning the lake, throttling down as he passed bleak islands of rock and pine. Hopeless, he realized. Kathy was not to be found. It was finished, obviously, and he had to take consolation in the fine line between biology and spirit.

Around mid-morning he crossed over into Canadian waters and continued north through a chain of thickly wooded islands. The Chris-Craft bounced along nicely: an expensive wheel-steered vessel, trim and fast. At moderate speeds, Wade estimated, the topped-off tanks gave him a two-hundred-mile cruising range. The emergency gas cans might tack on another fifty. Which was sufficient. Emergencies belonged to an earlier period. Now it was down to essentials. He leaned back, calm and relaxed, letting his thoughts mix with the overall flow of things, the sweeps of timber, the waves and water. Not so bad. Not at all. The day had turned mostly sunny, not warm but comfortable, and to the west little puffs of cloud animated a pleasant autumn sky. Twice he spotted deserted fishing cabins along the shoreline, but after an hour the forests thickened and the country went shaggy and unbroken. He used his new plastic compass to hold a bearing due north.

Very simple, really.

Lost was his forte. A lifelong pursuit.

It was close to noon when he moved into a series of channels that twisted capriciously through the wilderness. He swung to the northeast, where the woods looked deepest and most inviting, the channels splitting off and multiplying and then multiplying again. At one juncture he found himself thinking aloud. Nothing sensible. A little jingle in his head: *East is east and lost is lost . . .* He told himself to shut up. Don't lose it, he thought—not that, not yet—but soon he was singing against the throb of the engine: *You're much too good to be truuue . . .* Later, other songs came to mind, which he voiced to the afternoon, and for a considerable expanse of time he had the sensation of being adrift on a sea of glass, reflections everywhere, backward and forward. At times he found himself speaking to Kathy as if she were in an adjoining room, some secret hidey-hole just behind the mirrors. He told her everything he could tell about what had happened at Thuan Yen. The pastel sunlight. The machine-gun wind that seemed to pick him up and blow him from spot to spot. "Oh, Kath," he said quietly, "sweet lost Kathleen." The only explicable thing, he decided, was how thoroughly inexplicable it all was. Secrets in general, depravity in particular. He did not consider himself an evil man. For as long as he could remember he had aspired to a condition of virtue—for himself, for the world—yet at some point he'd caught a terrible infection that was beyond purging or antidote. He didn't know the name for it. Simple befuddlement, maybe. Moral disunity. A lost soul. Even now, as he looked out across the glassy lake, Wade felt an estrangement from the actuality of the world, its basic nowness, and in the end all he could conjure up was an image of illusion itself, pure reflection, a head full of mirrors. He laughed and thought aloud, *Won't you trust in me pleeease*, then paused to appraise the woods and water. Very natural. White-caps and plant life. Here was a region that bore resemblance to the contours of his own little repository of a soul, the tangle, the overall disarray, qualities icy and wild. Yes, and all the angles at play. This angle, that angle. Was he a monster? *Well?* he wondered, but it was inconclusive. A while later he yelled, "Hey, Kath!"

Not a monster, he thought. Certainly not. He was Sorcerer.

"Kath!" he yelled.

Some vacant time passed, an hour or more, and when he refocused, Wade saw that the sun had dropped off well to the west. Four-thirty, he guessed. There were clouds now, bloated and purply black, the sky pressing down hard. He smelled winter. Not snow, but the principle of snow—the physics. For a few moments he felt something approaching terror. If the object were survival, which it was not, he would now turn tail and put the throttle on flat-out flee and make a run for whatever was left of his life.

Instead, he chuckled.

"Dear me," he said, and turned in toward a low island a quarter mile to the east.

It was snowing by the time he'd made camp for the night. Nothing elaborate. A pair of pines. A blanket and a fire. He ate a sandwich, not tasting much, then pulled out the note Claude had left him and read it through by firelight. A grand old gentleman. Allegiant in an epoch of shifting loyalties.

"Whether you're nuts or not, I don't know," Claude had scrawled, "but I can honestly say that I don't blame you for nothing. Understand me? Not for *nothing*. The choices funnel down and you go where the funnel goes. No matter what, you were in for a lynching. People make assumptions and pretty soon the assumptions turn into fact and there's not a damn thing you can do about it. Anyhow, I've got this theory. I figure what happened was real-real simple. Your wife got herself lost. The end. Period. Nothing else. That's all anybody knows and the rest is bullshit. Am I right?"

Wade smiled.

He looked up at the sky, almost nodding, but there was no point in it. Points were hard to come by. He fortified himself with vodka and finished reading.

"A couple of practical things. You got a radio on board. It's set to the right frequency, just switch the fucker on and talk. I stuck the chart book under the rear seat—Canada's that hunk of dry land up at the top of most pages. Recommend it highly. I'm not saying you should change your mind, even if you know what your mind is, but at least there's plenty of space up there to evaporate. It's worth some thought. Luck to you. Love."

Wade read the letter through again, then lay back and watched the snow slanting across the yellow firelight. The old man was mostly right. Kathy was gone, everything else was guesswork. Probably an accident. Or lost out here. Something simple. For sure—almost for sure. Except it didn't matter much. He was responsible for the misery in their lives, the betrayals and deceit, the manipulations of truth that had substituted for simple love. He was Sorcerer. He was guilty of that, and always would be.

Just after midnight Wade woke to a heavy rain. He was drenched and cold. For the rest of the night he huddled under the pair of leaky pines, sometimes dozing, sometimes staring out at the dark. Here, Wade realized, he had come up against a few firm truths. The wet. The cold. His quixotic little war with the universe seemed pitiful indeed.

"Well, Kath?" he said.

Later he said, "*Well?*"

His tone was intimate, open to conversation, but nothing returned to him.

At first light he continued north. The rain had become fog, which was presently replaced by scattered flurries and a hard westerly wind. By nine o'clock the flurries were dense snow. The wind was light, the temperature not far above freezing. Visibility, he reminded himself, was not a problem. All morning he cruised at random through a maze of wide channels, zigzagging, no objective except to lose himself and stay lost. The snow helped. Once, in the early afternoon, he found himself surrounded by several sparkling white islands. The view was stark and beautiful. A Christmas card, he thought. Happy holidays. Despite everything, his mood was curiously festive, his morale high, and it occurred to him that happiness itself was subject to the laws of relativity. He took out his bottle and sang "I'll Be Home for Christmas," then other carols, and as he continued north the appropriate images began to take shape before him—wreaths and eggnog and stuffed stockings and big bowls of oyster stew. "Hey, Kath," he said. He waited, then yelled "Kath!"

Late in the day he switched on the radio. He listened for a moment and then switched it off again.

The world was elsewhere. All static.

And then a zone of white time went by, a mind blizzard, long drifting sweeps of this and that. He was conscious of the cold and little else. Sometimes he was Sorcerer, sometimes he wasn't. His grip on the physical world had loosened. Grip, too, was relative. At one point he heard himself weeping, then later he was back at Thuan Yen, clawing at the sunlight.

Toward dark he turned into a small sheltered bay and dropped anchor twenty yards offshore. He measured out two inches of vodka, drank it down, then tried the radio again. This time Claude's voice came back at him. "Read you weak-weak," the old man said. "Sounds like Alaska. Over."

Wade could think of nothing to say.

"You there?"

"Where?" Wade said.

"Yeah, very comic." Claude's voice came through frail and sickly. "Just so you know, Lux and company are probably monitoring this, so if you don't want nobody to . . . See what I mean?"

"Crystal clear."

"You're okay?"

"Snug as a bug. Lost as can be."

"You found the chart book?"

"I did," Wade said, though he hadn't looked for it. "I'm grateful. Thanks."

The old man snorted. There was some static before his voice returned. ". . .ripped up every board, right now they're prying off the shingles. Search and destroy. Vinny's down on his hands and knees with the sniffer dogs. Ain't found zero."

"They won't," Wade said.

"For sure."

"I appreciate that too. Listen, I didn't hurt her."

"Now there's a fact."

"I didn't."

Claude laughed. "Better late than never. I'll keep it between you and me." The airwaves seemed heavy with sentiment. "You read my little note? Winnipeg's not such a bad place. Calgary, I don't know."

"Thanks again."

"A possibility, don't you think?"

Wade was silent.

"Yeah, well," Claude said. "Try not to fuck up my boat."

Wade turned off the radio and sat still for a while. The afternoon had passed into dark. He took nourishment from his bottle and then found a screwdriver and spent ten minutes disconnecting the radio's twin speakers. Is there sound, he wondered, without reception? Do you hear the shot that gets you? How big, in fact, was the Big Bang? Do our pathetic earthly squeals fall upon deaf ears? Is silence golden or common stone?

He turned off the boat's running lights. In the twilight he ate half a sandwich, wrapped himself in a blanket, and curled up on the front seat with the vodka and his anthology of bad dreams.

The night passed slow and cold, with intermittent snow, and on occasion Wade was compelled to remind himself that misery was in part the point. Except the point sometimes eluded him. Current circumstances, he decided, were not explicable to the likes of a psychiatrist or clergyman.

The *point?*

To join her in whatever ways were possible.

To feel what she felt.

To harm himself? Certainly not. And yet harm was also relative. Happiness and harm. Clear as a bell, was it not? Had he been happy? Had he harmed her?

Well, no, but yes.

And then soon other thoughts intruded. If time and space were in fact entwined along the loop of relativity, how then could one ever reach a point of no return? Were not all such points contrivance? Therefore meaningless? So, again, what was the point?

Not to return.

Ipso facto, he reasoned.

Yet he could not stop returning. All night long he revisited the village of Thuan Yen, always with a fresh eye, witness to the tumblings and spinnings of those who had reached their fictitious point of no return. Relatively speaking, he decided, these frazzle-eyed citizens were never quite dead, otherwise they would surely stop dying. Same-same for his father. Proof of the loop. The fucker kept hanging himself. Over and over, the bastard would offer shitty counsel at the dinner table—"Stop stuffing it in"—and then he'd slip out to the garage and climb aboard a garbage can and leap out into endless re-turning, his neck snapped by no point in particular, all points unknown.

Late in the night Wade turned on the radio and broadcast these thoughts to the wee-hour ethers.

Emboldened with vodka, he pooh-poohed the notion of human choice. A scam, he declared. Much overrated. "At what point," he asked, "does one decide on rafters and a rope? Answer: No points to be had. There is merely what happened and what is now happening and what will one day happen. Do we choose sleep? Hell no and bullshit—*we fall*. We give ourselves over to possibility, to whim and fancy, to the bed, the pillow, the tiny white tablet. And these choose for us. Gravity has a hand. Bear in mind trapdoors. We fall in love, yes? Tumble, in fact. Is it *choice?* Enough said."

Once or twice his voice failed. He lay under an inch of snow, mike in hand, remarking to the airwaves on how hard and well he had fallen. Few fell farther.

Senator Sorcerer.

High ambition, eternal love.

"Did I choose this life of illusion? Don't be mad. My bed was made, I just lied in it."

He slept a brief numb sleep, waking to the danger of frostbite. It was a little past three in the morning when he switched on the radio. "Sinners and spinners, welcome back, you're tuned to WFIB, station of the stars, and we're socked in here at Storm Central on this treacherous Sunday morning. Traffic's light, roads are slick." He sneezed and wiped his nose. "As promised—and we deliver—here's our up-to-date list of closings. No services at Disciples of the Lost Shepherd. No mass anywhere, no velocity. Certainly no way out. Other cancellations to follow."

As dawn broke he was conducting a one-man talk show. The interview was going well. "My love, my life. The purpose of all deceit. She is what I had. Have I yet discussed her way of chasing me with a squirt gun? She did indeed. With a *squirt* gun. 'Squirt, squirt!' she'd cry. During a party once—this was years ago—we drove home and made Yum-Yum against the refrigerator and took a delicious little bubble bath and then drove back to the party in time for the speeches. Senatorial behavior this was not. It was her *way*. Did I tumble in love? I did. Did I remain in love? Oh, yes. Remember: a *squirt* gun.

The girl of my dreams. Her skin, her soul. So in this time of desolation, let us strive to be honest—would *you* not tell a fib or two?"

He went off the air at six-thirty.

His fingers were wooden.

It took twenty minutes to remove the radio from its mounting. He dropped it overboard. He fired up the twin Johnsons and swung north into Lake of the Woods.

29

The Nature of the Angle

It is in the nature of the angle that starlight bends upon the surface of the lake.

The angle makes the dream.

An owl hoots. A deer comes to drink in the topmost branches of a pine. From the bottom of the lake, eyes wide open, Kathy Wade watches the fish fly up to swim in the land of sky blue waters, where they are pinned like moths to the morning moon.

On a map of Minnesota, the Northwest Angle juts like a thumb into the smooth Canadian underbelly at the 49th parallel. A geographical orphan, stranded by a mapmaker's error, the Angle represents the northernmost point in the lower 48 states, a remote spit of woods and water surrounded on three sides by Canada. To the west is Manitoba; to the north and east lie the great dense forests of Ontario; to the south is the U.S. mainland. This is wilderness. Forty miles wide, seventy miles north to south. Gorgeous country, yes, but full of ghosts. A lone hawk circles in hunt. A mouse lies paralyzed in the blooded darkness. And in the deep unbroken solitude, age to age, Lake of the Woods gazes back on itself like a great liquid eye. Nothing adds or subtracts. Everything is present, everything is missing. Three middle-aged fishermen vanished here in 1941; two duck hunters lost their way in 1958, never to find it again, never to be found. Thickly timbered, almost entirely uninhabited, the Angle tends toward infinity. Growth becomes rot, which becomes growth again, and repetition itself is in the nature of the angle.

The history here is hard and simple. First the glaciers, then the water, then much later the Sioux and Ojibway.

The French came in 1734—men of adventure, explorers and Jesuits—converting or killing Indians, whichever seemed appropriate. Then fur traders and lumbermen and sawyers. And in 1882 the first settlers built their cabins along the southern and western shores of Lake of the Woods. A log church went up, later a granary and storehouse. A few hardy Swedes and Finns carved out their small square homesteads in the forest, but the land was never good for wheat or corn, and soon the farmers were gone and the wilderness reclaimed itself. For nearly four decades the Northwest Angle belonged once more to the mosquitoes. The Angle's border with Canada was not surveyed until 1925; until 1969 the area was accessible only by boat or float plane.

Even now, there are no highways. A single tar road runs through deep forest to the small community of Angle Inlet. The nearest city is Winnipeg, 122 miles to the west. The nearest bus station is in Roseau, 47 miles to the southwest. The nearest full-time law enforcement officer is in Baudette, the county seat, a 90-mile plane ride over Lake of the Woods.

And here, along the peninsula's northeastern shore, an old yellow cottage stands in the timber overlooking the lake. There are many trees, mostly pine and birch, and there is a dock and a boathouse and a narrow dirt road that winds through the forest and ends in a ledge of polished gray rocks at the shore below the cottage.

It is by the nature of the angle, sun to earth, that the seasons are made, and that the waters of the lake change color by the season, blue going to gray and then to white and then back again to blue. The water receives color. The water returns it. The angle shapes reality. Winter ice becomes the steam of summer as flesh becomes spirit. Partly window, partly mirror, the angle is where memory dissolves. The mathematics are always null; water swallows sky, which swallows earth. And here in a corner of John Wade's imagination, where things neither live nor die, Kathy stares up at him from beneath the surface of the silvered lake. Her eyes are brilliant green, her expression alert. She tries to speak but can't. She belongs to the angle. Not quite present, not quite gone, she swims in the blending twilight of in between.

30

Evidence

Everybody at the office, we used to talk about it constantly, we'd sit around at lunch and try to figure out if Kathy ever showed any signs of—like depression, problems at home, things like that. But you know what? Nobody ever came up with anything. She seemed just like everybody else. You got the feeling that she was basically happy, or that she thought she *could* be . . . Maybe she was just a great actress.
> —Bethany Kee (Associate Admissions Director,
>   University of Minnesota)

With missing persons, it's like digging a hole in this big pile of sand, the damn thing just keeps filling up on you . . . We looked every single place there was to look—the boathouse, the cottage, every inch. Brought in divers and a couple of State Police sniffer dogs. No luck. He was gone by then, of course. Didn't find a one thing.
> —Arthur J. Lux
>   (Sheriff, Lake of the Woods County)

So he dumped her deep. So what?
> —Vincent R. (Vinny) Pearson

The Bureau of Missing Persons in New York has handled, since its inception in 1917, more than 30,000 cases a year.[1]

—Jay Robert Nash (*Among the Missing*)

My plan, so far as I have one, is to go through Mexico to one of the Pacific ports . . . Naturally, it is possible—even probable—that I shall not return. These be "strange countries," in which things happen; that is why I am going.[2]

—Ambrose Bierce

Sometimes people just up and walk away. That's possible, isn't it? I don't see why everybody assumes the worst.

—Ruth Rasmussen

There *was* one clue, I guess. It was right after the primary, maybe a day later. Kathy was getting ready to head up north, and so naturally I asked when she'd be back in the office. Like a general date, I meant. Anyway, she goes over to this window. She looks out for a while and finally starts to laugh, except it wasn't real laughing. Like she *knew* something.

—Bethany Kee (Associate Admissions Director, University of Minnesota)

---

1. Jay Robert Nash, *Among the Missing* (New York: Simon and Schuster, 1978), p. 189.

2. Ambrose Bierce, letter, in Nash, *Among the Missing*, pp. 80–81. The flamboyant writer disappeared in Mexico without a trace. His last letter was dated December 26, 1913.

Whoever undertakes to write a biography binds himself to lying, to concealment, to flummery . . . Truth is not accessible.[3]

    —Sigmund Freud

Too bad I never got the chance to ask the man more questions. Vinny was right—some things just plain didn't add up. I don't care what Wade said, one plus one don't *never* equal zero, not in my book.

    —Arthur J. Lux (Sheriff, Lake of the Woods County)

I can't say Claude was too happy about the way they come in that day and ripped the whole place to hell. Wasn't called for, and the old man made sure everybody knew what he thought. A few times he got pretty mouthy—harassment, he kept saying—and he'd let out this cackle every time they came up empty. I miss that old-timer. Miss him bad. He had faith in people.

    —Ruth Rasmussen

All I know is, I know the guy gave me this weird look. The day before he took off, he comes in and pokes around and buys all this stuff—like I told you already, the compass and maps and all that—and he ambles up to the cash register and starts to say something and stops and just gives me this *look*. Soon as he was gone, I real quick locked the door.

    —Myra Shaw (Waitress)

---

3. Sigmund Freud, as cited in Alfred Kazin, "The Self as History: Reflections on Autobiography," in Pachter, ed., *Telling Lives: The Biographer's Art*, p. 74.

Yes, I shall go into Mexico with a pretty definite purpose, which, however, is not at present disclosable. You must try to forgive my obstinacy in not "perishing" where I am . . . I am pretty fond of you, I guess. May you live as long as you want to, and then pass smilingly into the darkness—the good, good darkness. Devotedly your friend.[4]

 —Ambrose Bierce

The Peers Commission people weren't looking for him. We were. Nothing to it really . . . Once we got wind of this so-called Sorcerer, it was only a matter of time. I put the boys on it. No sweat.

 —Edward F. Durkee (Democratic senatorial nominee)

Dear Sorcerer,

I'll keep this letter short because I figure you already know what happened. I didn't plan on talking, and that's the truth even if you probably don't believe me. They were slick, I'll say that. I barely even knew I was saying stuff until I was done saying it. So much for silent Indians. Either way, they already had you pretty much pinned down—the fact that you were *there* that day. I guess that's my excuse. I didn't mean to get anybody in trouble, and I feel bad, but there's one thing I know for sure now. Remember that night back at the ditch? I said we should get it off our chests and go report it, and you sort of blew me off. But I was right, wasn't I? Honesty's the best policy, that's for sure. I don't know how you stood it so long.

 —Richard Thinbill

---

4. Ambrose Bierce, letter to Mrs. J. C. McCrackin, in C. Hartley Grattan, *Bitter Bierce: A Mystery of American Letters* (Garden City, N.Y.: Doubleday, Doran & Co., 1929), pp. 75–76.

Yeah, we knew the story was coming. Couple days before, the *Star-Trib* calls, asks for a comment. John says, "Tell them April Fool." Couldn't fucking believe it, I swear to God, that's what he said, and then he gave me that blank dead-man look of his. Never said another word. That's when I decided to start job hunting.
    —Anthony L. (Tony) Carbo

Kathy read about it in the papers like everybody else. July, I think. Really hot. She asked me to drive over and so I did— still in my gym clothes—and I stayed with her all that day and all night. John didn't come home. I remember she was frantic, really frantic, and I kept saying, "Jesus, who *cares* if he comes home?" But Kathy was more upset about that than the fact that her own husband was a liar and a betrayer and . . . So the next morning he finally shows up. Walks in, gives us this don't-dare-ask look, goes off to take a shower. I knew right then she'd stick with him no matter what. It was obvious. So what the hell. I left. It makes me feel like . . . This is why I shouldn't be talking.
    —Patricia S. Hood

Brings to mind that old saw. Mr. Wade just wanted to crawl into a hole.
    —Ruth Rasmussen

Exhibit Eight: John Wade's Box of Tricks, Partial List
Mouse cage
Stand-up mirror
Military discharge, honorable
Book: *Marriage: A Guide*

I guess Claude was in on it. Never said as much, but after Mr. Wade went off with the Chris-Craft . . . Well, I could see Claude wasn't all that surprised. Kind of smiled, if you know what I mean. The two of them got to be pretty close in this quiet way, like they trusted each other, like they understood how things were and how there wasn't no choice finally . . . When the old man died last year, I kept waiting for a little note or something. Kept checking the mail. Nothing.
— Ruth Rasmussen

He had happened to dissever himself from the world—to vanish—to give up his place and privilege with living men, without being admitted among the dead.[5]
— Nathaniel Hawthorne ("Wakefield")

If you cannot believe in something produced by reconstruction, you may have nothing left to believe in.[6]
— John Dominic Crossan (*The Historical Jesus*)

For a while Mr. Wade was in radio contact, just a day or so. He didn't sound so good. Rambling Rose, that's what Vinny called him—the man didn't make a whole lot of sense. Anyhow, it didn't last long. Bang. Silence.
— Arthur J. Lux (Sheriff, Lake of the Woods County)

---

5. Nathaniel Hawthorne, "Wakefield," in *Twice-Told Tales* (reprint, Boston: Houghton Mifflin & Co., 1889), p. 162.

6. John Dominic Crossan, *The Historical Jesus: The Life of a Mediterranean Jewish Peasant* (New York: HarperCollins, 1992), p. 426.

They're gone and they're not coming back. Both of them. I mean, honestly, some things you best walk away from, just shrug and say, Who knows? I'm serious. You been gnawing on this a long time now, way too long, and sooner or later you should think about getting back to your *own* life. Don't want to end up missing it.[7]
—Ruth Rasmussen

Writers . . . have an obsession with missing persons.[8]
—Jay Robert Nash (*Among the Missing*)

Flies! You *hear* that?
—Richard Thinbill

We couldn't see the man—he was gone—nowhere! . . . his departure was a marvel.[9]
—Sophocles (*Oedipus at Colonus*)

---

7. Missing my life—she's right. But there is also the craving to know what cannot be known. Our own children, our fathers, our wives and husbands: Do we truly know them? How much is camouflage? How much is guessed at? How many lies get told, and when, and about what? How often do we say, or think, God, I never *knew* her? How often do we lie awake speculating—seeking some hidden truth? Oh, yes, it gnaws at me. I have my own secrets, my own trapdoors. I know something about deceit. Far too much. How it corrodes and corrupts. In her gentle way, I suppose, Ruth Rasmussen was trying to tell me something both hard and simple. We find truth inside, or not at all.

8. Nash, *Among the Missing*, p. 71.

9. Sophocles, *The Three Theban Plays*, translated by Robert Fagles (New York: Viking Penguin, 1982; reprint, Penguin Classics, 1984), p. 381.

My guess? I don't need to guess. He did it. Wasted her. That stare of his, the way he didn't even feel nothing. I seen it a zillion times . . . Who cares if we didn't never find no evidence? All it means is he sunk her good and deep.

—Vincent R. (Vinny) Pearson

I'm an optimist. Life after death, I believe in it. That big Chris-Craft, it could go forever, all the way to Kenora and then some. So I don't know. Maybe they're in Hudson Bay or someplace. I mean, they were in love. Honest love—just like Claude and me. You could see it plain and obvious. If you want the truth, I keep waiting for that note in the mail. And I bet someday it'll show up.

—Ruth Rasmussen

I'm not in the guessing game, but I'll lay out some basic facts. Number one, they were in debt up to their necks. Number two, there wasn't a dime left in their bank account. Cleaned out slick as a whistle even before they headed up north. Number three, nobody ever found *either* boat. Not a single scrap, no oars, no life vests. Number four, the man was a magician. Tried to wipe his name off the Charlie Company rolls, tried to vanish himself and damn near did it . . . Number whatever, Kathy had her own history. That dentist of hers, the way she used to take off now and then. I remember this time in Vegas, years and years ago, we had a talk about how sometimes you need to sort of unstick yourself. Maybe she finally did it. Maybe they both had it rigged up all along. When you think about it, they didn't have a damn thing to come *back* to—reputation shot, no more career, bills up the gazoo. Christ, I'd run for it too.

—Anthony L. (Tony) Carbo

Those tourist maps he bought. If he's out to zap himself, why tourist maps? Sounds to me like a tour.
——Myra Shaw (Waitress)

Well, sure, the possibility occurred to me. I can buy one missing person, I get antsy when it's two in a row. Certain stuff always bothered me. Like on the day she disappeared, Wade spends the whole afternoon paying bills, getting his affairs in order. Only thing he *didn't* do was make out a will. Makes you wonder. Mainly, though, it's how he *acted*, if you know what I mean. The man just didn't seem all that upset or anything. Just sat around. His whole attitude didn't strike me — it didn't seem normal.
——Arthur J. Lux (Sheriff, Lake of the Woods County)

At first I thought she probably drowned. An accident, I thought, but now I'm not even half sure. I told you how we used to sit around in the office and sort of brainstorm, how we all thought she seemed perfectly fine. Right after the election, she was almost carefree. Incredibly happy. Like I'd never seen her before. At the time I figured it was just relief or something. But maybe it was more than that. Maybe they decided . . . Hard to say. But I know this much. She had the guts. And she wanted changes.
——Bethany Kee (Associate Admissions Director,
University of Minnesota)

A person has to hope for *something*. So I hope they're happy. They deserved a little happiness.
——Eleanor K. Wade

Yeah, if I know Sorcerer, he had *some* slick shit up his sleeve. Guy had a million moves. No matter where he is, though, I bet he's still got nightmares. I bet he's out there swatting flies.[10]

—Richard Thinbill

---

10. Swatting flies—yes. Maybe. But still, it's odd how the mind erases horror. All the evidence suggests that John Wade was able to perform a masterly forgetting trick for nearly two decades, somehow coping, pushing it all away, and from my own experience I can understand how he kept things buried, how he could never face or even recall the butchery at Thuan Yen. For me, after a quarter century, nothing much remains of that ugly war. A handful of splotchy images. My company commander bending over a dead soldier, wiping the man's face with a towel. A lieutenant with a bundled corpse over his shoulder like a great sack of bird feed. My own hands. A buddy's bewildered eyes. A kid named Chip Merricks soaring into a tree. A patch of rice paddy bubbling with machine-gun fire. Everything else is a smudge of hedgerows and trails and land mines and snipers and death. We moved like sleepwalkers through the empty villages, shadowed by an enemy we could never find, calling in medevac choppers and loading up the casualties and then moving out again toward the next deadly little ville. And behind us we left a wake of fire and smoke. We called in gunships and air strikes. We brutalized. We wasted. We pistol-whipped. We trashed wells. We kicked and punched. We burned all that would burn. Yes, and these too were atrocities—the dirty secrets that live forever inside all of us. I have my own PFC Weatherby. My own old man with a hoe. And yet a quality of abstraction makes reality unreal. All these years later, like John Wade, I cannot remember much, I cannot feel much. Maybe erasure is necessary. Maybe the human spirit defends itself as the body does, attacking infection, enveloping and destroying those malignancies that would otherwise consume us. Still, it's odd. On occasion, especially when I'm alone, I find myself wondering if these old tattered memories weren't lifted from someone else's life, or from a piece of fiction I once read or once heard about. My own war does not belong to me. In a peculiar way, even at this very instant, the ordeal of John Wade—the long decades of silence and lies and secrecy—all this has a vivid, living clarity that seems far more authentic than my own faraway experience. Maybe that's what this book is for. To remind me. To give me back my vanished life.

31

Hypothesis

If all is supposition, if ending is air, then why not happiness? Are we so cynical, so sophisticated as to write off even the chance of happy endings? On the porch that night, in the fog, John Wade had promised his wife Verona.[1] Deluxe hotels and a busload of babies. And then for a long while they had cradled each other in the dark, waiting for these things to happen, some sudden miracle. "Happy," Kathy had whispered. "Nothing else."

Does happiness strain credibility? Is there something in the human spirit that distrusts its own appetites, its own yearning for healing and contentment? Can we not believe that two adults, in love,[2] might resolve to make their own miracle?[3]

"If we could just fall asleep and wake up happy," she might've said, and Sorcerer might've laughed and said, "Why not?"

---

1. Even this is conjecture, but what else is there? See Crossan, footnote 6 on page 194.

2. See Chapter 10.

3. See Parrish, footnote 1 on page 94: "It has been said that a miracle is the result of causes with which we are unacquainted."

and then for the rest of the night they might have held each other and worked out the technicalities. Improbable, of course. More likely they drowned, or got lost, or lost themselves. But who will ever know? It's all hypothesis, beginning to end. Maybe in the fog Kathy said, "We could *do* it—right *now*" and maybe Sorcerer murmured something about a pair of snakes along a trail in Pinkville, how for years and years he had wondered what would've happened if those two dumb-ass snakes had somehow managed to gobble each other up. A tired old story. If Kathy smiled, it was out of politeness. But maybe she said, "I *dare* us."

Too sentimental? Would we prefer a wee-hour boiling? A teakettle and scalded flesh?[4]

Maybe so.[5] Yet the evidence does not exclude the possibility that they ran for their lives. John Wade was a magician. There was nothing to call him back. And so one chilly evening he might have joined her on the shore of Oak Island, or Massacre Island, or Buckete Island. Maybe she scolded him for being late. All around them there was only wilderness, dark and silent, which was what they had come for. They needed the solitude. They needed to go away together. Maybe they spent the night huddled at a small fire, celebrating, thinking up names for the children they wanted—funny names, sometimes, so they could laugh—and then later they would've planned the furnishings for their new house, the fine rugs they would buy, the antique brass lamps, the exact colors of

4. Finally it's a matter of taste, or aesthetics, and the boil is one possibility that I must reject as both graceless and disgusting. Besides, there's the weight of evidence. He was *crazy* about her.

5. Because, on the other hand, there's no accounting for taste. It's a judgment call. Maybe you hear her screaming. Maybe you see steam rising from the sockets of her eyes.

the wallpaper, all the details. They would've listened to the night. They would've heard rustlings in the timber, things growing and things rotting, the lap of lake against shore. Maybe they made love. Maybe they wrapped themselves in blankets and fell asleep and woke up happy, and maybe in the morning they set a bearing north toward Kenora, or west toward Winnipeg, where they would've ditched the Chris-Craft and made their way on foot to a bus station or to a small private airport.

Documents? Passports?

He was Sorcerer.

High over the Atlantic they would've levered back their seats and unburdened themselves of all secrets. Good things and bad things. "Kath, my Kath," Sorcerer would've whispered, as if to summon her spirit, feeling the rise and fall of her breath against his hand. For both of them it was a wishing game, except now they were inside their wishes, and maybe one day they discovered happiness on the earth—in some secret country, perhaps, or in an exotic foreign capital with bizarre customs and a difficult new language. To live there would require practice and many changes, but they were willing to learn.[6]

6. My heart tells me to stop right here, to offer some quiet benediction and call it the end. But truth won't allow it. Because there *is* no end, happy or otherwise. Nothing is fixed, nothing is solved. The facts, such as they are, finally spin off into the void of things missing, the inconclusiveness of conclusion. Mystery finally claims us. Who are we? Where do we go? The ambiguity may be dissatisfying, even irritating, but this is a love story. There is no tidiness. Blame it on the human heart. One way or another, it seems, we all perform vanishing tricks, effacing history, locking up our lives and slipping day by day into the graying shadows. Our whereabouts are uncertain. All secrets lead to the dark, and beyond the dark there is only maybe.

———

John Wade made his last broadcast in the early morning hours of Sunday, October 26, 1986. He offered a number of rambling incantations to the atmosphere, apologies and regrets, quiet declarations of sorrow. His tone was confessional. At times he cried. At dawn, just before signing off, he seemed to break down entirely. Not his mind—his heart. There were garbled prayers, convulsive pleas directed to Kathy and to God. He spoke bluntly to his father, whose affection he now demanded, whom he begged for esteem and constancy, and then near the end his voice began to sink into the lake itself, barely audible, little bubbles of sentimental gibberish: "Your tennis shoes. Those hearts I drew . . . Only for love, only to be loved . . . Because you asked once, What is sacred? and because the answer was always you. Sacred? Now you know . . . Where *are* you?"

A murderer?

A man who could boil?

At no point in this discourse did John Wade admit to the slightest knowledge of Kathy's whereabouts, nor indicate that he was withholding information. Which brings me to wonder. Is it possible that even to John Wade everything was the purest puzzle? That one day he woke up to find his wife missing, and missing forever, and that all else was unknown? That the clues led nowhere? That explanations were beyond him?

Sorrow, it seems to me, may be the true absolute. John grieved for Kathy. She was his world. They could have been so happy together. He loved her and she was gone and he could not bear the horror.

Winter came early that year. By late afternoon on October 26 a half foot of snow covered the islands and shores of Lake of the Woods. The birds were gone, wildlife was in retreat, the pine forests stood silent in their wrap of white. To the horizon, in all directions, there was only the vast ongoing freeze, everything in correspondence, an icy latticework of valences and affinities. John Wade had lost himself in the tangle. He was alone. The throttle was at full power. He was declaiming to the wind—her name, his love. He was heading north, weaving from island to island, skimming fast between water and sky.

Can we believe that he was not a monster but a man? That he was innocent of everything except his life?

Could the truth be so simple? So terrible?

TIM O'BRIEN received the 1979 National Book Award in fiction for *Going After Cacciato*. His novel *The Things They Carried* won France's prestigious Prix du Meilleur Livre Étranger and the *Chicago Tribune*'s Heartland Prize, and was chosen as one of the best books of 1990 by the *New York Times Book Review*. *In the Lake of the Woods* was named the best work of fiction in 1994 by *Time* and selected by the *New York Times Book Review* as one of the best books of the year. It was also awarded the 1995 James Fenimore Cooper Prize for historical fiction.